Wendy Jones was the first person to do an MA in Life Writing at UEA and has a PhD from Goldsmiths, where she teaches. She hosts *Interesting Conversations*, a literary programme on Resonance FM, and lives in London.

THE WORLD IS A WEDDING

It is 1925, and Wilfred Price, purveyor of superior funerals, is newly married to the beautiful Flora Myffanwy. His brief and painful marriage to Grace is in the past. He's busy with funerals — and preparing for fatherhood by reading a philosophy book and opening a paint and wallpaper business. As much as he loves Flora, he senses her distance from him — are marriage and fatherhood going to be very different from how Wilfred imagined? Meanwhile, Grace has fled from Narberth to London, where she is working as a chambermaid at the Ritz Hotel. But she has a secret — one that cannot be hidden forever, and which binds her to her old life in West Wales . . .

Books by Wendy Jones
Published by Ulverscroft:

THE THOUGHTS AND HAPPENINGS
OF WILFRED PRICE, PURVEYOR OF
SUPERIOR FUNERALS

WENDY JONES

THE WORLD IS A WEDDING

In Which the Unexpected Nature of Reality Surprises Mister Wilfred Price

Complete and Unabridged

CHARNWOOD
Leicester

First published in Great Britain in 2014 by
Corsair
an imprint of
Constable & Robinson Ltd
London

First Charnwood Edition
published 2016
by arrangement with
Constable & Robinson Ltd
London

A catalogue record for this book is available
from the British Library.

ISBN 978–1–4448–3070–5

This book is dedicated to Solly, who thinks it should be dedicated to J. K. Rowling.

'The world is a wedding.'

The Talmud

'And the man said, Let me go, for the day breaketh. And Jacob said, I will not let thee go, except thou bless me.'

Genesis xxxii.26

1

The Secret of a Happy Life

Narberth, late summer 1925

Wilfred Price, undertaker, purveyor of superior
funerals, was up with the larks and off for his
morning constitutional. And no time, today, for
a cup of tea first. Wilfred strode out of his house,
put his hands on his hips and breathed in the
watery Welsh air that smelled of turned earth. He
felt affection for Narberth, the small town
— green as a bean — five miles from the crinkly
coast of Pembrokeshire, where he had lived all
his life.

'Morning, Jeffrey,' he called to his friend above
the sound of a cleaver splitting a rib in half, as he
passed Lloyd the Butcher. 'Sunny day, today.'

'Talking sense you are, Wilf.'

'Good morning to you, Mrs Evans,' he greeted
Mrs Annie Evans, who was heaving a sack of
oatmeal on her tiny back up the steps of the
Conduit Stores.

'Beautifulest funeral yesterday,' she replied.

'Wonderful funeral,' Wilfred agreed. It had
been the simplest of funerals yesterday for Mrs
James — as it often was for elderly ladies. Half
the time the whole town had been expecting
them to kick the bucket for decades. But some

1

old ladies were surprisingly enduring; they could be very determined about not dying, despite a whole host of ailments, including sugar diabetes. Though when they finally fell off the perch, the family were prepared, and simple grief made for simple funerals.

'And *beautiful* weather it is for you today,' Mrs Evans added. Wilfred raised his hand in acknowledgement.

In the High Street, Willie the Post, carrying his bulging mailbag, waved at Wilfred cheerfully. Mrs Cadwallader was singing opera in her steamy bakery. Wilfred heard Handel Evans, the organist, playing Bach in the Bethesda Chapel as he did every morning of the week, crashing chords and hitting harmonies. Meanwhile, no doubt, the Reverend Waldo Williams MA (Oxon.) sat hunched at the lectern beneath the organ, suffering perturbations over the Psalms in the big black King James Bible he so earnestly studied. Shiny-faced schoolboys scampered around Wilfred, and outside Dai the Mint's a baby in a broken perambulator cried.

Wilfred climbed the hill to Narberth's ruined castle, flattening the dewy grass with his feet as he walked. He stood between the roofless towers and the vaulted cellar, gazing over the hushed and splendid land where Pwyll, Prince of Dyfed, was said to have struck his bargain with Arawn, Lord of the Underworld. Wilfred saw the fields of barley; St Andrew's Church, where the gravestones stood like wonky gentlemen; and the wide circle of trees surrounding Narberth, tree after tree with great, round crowns, standing like a

2

chapel congregation, neither ostentatious nor afraid to be what they were.

He rested on an ancient stone wall, listening to the wind, then took the *Narberth & Whitland Observer* out from under his arm and glanced at the front page.

Popular Narberth Wedding
MISS DAISY PRIOR AND MR J. HEATH

The Tabernacle Chapel was the scene of a pretty wedding on Saturday morning . . .

He was eager to read on, couldn't help wondering what was inside the newspaper. There would be births, deaths, marriages, scandals, and the umpteen things in between of which he knew nothing and would be surprised to learn about. And there would be news of the prime minister in London, Mr Stanley Baldwin, along with an account of Mrs James's funeral. But there wasn't time to read — or to think, much as he loved to. He must go straight home to 11, Market Street right this moment and prepare himself. He folded the paper in half and set off across the hummocky grass. There wasn't time to read the newspaper, not today.

★   ★   ★

'It's mighty tidy in here,' Wilfred announced confidently, arriving back in the house and looking around the scully. But as Wilfred and his da stood in the cosy kitchen they'd shared for twenty-nine years, both had the same thought: the kitchen didn't cut the mustard.

'Let's get rid of that old flour sack,' Wilfred suggested, lifting up the frayed sack on the floor to reveal tea-leaves, grit, bits of grass and a dog-eared playing card.

'*Ach-y-fi*. Didn't you sweep under the rug?' Wilfred's da asked.

'No,' admitted Wilfred. 'It didn't occur to me.'

'Well, quickly then — get the brush.'

Wilfred collected the dustpan and brush from the yard next to the cabbages where it had been left a few months ago and swept the floor, but the brush kept shedding bristles and he had to sweep up those as well.

'That dustpan and brush,' his da said, watching, 'was a wedding present from Auntie Blodwen for your mam and me. Long time ago now.'

Wilfred stood up from all fours and put his large hand over his da's gnarled, soil-stained hands and squeezed gently. Summer sunlight streamed through the window and lit up the humble and dishevelled room, and brought it into vivid relief.

'We have lived very well, you and I, in this room, and this house, *boy bach*,' his da stated. 'I hope I have been wise,' he added. 'The only thing I ever prayed for was to be a good father.'

There was a gentle pause.

'Do you think you should have cleaned the stove?' his da asked.

'I did,' Wilfred replied. He took the blackened, encrusted frying pan with its inch of white lard

4

from the stove and put it in the higgledy-piggledy crockery cupboard. 'That's looking better now,' he stated. 'And you won't be able to keep your spade in the kitchen sink any more. I don't think that will do.' Wilfred's da rubbed his chest in silent contemplation.

'There are momentous changes ahead,' Wilfred said, attempting to console his da but succeeding only in unnerving himself. Then, from nowhere, Wilfred remembered, as a child, waking from a nightmare and running with all his might to his da — out of bed, across the tiny landing and under the scratchy blankets of his da's bed, where he clung resolutely to his father's back, which was naked and strong.

'I dreamed a saint nibbled me.'

'Whoever heard of a saint in a bedroom?'

Tumbling into the deep dip in the middle of the old mattress, Wilfred was soothed by his da's presence.

'Keep still, *boy bach*. You've got St Vitus's Dance.'

'Who's St Vitus? Is he dead?'

'Not yet,' his da replied. And then Wilfred had fallen asleep, warm and safe — safe as houses.

Wilfred straightened the chairs around the kitchen table and closed the cutlery drawer.

'That's looking better again. Are you going to comb your hair?' he asked his da.

'Aye aye,' his da replied, smoothing his halo of white hair down. 'Now, you's better go and get yourself ready.'

Wilfred nodded, rubbing his bristly chin. He must have a shave.

5

'I've put petrol in the hearse,' he mentioned, adding, 'It's not ideal, is it?'

'What?' his da said, alarmed.

'You know.'

'No! I's thought you were happy this time.'

'Not that, Da,' Wilfred explained. 'This time I couldn't be happier. I meant it's not ideal, going to my own wedding in a hearse.'

'Once an undertaker, always an undertaker,' his da replied.

* * *

'Now, *cariad*,' said her mother, bending down and cutting the stems of some dahlias, separating forever the flower heads from their roots. She stood up and handed the freshly cut flowers to Flora Myffanwy. 'Let bygones be bygones.'

Flora nodded. Her mother was talking about Albert. It seemed an obvious comment, but Flora knew what her mother meant. She was to let go of the past, no matter how golden it had been.

'This is a new beginning for you,' Mrs Edwards continued. She reached for the white, trumpet-like lilies. 'Shall I cut you some of these?'

'Yes, I'd like some lilies.'

'Your father planted these earlier this year.'

It was still so raw. Flora saw an image of her father slumped on the hall carpet. It was a very fresh memory. She gazed at the line of metallic blue sea in the distance. The air was full of insects flitting and a rabbit hopped in the apple orchard at the end of the garden.

'He would have wanted to give you away,' her

mother stated, cutting four of the tallest, most beautiful lilies.

Her father had died in the spring; she had first seen Wilfred at the funeral, met with him across the summer and they were marrying before harvest. Much else had happened besides, but at its simplest and most pure, they had come together over the year. Today was her wedding day, not to Albert, but to Wilfred. She loved Wilfred, but she was marrying him because Albert had died.

'Perhaps a few sprigs of laurel?' her mother enquired.

'Shall we find some ivy?' Flora said.

'Let's walk to the front garden,' her mother suggested, 'and see if we can find some. I'm sure there's some ivy clinging to the silver birch.' They ambled across the dappled lawn, passing the pink and lilac hydrangeas growing bushily in the borders and heading towards the iris beds.

'I like irises,' Flora said, gazing at the elegant, indigo flowers leaning giddily against the garden wall.

'But I couldn't imagine them in a bouquet,' her mother responded. 'The trailing ivy will go lovely with the lilies.'

Flora unbuckled her sandals, took them off and began walking barefoot on the cool, fresh grass. The lawn had not been cut regularly since her father passed away so the clover had long, wilting stalks.

At the silver birch Flora began pulling the ivy away from the tree. The sun beamed down, the sky was cloudless and it was a hot, almost oppressive day. Flora ran her hand round the back of her neck and lifted up her long brown hair.

'It will be time soon for you to put on your dress. I will help you with the lace veil,' her mother said, watching. 'That ivy's proving difficult.'

Flora tried to pull a young piece of ivy away from the bark but it was tangled and stuck too tightly to come away in one piece.

'Married life . . . ' Mrs Edwards began, then stopped. Flora knew her mother would not advise her on married life; she would be more sensitive than that. 'I only want you to know that I had a lot of pleasure from married life.' Her mother was allowing Flora into an aspect of her life that she had not revealed before. 'And I learned that there was nothing to be gained from holding back.'

Flora tugged at a different frond of ivy. She didn't know if she could let go of the past. Time had passed but the ties of her heart remained. Flora tried to feel within her her love for Wilfred, but it felt hidden quietly beneath the preparations for the wedding and moving to Narberth. She needed a still moment to feel her love for him clearly and strongly again.

'And to think you are wearing the same muslin dress as I wore, the one belonging to your great-grandmother,' her mother said, arranging the flowers in her hand. 'That reminds me, I have a small gift for you.' She went into White Hook and Flora stood waiting, looking at the large, old house that was her home, and could not imagine having another home. Her mother returned with a neat box wrapped in dark green ribbon. 'It is for you, now you are almost married.'

Flora carefully removed the ribbon and brown paper, opened the glossy black box and pulled out a lipstick in a pale, pearly pink.

'It's for you to wear today,' her mother explained. 'Something new to go with the something old — the wedding dress — if you think you would like to use it.'

'I'll try it,' Flora Myffanwy said, carefully dragging the lipstick across her lips.

'If ever there is a day a woman can begin wearing lipstick,' her mother said, 'it is surely her wedding day.'

★ ★ ★

'Tell out my soul, the greatness of the Lord,' the reverend roared, and Handel Evans hit the organ chords as if his life depended on it. Wilfred stood at the altar next to Flora Myffanwy and sang, strong and deep, with his shoulders back and head high, losing himself in the voices of those he loved surrounding him. He sang with all his might so that his heart was full of lightness and he felt he could float above Stepaside and Narberth and be singing with the stars. His joy was as plain as the written sign.

When the final thunderous organ chord had faded to a slow echo and the Benediction had been given, Wilfred, beaming, held out his arm for Flora to take and they walked together down the aisle to the church door. These are our first steps, he thought, of a long journey.

Wilfred and Flora Myffanwy stepped out into the sunlight to the sound of voices raised in a cheer. A shower of rice confetti landed with a pitter-patter on Wilfred's top hat and tails. The rice fell helter-skelter onto his shoulders and into Flora Myffanwy's bouquet, nestling among the lilies and the ivy. Small children from the local cottages strewed wine-red camellia and rose petals at their feet for the bride and groom to walk on.

'Here's the bride and groom,' Jeffrey announced. 'They look a masterpiece.'

Wilfred and Flora stood outside the small chapel in Stepaside. Wilfred noticed the quivering aspens and wild rambling roses. It was a glorious day, the sun was shining and the sea in the distance was still. A blackbird was putting loops and twists in his voice and a solitary plump bee hovered about the honeysuckle. The black clothes and the white linen of the guests were very plain against the green of the trees and the silvery-grey of the chapel.

'There's one thing I will say, and it is this,' Mrs Annie Evans stated. 'There's children you'll have, with all this rice thrown.' Men in bowler hats and top hats nodded in agreement, as did the ladies in bonnets with feathers in them.

'It's better than the old shoes of tradition they threw at my wedding,' Willie the Post called, pulling Mrs Willie the Post towards him. 'We're only happy because I'm deaf and my wife is blind.'

'Wondrous sermon. The reverend is like Milton and Cromwell rolled into one,' Wilfred overheard Handel Evans comment.

'Aye,' Dai the Mint replied. 'There's no flies on that bugger.'

Arthur Squibs of Arthur Squibs Studios of Tenby emerged from the gathering, lugging his cumbersome camera.

'Good afternoon, Mr Price. Good afternoon, Mrs Edwards. Good afternoon, Mr and Mrs Wilfred Price.' He doffed his bowler hat in greeting. He gazed up at the light of the sun, then set up his heavy wood and brass camera on a tripod.

'Now, Mr Price and Mrs Melbourne Edwards, if you would stand next to your son and daughter respectively.'

His da, smelling of mothballs and boot polish, stood beside Wilfred, his fine hair fluffing out around his hat, as white as if the snow had fallen in it. Mrs Melbourne Edwards, holding a new handbag, stood next to Flora. Wilfred watched his da attempting to straighten up.

The Reverend Waldo Williams MA (Oxon.) sashayed forward, his cassock swaying about him freely, with two simple wooden chairs for his da and Mrs Melbourne Edwards. His da sat down, as if resting from a long journey taken and completed.

'Wilfred, move closer,' Arthur Squibs said. Wilfred leaned towards Flora. Flora smoothed the wisps of brown hair springing loose from the delicate white veil placed over her head.

'There's beautiful the bride is,' said Mrs Bell

11

Evans with admiration.

'Thank you, Mrs Evans,' Flora replied quietly.

'There's proud you must be of your daughter, Mrs Edwards.' Mrs Edwards swallowed visibly, unable to reply.

'Look straight ahead,' the photographer advised, clapping his hands to attract their attention. Flora Myffanwy stood by Wilfred, her shy eyes smiling. Wilfred stood tall and upright in his best suit.

'Stand still, if you please.' Mr Arthur Squibs moved his large camera and tripod slightly to the left, hid his head under the thick cloth and emerged, moving the camera nearer again. He stood beside the camera, like a magician about to capture their souls. The photograph was eventually taken.

'There are photographs, and then there are . . . photographs,' Mr Squibs said enigmatically, 'and *that* was a photograph.' Then: 'One more picture, please. It is important to have two of everything that is important to have,' he announced to the baffled gathering, adding, 'like kidneys.' He took a cloth from his waistcoat pocket and rubbed the camera lens vigorously. 'Now, keep still, don't move a muscle,' he instructed. 'This is a ten-second exposure. Talk among yourselves, ladies and gentlemen . . . ' Arthur Squibs pressed the shutter. 'One second, two seconds . . . '

Wilfred stood as still as he could. This was a proper wedding in an ancient chapel, and standing next to him was the woman he wanted as his wife. Out of the corner of his eye he looked at Flora Myffawny — beauty was around her like lavender — and thought to himself that this was the happiest day of his life. And there was the night to come as well. He felt the muscles in his belly contract and the long muscles heat and flare inside him. It would be the happiest night of his life, too, when the air between them was hot. He had not yet had conjugal relations and did not know the exact ins and out of these things, but he had lain in bed with a woman before and he felt confident this practise would hold him in good stead tonight. He glanced at Flora Myffanwy.

'Wilfred, you're twitching!' Arthur Squibs reprimanded. 'Six seconds and seven seconds . . .'

Flora was looking at the camera lens with her solemn beauty and serious eyes. It wasn't always like this at a wedding, Wilfred knew. But he wouldn't think about that today. That was the past. Whomever else he had professed to love, honour and obey was gone. He would dwell on it no more. He would put it behind him. Flora was his wife now and he couldn't be happier. To think that the days earlier in the year had been so dark, so imprisoning, when all had seemed lost . . . and now here he was.

And Flora had loved before, but the chap had died in that dreadful war and so that was all over and they could both begin a new life. The past was gone for Flora, too. She loved *him* now. He must remember Mr Ogmore Auden's advice. Mr Auden had asked him, when he was an apprentice undertaker: 'Do you know the secret to a happy life?'

'No, Mr Auden,' he'd replied.

'Two words: 'Yes, dear'.'

13

Wilfred decided, there and then, that he would call Flora Myffanwy 'dear' and he hoped that she would like that. It was important to call one's wife 'dear'. It was called a term of endearment, Wilfred knew, and was the opposite of a term of abuse. One would never call one's wife a term of abuse. That was unthinkable.

'Nine seconds and ten seconds,' Arthur Squibs counted. There was the fat click of the camera then a fizz of the photograph being taken. A dignified round of applause broke out.

I will kiss her cheek, he thought to himself, and felt the gentle warmth of her skin.

'There is good to have flowers so near you,' Wilfred remarked on Flora's posy. 'Dear,' he added. Flora looked up at him quietly. Still waters run deep, he thought to himself, though she had said the only words that mattered to Wilfred: 'I do,' and in the gentlest voice he could ever imagine. Wilfred put his hand tenderly around her small warm waist and looked at the woman he could almost barely believe existed. And he could see the smile coming in her eyes. Wilfred was aware that he knew very little about women, as his mother had died on the fourth day of his life. Women were different from men. He had already noticed, and he'd only been married five minutes.

'Shall the bride throw the bouquet?' Mrs Willie the Post suggested.

'Those flowers are more beautiful than poetry,' Mrs Cadwallader remarked.

'There's an abundance of lilies for you,' Mrs Annie Evans agreed, 'and with the smell of the scent of paradise.'

'Jeffrey, if you catch the bouquet it will be your wedding next,' Mrs Willie the Post encouraged.

'Good God Almighty, there's a thought!' Handel Evans retorted.

Flora smiled, turned her back to the expectant crowd but the bouquet slipped from her hands, falling onto the soft grass. Wilfred, removing his top hat, bent down to pick it up.

'Oh,' she said, blushing a little.

'Let me. Dear,' he offered, picking up the bouquet and handing back the slightly crushed lilies. Flora took the flowers and threw them carefully behind her to a cheer of joy and excitement from the anticipating crowd.

2

Tea at the Ritz

London, midsummer 1925

'The Ritz is a machine that manufactures tranquillity.' The butler pulled a fat gold watch from his waistcoat and noted the time. He continued: 'A beautiful, purring machine oiled by money and cleaned by maids. Guests create chaos, the maids provide order.'

Grace held her hands protectively in front of herself and watched while the butler smoothed the shining bald dome of his head with a starched handkerchief, then drew the blinds to cut out the summer sun.

'So you want to work in the Ritz.'

Grace nodded.

The butler leaned back on his mahogany desk-chair and peered at Grace over his half-moon spectacles. 'You are not alone. In these times of increasing unemployment,' he pontificated, 'many girls come from the provinces — and the Valleys,' he flicked a hand at her, 'to earn money so their brothers and sisters can eat. And,' he folded his arms, 'because a certain breed of young girl likes to serve — and ape — the rich.' He asked sharply, 'Have you worked as a servant before? Are you a servant?'

'No.' Grace waited while the butler refolded his handkerchief and dabbed the sweat on his jowls.

'What have you done?'

What, indeed, had Grace done? She had cooked and cleaned under her mother's critical eye, she had read novels and she had kept bees, and the keeping of bees was what she was most proud of. The honey she'd collected from her hive, then sold, was a rich amber and flecked with pollen, but she had no illusions: beekeeping was fruitless to her here. She had been in the city only a few days but she doubted there were any honeybees in London; there were so few flowers. But she was alone and must earn her own money.

'Are you in good health?' the butler enquired, in response to her silence.

'Yes, sir.'

'In which case, Mrs . . . ?' He looked down at his papers and straightened his glasses.

'Rice,' Grace mumbled, feeling herself tense from telling a lie.

'And am I to suppose that you are a war widow?' he asked with a weary sigh.

Grace nodded.

'In which case, Mrs Rice, you will be a chambermaid. You'll work six and a half days a week. One week's holiday a year — unpaid, of course. Stand up straight, girl.'

Grace stood up straighter.

'Report to the head housekeeper's office in two hours' time, at six o'clock sharp. She will apportion you your uniform. You will sleep in the maids' dormitory from tonight and begin work in the morning.'

17

'Yes, sir.'

'No visitors in the dormitory. On pain of immediate dismissal.'

Grace nodded; she expected no visitors.

'You are dismissed.'

★ ★ ★

Grace wandered the labyrinthine, muggy streets behind the Ritz, unwilling to venture far, frightened she would be late returning to the hotel. As she walked along the pavements, Grace thought how much had happened, and how quickly: within a matter of weeks she had married, divorced, left home and now become a maid. It was as if her life had been suddenly concertinaed, when before it had been an expanse of sameness. Grace was bewildered, numb and in shock, and amidst these changes, all she seemed able to understand was the unstoppable forwardness of life.

She walked until she found a small ladies' dress shop squashed between a tobacconist's and an Italian café. The bell above the door rang shrilly when Grace entered and she tentatively browsed while the assistant finished serving a woman with a Pekingese dog, who was purchasing a clutch bag embroidered with King Tutankhamun.

'Customers are asked to refrain from opening the cabinet drawers,' the shop assistant announced with a tight smile. 'Madam is looking for a corset?'

Grace wanted to turn and walk out of the door, away from this shop hidden behind Piccadilly, its window crowded with mannequins — armless, legless, headless figures which suggested that a

18

butchering of the body was needed to buy clothes here — but the shop assistant quickly steered her into a changing room, in which stood yet another mannequin, like a cloth Venus de Milo.

'Madam should try a Rayon Corset first. It has steel stays,' pronounced the woman, standing close to the curtain dividing them. Shortly, a hand poked through the dusty, rûched curtain and gave her a corset. Grace yanked her dress down and took the rolled-up piece of elasticated fabric.

'Thank you,' she said automatically, heat flushing over her. Grace dragged on the corset; it was too tight over her hips and stomach, forcing her to breathe in and stand bolt upright.

'And would madam like a brassière as well? Perhaps a Symington Side Lacer, which flattens the bust and is lined with net?'

'Madam' sounded incongruous in this cramped shop selling coarse, drop-waist dresses: cheaply-made copies of *Vogue* fashions for poor girls who wanted to wear the chic styles but could not afford them. Was the woman being sarcastic? Grace didn't like the complexity of sarcasm, the amount of thought it demanded. It reminded her of her mother: 'Were you thinking of cleaning the hearth, Grace?' 'Were you thinking a man would look at you in that frock?' and the accompanying laughter that wasn't funny.

Grace fiddled with the stocking suspenders so they hung straight and barely dared look at herself in the mirror.

'Or perhaps madam would prefer a larger size?'

Grace squirmed. 'Is this the biggest corset you have?' she asked, closing her eyes when she spoke, emboldened by the curtain that hid her from the prim woman standing on the other side.

'Would it be of use, madam, if you adjusted the corset? Let the buckles out?'

'No,' said Grace, something new and stronger — an instinct to survive — rising within her.

'I will check the cabinet drawers.'

While Grace waited she thought of the print of the *Old Lady of Salem*: it was of a woman in Capel Salem who was committing the sin of Vanity, and so the devil hid in the folds of her shawl. It was her mother's favourite painting — she had collected nine tokens from Sunlight soap powder to receive a free print — and it hung in the drawing room above the fireplace. Her mother said that when Grace looked at the woman, if she saw the devil's face, then Grace had the devil in her.

'Here,' the woman pronounced with a distant contempt and thrust another thick corset through the curtain. 'This is the Spencer Corset, which corrects ptosis. Seventy women in one hundred suffer from ptosis,' the shop assistant declared, 'and the Spencer Corset cures it. It will prevent your intestines sagging out of place, resolve your figure faults and control your diaphragm.'

Grace tugged on the new corset, which reached from under her ribs to the top of her thighs.

The woman was waiting impatiently on the other side of the curtain. 'The whalebone provides considerable support for the spine,' she added pushily.

The corset was tight and hard but it would do. She would buy it and she would be a chamber-maid. She was binding her body and binding her life.

Grace dragged the undergarment off, pulled her dress on, drew the curtains apart and there, standing too close, was the woman. Grace stepped back into the changing room.

'Is madam going to take the underbust corset, the one in blush pink?'

'I will,' said Grace.

'Certainly, madam.' The woman held out her hand to take the garment, showing Grace she hadn't yet paid for it so it wasn't yet hers, trotted behind the counter, wrapped the corset in crisp brown paper and tied it with string. Then she wrote out the bill with exactitude. Grace paid the nine shillings with a sense of anxiety, which she tried not to show. It was some of the money she had been given when she left Narberth.

'Thank you,' she said, from habitual politeness rather than gratitude.

'I hope you will find your purchase of use, madam. One mustn't let oneself go, must one?'

★   ★   ★

Grace sat on a bed in the maids' dormitory. She had returned to the Ritz at six o'clock sharp, collected her uniform from the housekeeper and spent the rest of the evening embroidering her initials onto the two black dresses and four white aprons she would be expected to wear from tomorrow. When she had finished, she glanced

21

down at herself. She had thought she would have put on weight and was starving herself so as not to do so. She focused on her feet, the bones jutting out as she unrolled her threadbare stockings. Her toenails needed cutting. She used the scissors from the cheap manicure set she had bought earlier in the tobacconist's next to the dress shop; she had forgotten to pack scissors in her rush to leave.

Grace looked around at the white room with the black iron beds and the modern electric light-bulb hanging starkly from the ceiling, shocked to find herself here, somewhere so strange to her and far from home. But this stuffy dormitory under the hotel roof would do for tonight, perhaps a few weeks, a couple of months at most. Then . . . she didn't know. A time would come when she would need her own bedroom but she didn't know where to find privacy in this populated city.

A maid turned over, pulled a blanket over her head and Grace heard muffled sobs.

'Don't mind her.' The girl sitting opposite indicated the shrouded outline of the weeping maid. 'She's homesick. Cries herself to sleep every night. She's from the Lake District. Says Windermere isn't like London.' The girl pulled off her cap and let down her black plait, slipped out of her uniform, undid her brassière and was soon naked. Grace looked away, shocked.

'You new? Did you answer the 'Maids Wanted' advertisement in the *Evening News*?'

Grace nodded.

'My feet are killing me,' the girl moaned, hopping into bed, her breasts wobbling freely.

'Right, switch the electric light out. Go on, new girl.'

Grace went to the Bakelite switch on the wall and then fumbled her way across the cramped, darkened attic into bed. The lyrics of a swiftly paced song and the sound of a saxophone, full of longing, drifted upwards.

> 'He landed with a splash in the River Nile
> A-ridin' a sea-goin' crocodile.
> He winked at Cleopatra, she said,
> 'Ain't he a sight!
> How about a date for next Saturday night?'

'Not going to cry yourself to sleep, are you?' the girl asked. 'I don't think I can take any more snivelling.'

'No,' Grace said.

'Good,' the girl retorted. 'It only stops you sleeping.'

⋆ ⋆ ⋆

'You have a problem with beds,' the girl with the plait stated the following morning, lifting the mattress for Grace and folding the sheet in one practised, mechanical gesture. It was Grace's first day of work at the Ritz. They were bending down to do hospital corners on a bed in the Louis XIV Suite but Grace's did not have the origami exactness of the other maid's: Grace's sheet was pleated like the edge of a puff-pastry confection. They finished the bed in silence, Grace following the other maid's lead.

23

'Watch,' the girl ordered. 'Keep copying me.' She dropped a dented yellow cushion with a plop onto the Persian rug, picked it up, thumped it and arranged it on the chaise longue. 'That's how you plump up a cushion properly,' she explained, flicking her plait over her shoulder. 'And the guest who's worn this,' she said, grabbing a shimmery Flapper dress abandoned over an armchair, 'has the whole suite next door for her clothes. Can you imagine? Just her glad rags: as if they were a group of people. We'll clean that suite next. At least we don't have to change the beds because no one sleeps in them — so you'll be all right there.' The girl nudged Grace. 'Hilda,' she said. 'Hilda Bell.'

'Grace. Gracie . . . ' replied Grace, fumbling to find a new name for herself.

'Where are you from?' Hilda asked. 'You sound like you're from America.'

'Wales,' Grace answered, immediately regretting it.

'Is that a Welsh accent?'

Grace didn't know she had an accent. She spoke how everyone spoke in Narberth. But if she had a Welsh accent then she couldn't pretend she came from somewhere else. Where would she pretend she came from? She only knew her tiny corner of Wales, and the countries she had read about in books.

'What's Wales like? Is it like London?'

'No,' Grace admitted, straightening the tangled fringe on a silk lampshade.

'You don't talk much, do you?'

Not any more, Grace thought to herself. 'I'm

24

shy,' she said by way of an answer.

'Me, now, I come from Battersea. That's over the river. Me mum, she's never even been across the Thames, not in forty-two years. But not me, I want to be a chambermaid on a cruise liner.' Hilda twirled around, duster in her hand, white ostrich feathers waving. 'But not on the *Titanic*!' She smiled guiltlessly at her own joke, but Grace felt embarrassed by the girl's affectation. Hilda seemed suddenly self-conscious, aware of showing off.

'Well, it's better than living in Battersea all me life,' she whacked a lilac cushion roughly with the feather duster, 'being born and dying in the same place, like me mum and her mum before her. You got any brothers and sisters?'

'A brother,' Grace replied.

'They're the worst. Right: you and me, next door.'

Grace followed Hilda to the next room, their footsteps muffled. She had never seen so much carpet before, nor experienced the softness and silence it created. It wasn't slate, it wasn't grass, it wasn't wood; it was thick, sumptuous, almost-bouncy carpet. Grace thought of her parents' house, which was large alongside the crouching cottages that encircled Narberth, cheek by jowl, and which were painted in hopeful pastels. The framed print of *The Prodigal Son in Misery* that hung in her childhood home, and the heavy sideboards seemed burdensome compared to this glassy, modern lightness. Her parents' house was less sophisticated than she thought; less refined than her mother's pretensions had ever led her to believe.

'Get a wiggle on,' Hilda whispered, as if talking among themselves was a conspiratorial act and they oughtn't to be speaking. Grace followed Hilda along another long quiet corridor. She pushed the trolley in front of her; it was heavy with crumpled white linen, the remains of expensive nights of tranquil sleep. Grace understood that maids were to remain unseen, like mice, busy at the business of earning a crumb, living in the hotel but unwelcome, creeping by when no one was looking.

'Room service!' Hilda parroted politely, tapping on a door with professional obsequiousness. 'You must always knock,' she warned Grace. 'Don't want to find them doing *it*.' She plucked a key from a huge ring of keys in her pocket and unlocked the door, like a thief without guilt. Inside, the room was in disarray. Trunks stencilled with *P. A. Lytton* lay open — one with a fur coat half-tumbling from it — and lingerie and Chinese pyjamas were splayed on the bed. Draped over the headboard was a Poiret black and white fancy-dress costume. Someone, a lady of means, had been trying on dresses and discarding them, considering ensembles of her clothes until she came to the right one, the dress she had chosen to wear, a dress which — inconceivably to Grace — must have been even more beautiful than those lying crumpled and abandoned on the unmade bed.

'See?' murmured Hilda, indicating the umpteen trunks, hat-boxes and rails of exquisite clothes.

'So many dresses,' Grace stated, and wondered how life would approach a woman who

26

wore dresses like these. She imagined débutante balls, grand invitations, opulent dinners, proposals of marriage and promises from men — promises kept. Grace only had one lovely dress — a yellow one; beyond that, her wardrobe was a selection of routine skirts and drab jerseys. She had been proposed to in her yellow dress. She liked her yellow silk dress, she felt beautiful in it, and it had been easy to laugh when she was wearing it. Grace remembered sitting on the picnic blanket, serving the trifle when he asked her. Clothes could change a woman's life. She recalled afterwards, taking off her yellow dress in her bedroom, and how she saw her future as a wife, which was what she had always wanted — a home of her own and a kind husband, perhaps time to read books. She remembered her reflection in the looking glass, her girliness in her chemise. Then she felt her breathing tighten.

'Stop gawping. Start working,' Hilda ordered.

Grace picked up a pearly-white dress, its underslip dangling out, turning it into two garments, like two bodies sewn together at the shoulders. The inside was on the outside and the outside was on the inside. She tried to unravel it but the dainty crystals and taupe sequins caught in each other. It was like a puzzle of right-way-roundness. Grace felt overwhelmed by so many new impressions, and of having so many new skills demanded of her.

'Give it here.' Hilda held the dress with her reddened fingers, shook and unravelled it and slipped a silk-padded hanger through the neck. Then she hung it in the wardrobe that stood in the room as if it was a stern chaperone assigned to the protection of delicate clothes belonging to ladies.

'Like this,' she said, picking up another garment and putting it neatly on a hanger.

Grace watched Hilda's deft fingers. It occurred to her that swollen red hands were capable hands; the hands that made the world go round. Hilda had strong square fingers that could do what they needed to do and would put the world to rights.

The Louis XIV Suite was cleaned as swiftly as possible, the carpet swept with a *Eureka* cleaner, the gold-plated taps buffed and the sinks scrubbed and swilled, and Grace followed Hilda on to the next room in a long corridor of guest rooms, all in need of order and cleanliness.

★ ★ ★

'Wait!' Hilda whispered, later that afternoon on Grace's first day. Grace stood behind a doorway in the foyer of the Ritz while a bride passed, walking jauntily, followed by three men in military uniform, officers perhaps. A grand piano tinkled both elegantly and jerkily — maybe it was Jazz music the pianist was playing. Grace peeked out from behind the door and saw the hotel foyer for the first time. Everything glimmered as if it had been washed in the cleanest, freshest water and then lit with pearly starlight when it was still moist and glistening. Oval mirrors were painted with leaping deer and golden harts. The chandeliers were like transparent jellyfish floating on the ceiling. She saw Pan playing his pipes in the

Lalique glass, and thought it was like the Elysian Fields in Homer's *Odyssey*: a quiet heaven where the worthy might come when they died, should they so choose, and, to the accompaniment of the grand pianoforte, sip exotic tea from exquisite bone china.

'Stop ogling again,' Hilda admonished. 'Quick, follow me.' She clomped down the staircase to the Ladies' Powder Room. 'Clean in there,' she instructed Grace, pointing to a line of cubicles.

Grace, the whalebone in the corset straining against her, began wiping the first lavatory. She didn't like to do it; it made her feel nauseous and humiliated. Her father, a doctor, would disapprove of her not wearing Indian rubber gloves, for reasons of health. He vouched clean hands made for a long life, and he had spoken with admiration of Joseph Bazalgette who'd engineered the London sewage system — although Grace doubted he had ever imagined that his daughter would be cleaning some of it. That would *not* have pleased him.

'There are rats in the Ritz,' Hilda said, getting down on all fours to clean under a lacquered cabinet. 'The kitchen lads swing them by their tails at the kitchen maids. The rats run up from the Thames.' She pulled a dusty and forgotten comb out from beneath the cabinet, examined it and put it in her apron pocket.

'Your hands are dripping on the floor!' Hilda exclaimed. Grace's hands were wet from cleaning the rim of the toilet bowl. 'You are a ragamuffin. Here, look what I've got.' Hilda took a heavily starched and perfectly folded napkin from her apron pocket to reveal one piece of shortbread, dusted with exceptionally fine sugar. She held the biscuit, cupped in both hands, as one might cup the face of a small and precious child. 'Don't tell. It's from the Rivoli Bar. They serve it with the tea. Jack, one of the kitchen lads, gave it to me — he's goofy on me. Pinched my bum!' She smiled ebulliently. 'Says he'll marry me.' She checked the door to see if a guest was coming. 'One of us break it in half, the other has first pick.'

'You have it,' Grace replied. But Grace was hungry; she wanted it. She quickly rinsed her hands.

'Are you on a weight-reduction diet?'

'Yes.'

'You are quite stout. Here.' Hilda broke off a small piece and Grace put it in her mouth. The white sugar sprinkled down her front and she tried to flick it off but it clung stickily to her. The shortbread was like a mouthful of crunchy butter, almost fudgey, and the cinnamon gave it warmth. Grace wanted more. Hilda put the rest of the biscuit in her mouth, laughed, spluttered and then wiped her saliva-splattered hands on a dirty hand-towel. She bent and picked up a large crumb from the toilet floor and popped it in her mouth.

'Stay here and clean the rest of them cubicles; I'm going to the linen room to get more hand-towels,' she said, the crumbs falling from her mouth onto the gold-veined marble, commenting, 'you've had tea at the Ritz now.'

★ ★ ★

30

When Grace had wiped the panels of all the lavatory doors with a damp cloth, she began to polish the glass door-handles. She felt uncertain of herself, surrounded by the opulence of the Ritz, but she did at least know how to clean a bathroom. Her mother had taught her that.

'Goodness,' an elegant woman in a navy dress commented, coming into the Ladies' Powder Room and putting her parasol down on a small dressing-table, 'one can still hear the pianoforte in here. Do you notice it?' she asked, seeing Grace's face for the first time and looking at her.

Grace did. Since she had arrived in London four days ago, she had been overwhelmed by the constant noise of the city. She was used to silence — a silence that deepened with the night and the dark and gave one space to think and expand. At night, at home — or what was once home — there were stars and starlight. Here, there were even occasional gas lamps in the street. So yes, she noticed the noise.

'Yes,' Grace replied, wiping a washbasin with the clammy cloth scrunched in her hand, Last night when she lay in the dark in the maids' dormitory, she could still hear the noise of the day; it filled her mind, surrounded it like a halo of chaos.

'I suppose one becomes familiar with noise working in Piccadilly,' the lady continued, regarding her reflection and patting the kiss curl at her temple.

Would she? Grace wondered. The Ritz — London — seemed busy. Always. Everywhere. Or at least, the fragments of the city she had seen. There were the throngs of people in the theatre

31

of the streets. She noticed the white marble, embedded with ancient fossils, on the steps and staircases, and the flat façades of modern buildings made of stone polished into slabs of milky pearl. And the poverty, too. London was not a parish that cared for its parishioners.

The woman adjusted her pink silk turban in the mirror, applied some lipstick and retied her red belt, although Grace was aware the lady was also watching her out of the corner of her eye. The guest appeared as shiny and sleek as the Ritz itself. Grace was flushed from working, whereas the woman looked serene and slightly dewy.

'Do excuse me, I have a cold,' the guest said. She took a House of Liberty handkerchief from her sleeve and gracefully dabbed her green eyes. She smiled brightly; her white teeth ordered and even. 'I've been waiting in the Rivoli Bar for a friend. I wonder where she can be?' She arched her eyebrows. 'Well, there's not much one can do but keep waiting, I suppose.' She smoothed her auburn hair, then looked at Grace. 'We're going to the meeting — in the Conway Hall,' she said confessionally. 'Do you subscribe?'

'To what, ma'am?' Grace asked, straightening her stained apron.

'To votes. For all women. My aunt says female emancipation is poppycock. She believes all a lady needs to know is how to make a gentleman do what she wants.' The woman clicked open the silver clasp on her clutch bag and put a leaflet on the dressing-table. 'Here. I'm supposed to distribute these. Do come.'

Grace picked up the leaflet out of politeness.

MASS MEETING
ON THE REPRESENTATION OF THE
PEOPLE ACT
SPEAKER MRS EMMELINE PANKHURST
WED NEXT 3–5
CONWAY HALL, RED LION SQUARE

Grace considered it irrelevant to her: a diversion for rich ladies, those who'd had governesses and those women — far and few between, and whom Grace envied — who were admitted to university to receive an education. As far as Grace knew, votes for women were for the most privileged; were something luxurious that only the wealthiest could afford, or would contemplate having in the first place. What use was that?

The woman put on a navy summer coat, buttoned the one enormous tortoiseshell button, glanced back at Grace and said, 'The vote is only the start. It's not all shorts and cigarettes, you know.' She straightened her silver brooch, lingering. 'If you don't mind me being so impertinent, it's only, I had an elder sister. She looked rather like you. I'm painting a portrait of her from a photograph.' The lady composed herself. 'Excuse me asking, but what's your name?'

'Grace, ma'am.'

The lady offered her hand to be shaken. 'Lady Penelope Lytton.'

Then Hilda walked in, carrying clean towels, and Grace surreptitiously put the leaflet in her apron pocket.

3

What Nature Does

'Are you sure?'

'Yes, Wilfred.'

'You are sure then?'

Flora Myffanwy nodded. She put her camera down on the chest-of-drawers.

'Well, I . . . Well, it's . . . Well, my dear, it's wonderful. Are you sure?'

'Yes.'

Women were a mystery to Wilfred; they appeared to know everything — and now here was his wife, Flora Myffanwy, saying this: she seemed certain and he didn't want to argue. They had been married seven weeks and now they were going to have a baby. Wilfred imagined a big, fat chubby boy in a wool bonnet and a white cardigan, sitting up in a perambulator, smiling at him and clapping gaily. A real, living baby, here in 11, Market Street, doing the things babies do. Wilfred wasn't entirely sure what babies did, but keeping itself busy, sleeping, drinking milk, gurgling happily. Well, it was wonderful. The bee's knees. The caterpillar's whiskers. A baby was a family — it was someone else to love.

'That's wonderful, my dear. Wonderful. I didn't know these things . . . ' Wilfred paused, not wanting to be indiscreet. They hadn't even talked about having a family, had been too shy to speak so frankly with each other. He had imagined it would happen, as it seemed to happen to everyone who got married in Narberth. 'You are very clever, dear,' he said, feeling unexpectedly quite proud of himself.

'Thank you, Wilfred.'

'Does that mean it will be born in the late spring?'

'Yes,' Flora said, in her quiet, dignified way. She looked delighted.

'That's a very good time to have a baby, that's what nature does.'

Wilfred took Flora's hand and looked down bashfully. He went and drew the flimsy curtains across the window of their tiny bedroom and pulled his wife onto the bed. He wasn't sure if an undertaker was supposed to lie down and hold his wife after breakfast on a Sunday morning, but that's exactly what he did because, he said to himself, this was a very special occasion.

★ ★ ★

As he lay quietly on the counterpane, holding Flora very carefully, her head pillowed on his arm, and trying to take in this most momentous of news, he heard a voice calling him.

'Mr Wilfred Price. Wilfred! You need to come quickly.' Wilfred heard the sound of someone rushing through the front door and the furniture clattering. Bad news has good legs, he thought to himself, getting out of bed.

'Oh Wilfred, Wilfred, whatever is to be done?' Mrs Emlyn Jacobs was standing in front of him, her stockings bunched round her ankles, her shawl awry.

'What is the matter, Mrs Emlyn Jacobs?' asked Wilfred, knowing exactly what was the matter. Mr Emlyn Jacobs was a stout gentleman who flushed mauve in the face with the slightest exertion and ate a surprisingly large number of pork pies, his false teeth clacking under his curled moustache. It wasn't good to be exceptionally fat.

'Oh, Mr Wilfred Price,' moaned Mrs Emlyn Jacobs, as if saying the undertaker's name was the answer to her predicament. 'Wilfred. Price.'

'Don't fret now,' consoled Wilfred, pulling himself up tall and assuming his undertaker's face, ready for Mrs Emlyn Jacobs to tell him what he had already surmised. She put her hands to her red round cheeks and started sobbing, her face crooked with pain. Yet there was something about Mrs Emlyn Jacobs that suggested to Wilfred that, along with her shock, there was a thread of shame. To relieve her of her embarrassment, he said consolingly, 'I'll take care of everything for you.'

Mrs Emlyn Jacobs told Wilfred she had gone to stay with her cousin in Wooden, only to return on the first train to find that, when she came through the front door, the house was silent with no sign of her husband. Unable to find Mr Emlyn Jacobs anywhere, she did the unthinkable and pushed open the closed door to the indoor water closet. And there, to her eternal surprise,

36

was her husband sitting down, dead.

That in itself wasn't unusual, Wilfred knew. Far more folk conked out in the water closet than was ever let on, though to hear people talk you would think it didn't happen. Relatives said, 'He was feeling unwell and passed away at home.' Wilfred knew from plentiful experience what that meant. But he could be relied on to be discreet about these things. He always was. Very few buggers died in a dignified way. His wise and experienced apprentice-master, Mr Ogmore Auden of *O. Auden, Wheelwrights & Cabinet Makers of Whitland*, had told him that the last words of the late Bishop of St David's — who was renowned throughout the whole of Pembrokeshire for the profundity of his sermons — were: 'Pass the spittoon.'

Wilfred reached for his top hat.

'Let me accompany you to the house,' he offered in an attempt to spare Mrs Jacobs the torment of detail, 'and I'll be able to oversee the situation.'

But when Wilfred arrived at 4, Market Square — the large house in the Georgian terrace where the Jacobs lived — and saw Mr Jacobs, he was rather taken aback. It wasn't the deceased's state of undress or frozen expression of consternation and straining, but that Wilfred knew immediately from the green colour of Mr Emlyn Jacobs's swollen face that he had sat in the same position for at least a day, perhaps two, and rigor mortis had already set in. Wilfred would be able to lift him — with some help from his da and his friend, Jeffrey, as Mr Emlyn Jacobs must be a good fifteen stone. But even if the three of them could carry the deceased down the stairs and made the short walk across Market Square into Wilfred's workshop, they would never be able to do it without anyone noticing. And it wouldn't do for people to see Mr Emlyn Jacobs — the long-standing accountant for Narberth who was famed for his almost supernatural ability to bend the books — carried upright, legs apart, dead as a dodo, across Market Square, even if he was covered with a sheet. There was nothing for it, Wilfred thought. They'd have to take him to the chapel of rest — his workshop — in the middle of the night.

'The utmost confidentiality is assured, Mrs Jacobs,' Wilfred promised, gently prising the *West Wales Guardian* from Mr Jacobs's clutching hand. Confidentiality was, according to Mr Auden, the golden rule of undertaking: 'Don't mention the unmentionable!' he'd ordered. 'And don't mention that you've seen the unmentionable.'

Mrs Emlyn Jacobs looked at Wilfred gratefully.

'Nobody need know the manner of his passing,' he reassured her, patting the widow's arm. Mrs Emlyn Jacobs dabbed her eyes, closing the door on her husband.

'Thank you, Wilfred. Mr Jacobs would have wanted that.'

'Yes,' Wilfred agreed, out of politeness rather than conviction. 'Don't fret, Mrs Jacobs,' he said quietly. 'There's nothing we can't handle and nothing I haven't seen before.'

Mrs Emlyn Jacobs nodded, then said 'Congratulations on your recent wedding, Wilfred.'

'Thank you very much, Mrs Emlyn Jacobs.'

★ ★ ★

The Reverend Waldo Williams MA (Oxon.), stood in the pulpit, raised his hands upwards and proclaimed, 'Every morning I wake and thank the Lord I'm Welsh!'

The reverend was very patriotic, Wilfred thought to himself, for a man who was born in Birmingham.

'But *Jacob*,' bellowed the reverend, slamming his palms on the huge Bible in front of him, 'was a Hebrew who fought, wrestled and boxed with the Angel of the Lord and . . . '

'Do excuse me, Mr Price, if you don't mind. There we are then, thank you very much.' Mrs Cadwallader from the Mozart Bakery was arriving late. Wilfred watched Mrs Cadwallader squeeze her curvaceous figure past him and Flora in order to reach her usual place on the pew, her maroon alligator handbag swinging from her arm as if it were a separate entity. She edged past two elderly ladies, the Misses Evans, poor, courteous and religious, whose fragile bones were clothed with translucent skin, and sat down next to Mrs Prout, the charmer, who was the great-granddaughter of Brangwen Prout, the last woman in Pembrokeshire to be hanged, rumour had it, for witchcraft.

'The Scripture reading this morning is taken from the Book of . . . '

The ululations of the sermon and the verses of the Bible washed over Wilfred and he rested in the ancient words, bored and reassured at the same time. Absentmindedly, he read the

Scripture painted in dove grey above the organ: *COMPEL THEM TO COME SO MY HOUSE MAY BE FILLED* and wondered if people who went to chapel accepted death better than Atheists. He didn't know. There was an Atheist in Carmarthen, Mr Auden had told him. There was a vegetarian in Carmarthen, too.

''Two hundred female goats and twenty male goats . . . '' the reverend read.

Wilfred liked a long sermon — it was a crackerjack of a time to have a good think. He settled back on the uncomfortable pew. If the rigor mortis didn't leave Mr Jacobs's body by this evening, he would collect him from his house, past midnight, and keep him in the workshop until the rigor mortis had left him, which should only take a couple more hours. He'd ask his da and Jeffrey to help.

Wilfred glanced at his wife: she wasn't translucent, thank goodness, like the Misses Evans. Her abundant brown hair was almost tidy beneath her hat and she sat with the distracted air of one who accepted Chapel yet knew there was a greater understanding of Narberth and its people. The beauty in her shone out. And she had a lovely bloom to her face.

''Two hundred ewes, and twenty rams . . . ''

He was going to be a father. It hit him with a jolt. He swallowed hard.

''Thirty milch camels and their colts . . . ''

Fathers, even more than undertakers, needed to know a lot. What was it Mr Auden said? 'Everything is interesting. And you will need what is in books.' He thrummed his fingers on his thigh.

"'Forty cows, and ten bulls . . . ''

He had been reading the A section of his red dictionary. Why did he stop? He had stopped when he got married. If only he had continued reading the dictionary! He would have been in the B section now. When he spoke to his son, he would have been able to educate him in all manner of B words to add to the A words he used. Words such as abundant, adamantine, alphabetise, *auf Wiedersehen*, even exotic words like avocado. He hung his head. How could he talk to his son about important matters when he didn't know the words for things? He had compromised his own son's intelligence and education, as well as his prospects, by being so lackadaisical as to give up on reading the dictionary.

"'Twenty female donkeys and ten he-donkeys . . . ''The reverend patted his temples with a folded handkerchief.

Should he start reading the dictionary again at the B section? Yes, he must. Indeed, 'baby' was a B word. But there were so many other things he knew very little about. Shakespeare — he hadn't even read *Hamlet*. Philosophy. He knew nothing of philosophy. What was right, what was wrong? That was philosophy and he should certainly know about that, now he was going to be a father. He ran his hand through his hair. Could he read a philosophy book and be a father at the same time?

"'And there wrestled a man with him until the breaking of the day'.' The Reverend Waldo Williams raised his fists and closed his eyes.

I know, thought Wilfred with inspiration. I will read a book about philosophy, and if — when

— I come across a word I don't know, I will immediately look up that very word in my red dictionary, and that way I will gain knowledge not only in philosophy but also in the King's English. And with that he gained some peace, knowing he would be more prepared for the immense role of fatherhood that awaited him.

''And he said, Let me go, for the day breaks',' the reverend pleaded.

But children cost money! Wilfred's chest tightened. What did a baby need? Many things: he was certain of it. Terry-towelling nappies, shoes, nightgowns, vests. And bonnets. Blankets, a coat, gloves — yes, perhaps they even needed gloves. He took a breath and suddenly found it hard to inhale. A baby needed socks. And socks cost money. Everything a baby needed cost money. A sponge to wash its face. A soft hairbrush to tidy its hair. If it had hair. Wilfred's chest tightened to tightness it had never before reached. And a highchair. And a perambulator.

''The sun rose upon him, and he limped upon his thigh',' the Reverend Waldo Williams whispered in a swoon of religious compassion.

The hessian bag of money he kept hidden in an empty coffin in his workshop was half-empty. He had given the other half of his savings to Grace; to keep her safe, to tide her over. It had been a lot of money, many years of savings. Had it been the best thing to do? Wilfred hung his head. Now he needed that money. He must provide for Flora — she was his wife now.

''Do not eat of the sinew which shrank, which is upon the hollow of the thigh'.'

People would always die in Narberth, but a lot of people would have to die every month to pay for the expenses involved in having a baby. A cot! And new shoes, because children's feet grow all the time. And food, because boys have hollow legs. A wave of panic came over him. He had grown up in poverty; his child would not do the same.

'"Therefore to this day . . . "'

Right, he'd been considering it for a while. This was the moment. He would turn the front room into a paint and wallpaper shop. If the people of Narberth weren't going to drop dead in droves, if they were going to stay alive, then they would have to decorate their withdrawing rooms and wallpaper their bedrooms and paint their hallways because Wilfred Price was going to have a son.

'We have been reading from the Book of Genesis,' the reverend announced, lifting his palms to the ceiling with untrammelled joy. Had they? Wilfred hadn't noticed.

'Now let us pray,' the reverend shouted, his eyes glassy with tears.

★　★　★

Flora Myffanwy leaned up in bed and looked at Wilfred. This large solid man, flat on his back, with his clipped black hair and closed eyes, snoring for Christendom, was her husband. He was released and relaxed. She watched as he rolled onto his side, flailing his arm out so that it lay across her, like a lion's limb, muscular and hairy and full of latent power: it was an undeniable weight.

This was marriage, she thought. This man here, now, forever, for the rest of her life and, if you believed the Bible, also for eternity. Flora lay back and Wilfred lifted his leg, and pinned down her legs.

She loved Wilfred, she knew that, but she was now a wife. When she was Flora Edwards, she had what felt like wings. Before she was married, when she had bicycled to Wiseman's Bridge to meet Wilfred in the cottage at the cove, she had not waited; instead, she had buckled her sandals and left the house in her own time. This morning when they left for the Tabernacle Chapel she had stood while Wilfred combed his hair in the hall mirror.

'Wallet?' he'd said. 'It's not on the dresser.' It had taken five minutes to find it — it had been under an egg box. Then Wilfred remembered that he had to tell his da something, while Flora had stood, handbag clasped in both hands, moving from one foot to the other, her stole quivering with her breath.

'Right, dear!' Wilfred had said, as they were about to leave. 'Just one more thing . . . '

To go alone was to go in your own time; to go with someone else was to wait, Flora Myffanwy thought. Those days of buckling her sandals and walking out of the door when she was ready had passed. That was how the unmarried lived. The married waited.

When she was engaged to Albert, she had felt unencumbered. She used to fly then — at least, she felt like she was flying. Now she felt heavier than she could ever imagine being — immeasurably heavy, rooted by marriage and the beginnings of motherhood.

Wilfred shifted and his breath flowed warmly over her. Was this something else women went through — this rootedness to the earth that came with expecting a baby? Flora didn't fully understand it, but she was beginning to experience it. She was quietly delighted she was expecting.

She lay back and fell asleep and dreamed a dream which was vivid and stayed with her in the morning when she awoke. It was of a stone angel floating over the cove, with a lightness and freedom Flora no longer felt she had. It was gigantic, many times larger than herself: the image of a woman who had the strength of a man or the strength of a lion. She was standing suspended in the air. Her wings were glorious, ascending like a stairway of feathers, higher and higher — and then she strode forth in the air, across the cove: a goddess, Aphrodite without a head. She was magnificent, pure in purpose, the creamy white drapes folding delicately on her hips and back and over her smooth, enormous limbs and torso. She was only feet and torso and wings — all else was lost. Her head had cracked and fallen away. She was full of purpose, striding forward through the empty air and the pure blue sky, with élan in her winds, élan in the surging of her legs across the silent cove.

4

'I'm Certain Everything is Very Proper in Heaven'

'Good morning, Mrs Annie Evans,' said Wilfred, striding into the Conduit Stores on Monday morning and looking around. He, too, would shortly be a shopkeeper. And he hoped his paint and wallpaper shop would have as many customers as the Conduit Stores.

'Morning, Wilfred. By damn, there's bad about Emlyn Jacobs.'

'Indeed.'

'Your da will be digging the grave, won't he? I don't know what we'll do in Narberth without Emlyn Jacobs cooking — I mean *doing* — the books! *Doing* the books.' The shopkeeper busied herself under the counter for a moment, before asking, 'What can I do for you, Wilfred?'

'Bunch of flowers please, Mrs Evans.'

'Flowers, Wilfred? Well, I never! And you a married man. You do know how to behave. By damn, your da has brought you up well.'

'Thank you, Mrs Evans.' Wilfred had not bought flowers before but knew that a gentleman bought flowers for a lady, and his wife was a lady. And they had reason to celebrate.

'Here you are buying flowers for your wife, of all people. And you being married two months

46

and everything now.'

But Wilfred had been married before, and was uncomfortably reminded of it. He remembered struggling with his forced marriage to Grace Reece, and how he could see no escape because she was expecting, and everyone — her father most notably — assumed the baby was Wilfred's because they'd been engaged briefly.

He looked at the jars of honey on the shelf and felt a pang of guilt: even though he had given Grace money when she fled Narberth, he had nevertheless left his marriage to her with a hard mind and an overriding desire for Flora. As much as he hadn't wanted Grace, he had wanted Flora. He had been the undertaker at Flora's father's funeral. The moment he saw Flora, as she stepped quietly out of the house, beautiful as a Pharaoh's daughter, then into the motor car — her head dipped, her face veiled, beads hanging loosely from her neck — it was decided: the way was made plain and the life of his heart formed. It had been done, never to be undone. He could barely believe that he was now married to this woman, the only woman he would, could, ever have. That she was his wife. Life had lavished on him a richness, a bounty of goodness such as he could barely comprehend.

'I'll have the pink carnations, please,' he said.

'You can never go wrong with carnations. Tell me, Wilfred, did Mr Emlyn Jacobs die in the toilet?'

'He died at rest in the hands of the Lord.'

'That's no answer, Wilfred. And was that Mr Emlyn Jacobs that Cuthbert Jones saw you and your da and Jeffrey carrying down Water Lane by the Salutation Inn on Saturday, gone midnight?'

'Hello-hello!' called Mrs Willie the Post, bustling into the Conduit Stores. 'Wilfred — there you are. I's just thinking about Mr Emlyn Jacobs.' She lowered her voice. 'You's learn a new thing every day.' She took out a shopping list. 'Now then,' she said briskly, looking up at the shelves of packaged goods, 'a jar of honey from the Reeces' hive, please, Mrs Evans. And some Symington's Lemonade Crystals.' She straightened her hat. 'Dear me to goodness, there's a thing, going to meet your Maker like that: very unprepared, your clothing all about you. That's the kind of to-do you hear of happening to the old Welsh of Carmarthen, but never in Narberth.'

'I expect you have some time between dying to arrange yourself,' Mrs Annie Evans suggested, 'before crossing the shining river and meeting Saint Peter at the Pearly Gates. Don't you think so, Wilfred?'

'I'm certain everything is very proper in Heaven,' replied Wilfred, who was unsure of the finer points of what happened to the souls of the recently deceased. Although he did often wonder if the dead climbed the ladder to Heaven cradling a piece of paper with the names of the people who had mattered to them in life. 'Here,' one might say to St Peter, 'these I have loved.'

'Best not speak ill of the dead,' continued Mrs Willie the Post. 'A tin of marrowfat peas, please. And a tin of Mock Turtle Soup — no, make that a tin of Thick Kidney Soup. Shame there is he didn't visit Mrs Prout; she could have charmed him with her magic eye.'

'Can you cure a heart attack with a charm?' asked Mrs Annie Evans.

'She cured John Jeremiah of liverandheartgrow. His liver and heart were stuck fast together. Packet of Lively Polly soap powder, please, while you're up there. And Mrs Emlyn Jacobs told me that she is giving the deceased's false teeth to his brother because he needs a new pair. Is that right, Wilfred?'

Wilfred nodded.

'There's kind. May his soul rest in peace,' commented Mrs Willie the Post, batting away a big bluebottle. 'Very warm weather still for the time of year. Hot as abroad.'

'Yes,' agreed Wilfred anxiously, thinking of Mr Emlyn Jacobs, who was sitting in the heat under the glass roof of the workshop.

★ ★ ★

Wilfred looked at the tarpaulin-covered lump stood in the middle of his workshop. Under the tarpaulin was Mr Emlyn Jacobs, sitting on a chair — the same one on which Wilfred had carried him across Market Square. It was an ornate Chippendale-style chair that had been French-polished and looked rather like a throne. Its crimson velvet cushion might become slightly stained, but there was little Wilfred could do about that. Mr Emlyn Jacobs had to sit somewhere until the rigor mortis left him. Indeed, he'd been sitting in Wilfred's workshop, like a deposed king, with a tarpaulin over him, for three days. Wilfred had put a vice and several heavy tins of varnish around the circumference of the material to hold it firmly in place and to keep the flies off. 'Only one fly,' Mr Auden used to warn ominously. 'That's all it takes.'

'Now then,' announced Wilfred, 'are you comfortable there, Emlyn? I'm sorry about having to cover you up, but what with my wife and visitors coming past the workshop, I'm sure you can understand.' The air was beginning to smell a bit sweet. Wilfred put his hand briefly on the tarpaulin covering Mr Jacobs's forearm. Stiff as a board.

'Come on, Emlyn,' he said exasperatedly, 'there's a good chap! You've got to settle yourself a bit. No good you sitting here stuffed up like a month of Sundays. Once you're dead, you have to lie down. I can't bury you on a chair. Nice chair, mind. Mahogany. Not less than two hundred years old, I expect.'

Mr Emlyn Jacobs had his arm out as if he were resting on an invisible shelf; indeed, he had been leaning on the dado rail of the indoor water closet when he had popped his clogs. Rigor mortis had crept through his corpse and frozen him in death in the position of his last moments on earth. And that was all very well and good. Rigor mortis was terrific, the canary's tusks. Wilfred liked to see his customers rigid and was relieved when it came over them, tightening first their heads, then necks, hardening their spine and fingers, finally stiffening their whole bodies for a couple of days.

'There was a to-do, Emlyn, getting you out of the house. Now, I'll call round and tell your wife later that you're not quite ready for a viewing yet.' Wilfred nodded at the rightness of his own comment and opened a tin of Lady Brand Varnish to begin varnishing Mr Jacobs's coffin.

Rigor mortis was the sign of death in a way nothing else was. Not breathing was no good. All manner of folk could stop breathing — lie stock-still and turn white as a ghost — and it didn't mean they were dead, especially if they'd had a stroke or drowned. An undertaker could poke them and prick them, hold a mirror-glass to their lips to see if it misted, then listen with an ear-horn for a heartbeat and be certain that the person had kicked the bucket, only to later hear a cough, moan or fidget from inside the coffin, and — for those left behind — it was a miracle beyond miracles. Bit unsettling for the under-taker, mind. There was the deceased, who everyone thought had gone to the sphere of celestial rewards, suddenly waking and talking — and only sleeping all along. No, it was hard to know if death had come without rigor mortis.

Wilfred smoothed the pig bristles of the small brush he used for varnishing and said to Mr Emlyn Hughes, 'Mind, your wife will give you a good send-off. 'No life without a wife!' That's what my apprentice-master said to me.' Then Wilfred was reminded how that phrase had inspired his proposal, his impulsive and wrong-minded proposal to Grace at a picnic, how he had been drawn in by her yellow dress and what was underneath it. The memory sobered him,

51

and he threw it from his mind. He turned to the hefty tarpaulin-covered mound in his middle of his workshop.

'I'm varnishing the lid for you right now,' he said. 'It's made of oak and fit for a king.' He dipped the bristles in the golden liquid. Mr Auden had said to Wilfred early on in his apprenticeship: 'Don't bury them until they're dead. Wilfred, are you listening? This is important.' It was good advice and he wouldn't want to contradict it. A fair few of his customers, the Dead Ringers they were called, asked in their last will and testament to be buried in a British Safety Coffin with a periscope to see above ground and a bell which the poor bugger could ring. It was less common these days, but he had to agree with the old-fashioned folk who requested it. It would be terrifying to be buried alive and to come round from the sleep of the dead to find you were six feet under with nothing to do but claw fervently at the lid of a coffin. You'd have to die all over again, as it were. No, not a pleasant way to go. On occasion, a coffin had been exhumed and the skeleton found curled up at one end and scratch-marks etched into the underside of the lid. At least there was no fear of that with Mr Jacobs.

Wilfred varnished the smooth underside of the coffin lid carefully.

'I've made your coffin slightly larger, so you should be comfy. I didn't want you crammed in: you'd have no room to breathe, as it were. We're getting you sorted, Emlyn — don't you worry. You'll soon be lying down. Better to be lying

52

down for eternal rest, more comfortable. And your wife will be wanting her chair back.'

He would forewarn the pallbearers of the weight they would be forced to carry at the — what was that? He listened. Ruddy hell. Was that what he thought it was? Was that the sound of dripping? He lifted the rim of the tarpaulin covering Mr Emlyn Jacobs. A pool of gluey, dark red liquid was growing alongside the corpse's black lace-up shoe.

Wilfred pulled the tarpaulin off. Mr Jacobs's stomach was bloated with gas and his trousers were straining at the seam: his testicles were swelling by the looks of things. His lips were swollen, his tongue was beginning to poke out between his gums and there was froth on his lips. His brain was being eaten by germs and seeping out of his mouth. The brain was always first to decay. And his eyes had leeched away. As Mr Auden said, 'When you die, you eat yourself.' Wilfred didn't know about all this modern embalming, but it would have to be better than this.

What to do? Mr Auden had taught him: 'A superior undertaker looks calmly at all the different and unexpected faces of death. And God only knows, Wilfred, *boy bach*, death has many faces. It isn't just old ladies ascending to the celestial realms.' Well, this must be one of the faces Mr Auden meant. There was something rotten in the centre of his workshop. Right. Wilfred must act. A good undertaker was decisive in the face of death. A purveyor of superior funerals knew exactly what to do when faced with the great unknown. And even if he didn't know what to do, he pretended he did.

'Emlyn, you're getting in that coffin now! This is enough. No more of you lounging around in my workshop as if you're having a pint in the Conduit. Come on, in that coffin!' He put his hand on Mr Emlyn Jacobs's rock-hard shoulder. 'You're going to have to help me here; you're a portly chap. I'm not going to be able to do this on my own. Right. Wait here.'

Wilfred stood on the steps of the workshop and bellowed, 'Da, give me a hand with Emlyn. Bugger weighs a ton. And he's not looking pretty. Hurry up, Da!' he yelled. 'Got to get him in that ruddy coffin now.'

Hearing no answer he bounded down the four steps of the workshop, across the small yard and into the house.

'Da, what are you — ' His da was speechless and sitting as if glued to the kitchen chair. Then Wilfred noticed that Flora was at the kitchen table, quietly sewing a button on the cuff of his cambric shirt.

'Oh, Flora,' said Wilfred. This was one of those instances when the way he used to talk and the way he spoke now that he was married was very different. 'Da, would you be so kind as to assist me in the workshop?'

His da nodded his reply while Flora Myffanwy, seemingly thinking nothing and seeing little, continued to take the needle through the button-holes. If she understood, and Wilfred suspected she did, she was contained enough to behave discreetly.

'Good God Almighty,' his da uttered once they were in the workshop and the door closed.

'He's dripping everywhere, Da. Got to put him in his coffin.'

'How are we going to do that?'

'We'll drag him on the chair till he's next to it, then lift him in.'

Wilfred's da looked at Wilfred with a lack of conviction but the two men started jerking the chair, which swerved indeterminately, its legs threatening to snap, across the floor. They shuffled slowly forward, Wilfred bending over and hugging Mr Emlyn Jacobs around his bulging stomach so that the corpse didn't topple over. Wilfred kicked a tin of Kingston Varnish out of the way. The accountant was eventually shunted, trailing rivulets of fluid, to beside the waiting coffin.

'Right — you take his legs, I'll take the top half.' Wilfred got hold of Mr Jacobs's hand but felt a sheet of skin begin to peel away. Mr Jacobs was gloving: the skin from his hand was falling off.

'Wait a moment,' Wilfred said, not explaining. He held Mr Jacobs under the arms instead. 'Don't strain yourself, Da. On the count of three: one, two — *three*,' and, with some grunting, they managed to raise the corpse and then near-drop him into the specially-widened coffin. Mr Emlyn Jacobs sighed deeply with what sounded like satisfaction as the air left his lungs.

Wilfred put his hands on his broad hips, his face dripping with sweat. He and his da looked down at Mr Emlyn Jacobs, who still had one arm sticking out and his knees bent. Wilfred would have to break that arm and both legs with a mallet; he had hoped not to have to do it. He took the gold-rimmed spectacles from Mr Emlyn Jacobs's jacket pocket and put them on him.

'I'll get a cloth and wash this . . . this . . . off our shoes,' he said.

'Can't you bury some lighter buggers next time, Wilfred *bach*?'

5

What Husbands Do

Wilfred ate his fried breakfast with a sense of satisfaction. The day was already bright and autumnal, and Mr Emlyn Jacobs was finally in his grave. It had been a pleasant funeral yesterday, although it had not been entirely true when the Reverend Waldo Williams MA said that Mr Emlyn Jacobs had been an honest Christian man who lived an upright Christian life — the reverend liked to say the word 'Christian'.

And tomorrow, Wilfred decided, taking a bite of some fried bread, he would empty the front room of furniture, sweep the floor, put up a shelf and start making a counter. Then he would order the paint and wallpaper.

He noticed the tip of his necktie was resting in some egg yolk on his breakfast plate: he pushed the tie between the buttons on his shirt then looked down at the piece of bacon on his plate and said to his da and Flora Myffanwy, 'Did you know 'Baconian' doesn't mean a man who likes bacon. It means 'pertaining to Francis Bacon'.'

'You're not reading that ruddy dictionary again?' his da asked.

'Indeed I am.' Wilfred put his knife and fork down. 'Right!' he announced, adjusting his necktie. Now he was a husband and going to be a father, he must sound confident.

'Right,' he repeated. Wilfred's da and his wife looked at him, slightly puzzled. 'It is a glorious Saturday morning. Flora Myffanwy and I will be making an early start in the hearse for a day at the seaside.' Flora Myffanwy smiled: Wilfred was delighted. This being confident was the right thing to be doing. He stood up and put on his Harris Tweed jacket.

'Tenby it is,' he declared. 'We won't be needing anything apart from a sunhat.'

'A sunhat in Tenby?' Wilfred's da asked. 'You're optimistic.'

'The sun always shines on the righteous.' Wilfred smiled self-consciously at his weak joke. Lines from the Bible never made very good jokes. 'Let us go. Dear.'

'I shall fetch my camera,' Flora replied.

He waited to pull out Flora's chair as she stood. That's what husbands did, although quite how they knew the perfect moment to do it was a mystery to Wilfred. If a husband's timing was wrong, his wife could end up on the floor — and that wouldn't do, to have your beloved splayed on the kitchen flagstones, all crumpled and bruised. Yet somehow husbands knew how to do these things. But he had only been married for eight weeks and would have time to learn, to the end of his life — *until death do us part*. Hopefully, that was plenty of time.

'Let me help you. Dear,' he offered.

'Thank you, Wilfred,' Flora replied politely.

The chair squeaked awkwardly as the spindly legs dragged across the slate flagstones and

Wilfred reached out a hand to help Flora regain her balance. Perhaps he should have been wearing bedroom slippers instead of socks, then he wouldn't have stubbed his toe. Perhaps *husbands* wore bedroom slippers. They definitely wore dressing-gowns and pyjamas at breakfast, of that he was sure.

'That'll be a nice day out for you young people,' Wilfred's da commented.

'Yes, Da. The weather looks clement.' Wilfred still didn't know how to talk naturally now that Flora was here. Usually on a Saturday he would have slouched at the table reading *The Undertaker's Journal* and eating a hunk of soda bread without a plate. It wasn't unheard of for Wilfred, on a sunny morning, to have his breakfast naked while doing a jigsaw of the Empire. That was unthinkable now. Life was different; Wilfred was married.

'And tomorrow I shall begin turning the front room into a paint and wallpaper shop,' he announced. His da and Flora looked at him in amazement. Last time he'd mentioned it to his da, his da had pointed out — correctly — that it was only seven years ago that he'd built the workshop in the yard, and that it was near-impossible to wallpaper the wattle and daub walls of Narberth houses. But this time Wilfred's mind was set.

'Right then, let's go,' he said quickly, before either of them could speak.

Wilfred drove down the hill beyond Templeton, the hearse purring like a sleek black panther. The land was deep in peace and they were the

59

first ones to motor through the day; as if the day was still a secret to the people sleeping in the cottages they passed.

'We're steaming along nicely,' said Wilfred, turning to Flora, who was holding her straw hat with one hand and the dashboard with the other. Flora laughed as her hat almost blew away and Wilfred smiled because she was happy. His wife was happy. She said yes, Wilfred thought to himself with a rush of joy. She said yes to me, Wilfred Price. I am the husband of Flora Myffanwy, and Flora Myffanwy is my wife. And I vowed to worship her. Because if ever there was a woman to worship it was Flora. Flora Myffanwy Price.

He accelerated with verve through the autumnal lanes towards the sea, the fresh air blustering through the hearse windows, and if his hair hadn't been oiled it would have moved in the wind. It was a good day — a splendid day — and Wilfred in his optimism and joy could only imagine days of happiness amounting to years of joy for both of them. Please God, let us live, he thought, closing his eyes tightly, for years and years. Let us keep on living now that we have found each other. Especially now. He stopped praying — it was important to keep one's eyes open while driving. He had read in *The Undertaker's Journal* that there were fourteen fatal automobile accidents every day. One wouldn't want an automobile accident, especially not one caused by praying for a long life. He opened his eyes, his heartfelt prayer having, he hoped, ascended to the heavens where it would be heard. He looked at his wife and wanted to tell her all this.

'Mind the door doesn't fling open,' he said as an attempt to explain. 'It's a magnificent day,' he added, 'to go for a spin in the hearse to the seaside. And the weather is very clement.'

'Yes,' said Flora.

'It is particularly temperate weather for autumn.'

'Yes,' Flora concurred.

'It is very clement indeed,' Wilfred repeated.

'Yes, it's clement,' she acquiesced.

Wilfred was reminded of the spring when he met Flora on Saturday afternoons in the empty cottage by the cove; when her presence had almost overwhelmed him, and the reality of her and her beauty left him floundering so that he didn't know what to say. There were pauses then, like these pauses now. Wilfred turned and smiled at Flora and she smiled back. He reached out his hand and put it over hers. Both of their hands were warm.

'Wilfred,' Flora Myffanwy said, straightening her pearls, which had twizzled around in the breeze.

'Yes, dear?'

'Might it be possible not to call it a hearse?'

'But it is a hearse,' Wilfred announced pragmatically. 'It's a Super Ford hearse. I bought it from Mr Ogmore Auden, my apprentice-master. It is most definitely a hearse.'

'Yes,' agreed Flora, 'though it sounds so much nicer if we say we're going for a drive in a motor car.'

'I see what you mean,' said Wilfred, under-standing. He glanced at his wife's fresh skin and the pink lipstick on her lips, then down at his own strong thighs, and his feet covering the pedals. 'We don't look dead,' he replied.

'No.'

'And I certainly don't feel dead — no disrespect to the deceased. Indeed, these days I feel very much alive.' He winked at Flora, who smiled shyly. Wilfred felt emboldened by her response. 'Right then — so it is. On every Saturday morning of our married life, Mr Wilfred Price will take his wife, Mrs Flora Myffanwy Price, for an outing in the *motor car*.' He undid the belt on his jacket then slapped his knee. 'I know!' he said thinking out loud. 'Let me take you to Fecci's Ice Cream Parlour.'

'And Wilfred?'

'Yes, dear?'

'I would like to learn to drive.'

★   ★   ★

Flora dipped her long silver spoon into the spiral of cream. It was the first time she had eaten a Knickerbocker Glory. She looked around her. The walls of Fecci's Ice Cream Parlour were decorated with hand-tinted photographs of ice cream concoctions which customers could order: Knickerbocker Glory, Black Cherry Supreme, Banana Boat, Banana Split, Peach Melba, Strawberry Melba and Fair Lady.

'That's a Cadbury's Flake,' remarked Wilfred, who had ordered a Banana Boat decorated with a stick of rippled chocolate. 'Sometimes I eat them after a funeral, but if I'm not careful, they crumble all over the place. I get chocolate splotches on my morning suit and have to wipe them off with the dishcloth.'

'The dishcloth?'

'Is that not right?'

'I should think so,' said Flora diplomatically, picturing the slimy grey cloth slumped on the wooden draining-board. She ate the glacé cherry balancing on the tip of the cream and noticed her wedding ring on her finger. Flora remembered the delicate engagement ring Albert had given her. She thought back to Alfred, who had been killed in the war seven years ago, and her father who had died in the spring. She had met and married Wilfred, perhaps too quickly — perhaps because he was devoted to her, perhaps because she had wanted to lay aside her mourning and live again. Flora looked into the glass at the whirls of fruit and strawberry syrup mixed together in no particular order. Sometimes she wondered if she had married Wilfred because she was so very shocked by the sudden death of her father.

'It's cold enough to make my teeth chop,' Wilfred commented, putting a chunk of vanilla ice cream in his mouth then a moment later pressing his hand across his forehead and closing his eyes. 'The ice cream's touched my brain,' he groaned.

I have married Wilfred, Flora Myffanwy thought to herself, watching him take his jacket off and place it over the back of the chair. I said yes when he proposed in the cottage by the cove, a plate of blackberries between us. I would have married Albert, had he lived, would have been a farmer's wife in Pleasant Valley. And I would be carrying a different child. Instead I am an undertaker's wife in a town. I have chosen my husband and I have chosen a life, she thought to herself. She could never have imagined the life she had now.

'I was thinking that for our first wedding anniversary next year we could share a Black Cherry Surprise,' Wilfred suggested, loosening his tie, 'seeing that we are baccivorus.'

She watched Wilfred lean back and rub his chest contentedly. Wilfred had been married before, to Grace. The marriage had been brief, lasting only weeks. It had been — Wilfred told her — unconsummated and she believed him. Certainly the Narberth courthouse had believed him. Although this surprised Flora in that Wilfred was eager to consummate their marriage — unable to hold back. Flora would rather not have been Wilfred's second wife; some would consider it deeply shameful that he was divorced, and she would have preferred to have been his first wife, although in a way, she was.

'You could have taken a photograph of the Knickerbocker Glory, my dear,' Wilfred commented, eating his last slice of banana.

'Yes,' she agreed.

She would like to take a photograph of the statuesque glass, the small helter-skelter of ice cream with the orange paper parasol sticking out of the top at a jaunty angle. Her camera felt like the only thread of constancy in her changed life: and the photographs she took of trees, shells and the jugs of flowers she arranged and snapped. Her Box Brownie was the way she framed the world and showed the world what she saw. She would like to work as a photographer, but she was a woman: it was almost impossible.

'That Banana Boat was most satisfying,' Wilfred declared.

'Wilfred . . . ' Flora asked.

'Yes, dear?' he replied, putting his spoon down.

'Now that we're married, is it still the same?'

'No,' said Wilfred. 'It's not the same, it's completely different.'

He straightened his tie, adding, 'And now there is something special to look forward to.'

'It's only that,' she ate some cream sprinkled with hundreds and thousands and thought back to their wedding day — her posy of lilies and ivy, the daub of lipstick on her lips, 'it's as if we don't know how to be together, now we are married.'

'We are very polite,' Wilfred agreed. 'Do you think that we will always be this polite to each other, Mrs Price?'

Flora laughed. 'I don't think so at all, Mr Price.' She watched as Wilfred picked up his long spoon, scooped up some Knickerbocker Glory and offered it to her. Their eyes met.

'It is funny, isn't it?' she said. 'We are married and we don't know how to talk to each other.' They had been more at ease together before their wedding. It seemed that marriage, living in the same house, along with the news that she was expecting, had made them shy with each other. Her life was intimately woven with a man she knew so little about.

'Have you had an ice cream before?' she asked.

'Once. My Auntie Blodwen bought me a tub for my sixth birthday from the ice-cream tricycle at Cold Blow. I was sick in the charabanc on the way home.'

There was so much, Flora realised, that they didn't know about each other, years when they hadn't known the other even existed, years which had been filled with other people and experiences. Wilfred was twenty-nine and Flora twenty-seven; between them they had fifty-six years of life to tell each other about.

'We could go on drives,' she suggested, 'and walks on Saturday mornings and tell each other about ourselves, so that I know you and you know me.'

Wilfred considered her suggestion solemnly, then nodded in agreement. He summoned the waitress, who handed him the bill. He looked at it calmly, pulled a note from his pocket, placed it in the leather wallet that the bill came in and looked at Flora.

'Thank you,' she said.

'My pleasure, dear. Shall we go?' he said, adding, 'It's your turn to tell me something now.'

★ ★ ★

'I am reading, dear,' Wilfred announced to Flora Myffanwy. He rested back in the armchair in

66

their small bedroom; it was the end of a very enjoyable day in Tenby but he didn't like to waste a moment. 'Preparing for fatherhood.'

Flora was sitting up in bed in her nightdress, smocking a baby's gown. Wilfred would rather be in bed with his beautiful wife, his *bathykolpian* wife, but he did not want to let Flora Myffanwy or their son down by his ignorance of philosophy.

'It's *The Last Days of Socrates*. I've borrowed it from the Narberth Mechanics' Institute Library.'

'What's it about?'

'Chap called Socrates. He dies. It's very learned,' said Wilfred, hoping his wife was impressed. 'I thought I had better know about right and wrong and things like that, you know . . . now that I'm going to be a father.'

'I see,' said Flora, smiling and threading a needle with green silk. Her smile had a lot of woman in it.

'I imagine it might have a bit about the funeral trade, which would be of particular relevance to me.'

'Indeed,' replied Flora.

'And I will endeavour to read it before the spring, but right now I'm feeling somewhat tired and I think I may put the book down.' He was, after all, in a bedroom and not a library. And with that thought he put the book next to his red dictionary on the chest-of-drawers and got into bed with his wife.

★ ★ ★

Stanley Baldwin. Stanley Baldwin. Stanley. Baldwin! It was imperative that Wilfred thought about Stanley Baldwin. He screwed up his eyes and tried to see a picture of the leader of the Conservative Party, and Prime Minster of England, Wales, Scotland and Ireland. Stan. Ley. Bald. Win.

Wilfred was hot and covered in sweat. He shifted his weight to the other arm and lay very still. The irony of the situation was not lost on him. As a bachelor he had spent so long, far too long, thinking about this — and now, in the very moment when he was almost doing it, he had to force himself to think about something else entirely. Stanley Baldwin flashed into his mind — his upright stance, his neat centre parting, his purposeful demeanour.

He rolled onto his side and pulled Flora to him. On his wedding night he had thought about the Royal Family and the fusty old Queen, but even with the image of the late Queen Victoria he had fallen apart and let go. And it had all been over in a moment or two, perhaps less. He was disappointed with himself. He had yearned for this occasion since the moment he had first set eyes on Flora Myffanwy. And had waited months, when waiting hours had felt like a long time. Even seconds felt like a long time when confronted with the physicality of Flora Myffanwy. Now he had a new frustration — this time with himself.

He reached down, put his hand on Flora's nightdress and began to pull it up. On the second Saturday night of his married life he had tried thinking of cricket, but had found it too *abstract* — that was an *A* word from the dictionary — and so cricket had also failed him in the performance of the duties of his married life. It was hard to think of something specific about cricket, and this had made his mind wander from the task at hand, so to speak, and that had been that.

If he moved his hand any higher up Flora's thigh, he would need to think about Stanley Baldwin again. He paused. It was a mystery to Wilfred how long these things were supposed to last — but he felt certain it should be more than a couple of seconds. He thought perhaps around two minutes. That was a long time and would demand an exceptional level of control, and political thought.

He stroked and kissed Flora's hair. He didn't know if Flora enjoyed the conjugal act. He could ask, but that would be very ungentlemanly. She appeared to like it because she smiled after-wards. He wasn't sure if ladies liked these sorts of things. Perhaps ladies didn't think about these matters as much as men — otherwise they would need to go, like men, to the Narberth Rugby Club to get things off their chest. And he had never heard a lady make mention of marital relations, so perhaps they didn't think about it at all. Although Flora Myffanwy had once said something: 'You're on my hair,' and when Wilfred had looked he saw that his forearm was leaning on her long thick curls so that her head was being pulled to the side at an odd angle.

Wilfred shifted and arranged himself in the

bed. What he hadn't understood was how much geometry there was in the conjugal act — it was not unlike trying to get a corpse in a coffin at the right angle. Things had to go in the right place in the right way, so to speak, and he was glad of his training in undertaking. It had unexpected benefits because he was experienced in attempting to get bits of other people's bodies to do what he wanted and needed them to do.

He lay still and paused in the proceedings for a moment. Wilfred had thought about his predicament a great deal while making coffins. What was the least exciting thing he could think of? Tax. But he was prone to getting hot and bothered when doing his book-keeping and getting in a fix about the figures. Politics? The Liberal Party? But then he might think about David Lloyd George, that Titan of a Welshman — though he was born in Manchester. Now there was a man to rile the blood. Stanley Baldwin? Very nice chap, no doubt commanded respect, what with him being prime minister, of course. Couldn't argue with that. Stanley Baldwin was a good choice — an *apposite* choice — and Stanley Baldwin cut the mustard.

By the eighth Saturday night of his married life, Wilfred Price was happy to acknowledge to himself that he had performed his matrimonial duties with the requisite level of control demanded by a husband for the satisfaction of his wife. With the help of the prime minister.

6

The Apple Never Falls Very Far from the Tree

There were so many women in the Conway Hall. Grace glanced down at the leaflet the guest at the Ritz had given her: *Mass Meeting on the Representation of the People Act*. Grace had not seen this many women together before. She didn't know if she was unnerved or reassured. There were women swarming towards each other, greeting each other, turning this way and that, and friends in small circles. A huddle of Indian women, draped in bright saris, stood talking animatedly, and another gathering of women in coats as threadbare as her own looked at a pamphlet. There was hair in Eton crops, confident voices, fox-fur stoles, and embroidered handbags hanging from delicate forearms. Grace waited in this mêlée, alone and uncertain, yet something within her wouldn't let her leave, even though she sensed that, with a spark, the excited chatter could burst into hysteria. But Grace noticed she wasn't frightened; she merely stood in the middle of this strange, foreign scene in her strange, foreign life.

She thought back to how she came to be here, in London, and the beginning of her journey several months ago. She remembered the station

71

in Narberth: the two well-kept platforms with hanging baskets and ironwork that was regularly repainted white. When the steam train came round the corner, curling through the grassy hills, the platform was laid out like a well-considered tea-table, carefully set and waiting, a place where one might disembark and find repose. But that day she hadn't been arriving; she had been fleeing Narberth. Her train had passed through the green ancient fields of Narberth: there was Whitland, Carmarthen and then Neath, like a whisper of what was to come. Then Port Talbot: a valley of coiled pipes and thin chimneys puffing smoke that seeped into the train carriage. And dark clouds that cut out the sky. She hadn't known Wales was like that: the earnest mining and smelting by people who lived close to the soil, toiling within the earth, dwarfed by the mountains. She had only known Narberth, and it had been safer and more beautiful than she had been aware of. She was frightened — and she hadn't yet left Wales.

Grace looked around the Conway Hall and wondered if she should talk to someone. She had come to the meeting today because it was her afternoon off and, as usual, she had nowhere to go, nothing to do and no one to see, which was too much space for her mind to fill. She wished she'd brought some books with her to London — she had been reading *Silas Marner* — but had packed so hurriedly she hadn't thought to, taking only necessities — although reading kept her mind occupied, which was a necessity.

A woman approached, her Wellington boots

unbuckled and flapping.

'Come on!' She commandeered Grace by the arm, chaperoning her into the auditorium, her bobbed hair swaying. 'You'll want to sit near the front, won't you?'

It was loud inside the auditorium, with voices and the clack of shapely heels on the parquet floor. A banner worked in purple and green above the podium read:

Mrs Pankhust, Founder/Champion
of Womankind
Famed for Deeds of Daring Rectitude

'Take your coat off: you'll be blistering.'

'I'd rather not.'

'Whatever suits. Sit here. I'm Mary — Mary Richardson.' The woman whitened the large maroon birthmark on her cheek with face powder from a compact. 'If they extend the Reform Act I'm going to stand as a parliamentary candidate for Bury St Edmunds. Isn't it just ripping?' She snapped shut her compact and it closed with a clean click.

Grace smiled politely. All these women, what would it lead to? The only times she had been within a group of girls — and some of these women resembled girls to her — was at school when clusters of girls formed to skip with one long skipping rope, chanting:

'Bronwen and Llywellyn sitting in the tree,
K-I-S-S-I-N-G
First comes the love,

Then comes the marriage,
Then comes the baby in the baby carriage.'

And, as a small child, she had been taken to the Mothers' Union where she had played at the feet of matronly ladies with elaborate hair, dressed in milky-white cotton. To her child's eye, they looked like a circle of wedding cakes: sculptured, moral, firm and ornate. But this, here, was almost a rabble of femininity.

'Mary Richardson? The Window Smasher? I simply don't believe it!' a woman exclaimed. 'I haven't seen you since Holloway Prison.'

'Daphne Brimble!' the woman Grace had been speaking to replied excitedly.

Grace glanced around. She had seen what large groups of people — of men — did during the war. And what had been done to them: how they returned — her brother Madoc included — with a disturbed sanity. And a destructive arrogance. She had seen the stupidity of groups and the fantasies they could concoct. Were these women aping men, being called to arms for yet more violence, triumphant and expanded on the fantasy of victory? She had read in the newspaper that Christabel Pankhurst had said the Great War was God's vengeance upon the people who held women in subjugation. But, as in the War, Grace had no passion for this fight. She didn't understand what the Suffragettes wanted. What was the Representation of the People Act? And what did 'universal suffrage' mean? It sounded like universal suffering and rage.

'Look, there's Mrs Garrud.' The woman with

74

the birthmark tapped Grace. 'If you're going to join the Cause, it's simply essential to learn Suffragettes' self-defence from Mrs Garrud. You can't imagine what brutes the police constabulary can be. Do join us for a lesson. Be at Highbury Corner at three o'clock on a Wednesday . . . ' The woman suddenly leaped up. 'Sit here. I'll be back.'

The hall was filling and Grace was squashed in her seat; the rows of chairs were cramped together and three Alexandra Nurses in uniform, who looked like sisters, were sitting to the other side of her. They were jolly, buoyed by hope and moral purpose.

'Have you read *A Doll's House*? It's a play by Henrik Ibsen,' one piped up.

'Christabel is pregnant,' another whispered.

'No, she isn't,' the other replied conspiratorially. 'She only thought she was. Wished she were. It was a phantom.'

Grace stopped listening, entering into that state of awake sleepiness she existed in since she had come to London. London — this meeting — didn't disturb her. It was the backdrop to her somnolence, like a fantastical bedroom in which she was sleeping. What I do to forget myself, she thought, and closed her eyes.

'You came; you read the pamphlet. I'm glad I've recruited at least one girl for the Cause,' said a young woman with auburn hair, walking elegantly in front of the stage. It was Lady Lytton from the Ritz. She squeezed politely along the line of chairs towards Grace and the three sisters attempted to make space for her.

'Yes, ma'am,' Grace replied. Did she have to play subservient, served and server, now they were no longer in the Ritz? Yes, she decided. Grace couldn't talk to Lady Lytton in the way that Lady Lytton would be free to talk to her.

'Haven't been anywhere this cramped since I went camping in Sissinghurst with Lord Baden-Powell's Girl Guides. Eleven of us in a four-man tent.' She straightened an unusual silver ring on her finger. Grace looked down at her own hands, once fair and fine, but already reddening and becoming chapped. Before, when the nearest she had come to work was collecting honey, she had worn her brother's protective leather gloves; now there were no barriers between her skin and her work. Her hands were changing her and putting her into a lower class.

'That's Mary 'Slasher' Richardson, the lady with the birthmark standing by the pillar,' Lady Lytton said conspiratorially. 'It was she who attacked the Rokeby *Venus* in the National Gallery, with a meat chopper just before the war. That must have taken some doing.' She took a rosette from her pocket and pinned it to her velvet lapel. 'It is a rather lovely painting — or was.' She straightened the long green, white and purple ribbons hanging from the rosette, then took a small sketchpad from her coat pocket and began quickly sketching the outline of the stage.

'Don't the banners on the stage look colourful?' she remarked. 'I know what you think — that this is only for rich women. So we may occupy ourselves with more than needlepoint or watercolours.'

Grace smiled non-committally. There was a pause. They sat quietly, side by side, as the pause became more charged until suddenly the young woman said, 'You remind me of her. My elder sister. She was quiet and fair, like you. And had blue eyes. Oh, the peculiar things grief does. I am even talking to you, speaking with you as if you were her, with the same ease,' she said, seemingly embarrassed by her sudden self-revelation. 'Really, I shouldn't talk to anyone about it.'

'Yes, ma'am,' said Grace.

'I had a sister,' the lady explained. 'She died. Sometimes women do — in the most awful circumstances. It's all very hush-hush — the circumstances, that is.'

'Yes, ma'am.'

Lady Lytton put her hands to the row of pearls at her neck. 'If my fiancé's mother knew, I doubt she would allow him to marry me. They're Catholic, too. It's so utterly dreadful at home these days, I escape to the Ritz to get away.' She sighed and batted her hand, as if to clear her mind of painful thoughts. 'Are you going to become a Suffragette?' she asked Grace abruptly.

'I don't know, ma'am.'

'I've been coming to the meetings since my sister died,' Lady Lytton said, resuming her sketching. 'I expect the vote is incidental, but something useful might come of it one day.'

A dignified woman in a huge hat walked determinedly onto the stage, hit a gavel on the lectern and stood square on, waiting for the room to hush. A frisson ran through the crowd.

Lady Lytton began sketching with purpose. Without introduction or any to-do, the woman began to speak:

'What lies in the future, no one can tell. The women's movement will go forward, as all other movements for human progress will go forward. No woman of today would go back if she could to the conditions her grandmother suffered. No matron would agree to put on her cap and retire from life at thirty-five.'

Grace began to listen.

* * *

Back in the dormitory at the Ritz, Grace took off her coat and put her feet on the dormitory bed despite still wearing her shoes. It was a small rebellion; perhaps it was because of the Suffragette meeting she'd been to earlier that afternoon, with all those independently minded women. Grace lay back and felt the warm ache of her exhausted body.

She adjusted her corset, which was tight but fitted and did the job. She could have loosened it, but didn't — kept it on, even at night. *One mustn't let oneself go*, the shop assistant had admonished. No, one mustn't. She tore a piece from the loaf of bread she was keeping in her bedside cabinet drawer, hard now because it had lasted her five days. She was hungry, but she wanted above all things to keep her figure. The corset helped keep her flat and shapeless.

Hilda burst in: 'The housekeeper wants to see you now. You're to wait in her office.' She tutted

78

excitedly. 'You must be in trouble.'

Grace got up, put on her cap and went down the shabby servants' stairs to the housekeeper's office, uncertain of why she was being summoned. But then she knew from her mother that it wasn't necessary to do something wrong to be in trouble. The office was empty and the door open so she stood and waited in front of the small, sharply-cornered desk. There was a rap on the open door. She turned.

There was her brother Madoc. Grace leaped forward and slammed the door, her heart racing. Fear rode over her like wild horses stampeding; she thought she might faint. There was another knock at the door. The key wasn't in the lock.

'Grace?' her brother said quietly, his voice reverberating on the wood of the door. Her hands shook uncontrollably as she tried to shift the bolt, banging the bolt handle of it with her fist. The bolt was stuck fast.

'Grace, really!' she heard her brother's voice. She stood back from the unlocked door. Why had he come? What did he want? How did he find her? What would he do?

'Grace, don't be silly. Open the door! What if that housekeeper comes? You'll be in real trouble then. And I've come all this way to find you.' She heard the force and impatience in his voice. '*Grace!*' He said her name as if he owned it. She didn't want to see him. She didn't want him to see her . . . she didn't want to be in the same room as him, the same city as him, the same country. What was he doing here? She had thought he was in Egypt. He must be on leave.

'I was right,' she heard him say triumphantly through the door. 'I knew you'd come to London.' She heard what sounded like Madoc leaning against the doorframe, the buttons of his military uniform knocking against the door. 'Because you liked *Peter Pan* as a child and wanted to go to Kensington Gardens.' Grace had forgotten that. 'You made me play Peter Pan with you.'

There was a pause and the irritated thrum of fingers on the wood. 'Then it was a matter of finding the places a Welsh girl would go. I tried the Eglwys Jewin Chapel yesterday but they hadn't heard of you, then the hotels, and you'd stayed in the Pembroke Lodging House for a few days a couple of months ago. They said you'd left to work here. You were easy to find among the London Welsh,' Madoc said. 'Mam says the apple never falls very far from the tree.'

Grace stood staring at the door.

'Come on, Grace. Open the door. Let me in. Is it locked?' And with that he turned the handle and opened the door.

'There we are, see? That wasn't so bad, was it?' Madoc punched her arm lightly, jokingly. 'What a hotel you're working in, sis! It's not like the Dragon Inn.' Then Madoc looked around the housekeeper's stark, functional room. If I had a cleaver, I would bring it down on him now, Grace thought. But then an unexpected rush of vulnerability came over her: a wave of homesickness for her father, even her mother, her home, her town — everything she had left.

'Lost your tongue?'

'No.'

'You're as cool as a stream up the mountain.'

Grace stood there formally, her hands folded in front of her, her soul somewhere else, just a broken casket decorated with polite responses and gestures, like an empty vase mishandled by a previous owner.

'Back from Egypt last week . . . stationed in London for six months. Come on, Grace, can't you do better than this? I've come from the barracks in Chelsea, taken two days' leave looking for you. Father told me to, he was worried you hadn't written — and all you do is stand there like some . . . I don't know what, and not saying anything. Look, I brought you this.' He took a pink wooden box from his knapsack: Turkish Delight. The moment Grace saw the sweets she knew she didn't want them. In her mind's eye she saw a knife smash down on the confectionery.

'You look well.' Madoc put his arm around her shoulder. 'Good to see you, sis.'

Grace was repelled. Was this his way of saying sorry?

He looked around the room, assessing it, dismissing it. 'I came earlier; the housekeeper said to come back at seven o'clock when you'd be back from your half-day.' He put the third finger of his left hand to his mouth, bit down hard on the skin and looked down at his shiny black boots.

'Sergeant now,' he said, tapping the three gold stripes on his uniform. 'For Highly Responsible Behaviour. Mam's pleased. And I'm engaged.' He smiled and looked at the floor. Grace

81

examined him, stared at him defiantly, daring him to do something, giving him a chance to confess. 'Girl called Dorothy,' he said weakly. 'Army's good to me. You're looking well.'

She threw a glance over him. Why wasn't he leaving?

'Glad it all turned out well. Wilfred went, I heard. Good riddance to bad stuff.' He was dallying. 'Chambermaid?' Grace nodded. He nodded back. The clock chimed on the mantelpiece.

'Let the dead bury the dead,' he said with the authenticity of a false priest offering an olive branch that promised no peace. 'Looks like you'll be here a few months. You coming back to Narberth?'

Grace said nothing, did nothing.

'As I said, good riddance to bad stuff.' He pursed his lips together and frowned. 'Mam's furious. She won't even speak your name. She doesn't know Father told me to look for you.' He looked around the room disinterestedly, arrogantly. 'I'll tell Father I've seen you. Grace — '
He held out his hand to shake but Grace didn't take it. He stamped his feet, saluted cockily instead, the metal half-moons on the heels of his boots clicking frantically on the bare floor so that the lampstand oscillated violently on the desk.

'I could always come again soon — now that I've found you.' He turned around and walked out with a swagger, putting his hand up to wave behind him. Grace stood there looking through the opened door into the emptiness. 'Take you for tea next time,' he called.

* ★ ★

It was her first afternoon off since Madoc had turned up. Grace looked around Mrs Garrud's drawing room while she waited for the Suffragettes' self-defence class to begin. The drawing room was on the first floor of an elegant townhouse in a square in Islington. She had arrived with Mary Richardson, whom she'd met at Highbury and Islington underground station. Grace was curious about the Suffragettes, if uncommitted.

Grace noticed the stuffed birds petrified in a glass cabinet — the jade and turquoise of a bird of paradise, the kingfisher's feathers caching the light, the nightingales on a brittle, dusty perch.

'One should never have a glass case of dead songbirds — they're ghastly,' Mrs Garrud, a tiny woman, said to Grace. 'I know you're thinking it. But they belonged to my late Mama and she would simply turn in her grave if they were auctioned at Sotheby's. Many people collect taxidermy to display in their drawing rooms, but that's not why I keep them; it's from fear of being haunted.'

'With your reputation I wouldn't have thought you were afraid of anything,' Lady Lytton remarked.

'Ah, but one can't practise jujutsu on ghosts. Only policemen — and those who show violence against our Cause,' Mrs Garrud retorted. 'You're from Wales, Miss Rice, and so am I. The Valleys. Is that a Pembrokeshire accent?'

Grace nodded. Mrs Garrud smiled.

'Now, prepare yourselves for the class, ladies. If one is going to join a war, one needs to fight. If one is going to be a Suffragette, one must practise jujutsu.'

The group of eight women undid their shoes and slipped out of them.

'Come next to me, Grace,' Lady Lytton offered, shaking out her auburn hair and retying it into a loose chignon. Grace didn't move. One woman unclipped her drop pearl earrings and placed them in a cloisonné bowl.

'Yes, do remove your jewels,' Mrs Garrud encouraged.

Mary Richardson shyly patted face powder on her birthmark.

'One shouldn't be self-conscious about these things,' she admitted to Lady Lytton and Grace, who was slowly untying her shoelaces. 'Mummy says beauty is on the inside, but I feel — '

'Notice,' Mrs Garrud interrupted — her small stature meant she had to look up at the attentive women — 'we practise Suffragette self-defence in our everyday clothes, as one is not arrested breaking expensive pane-glass, setting alight haystacks, or indeed attacking the Rokeby *Venus* in Mary's case, wearing the customary jujutsu uniform. I forgot to say: one must not practise jujutsu during the monthly menstruation. If any ladies are so incapacitated, do please make yourself comfortable on the ottoman, and watch closely.'

'I will sit out,' said Grace quickly, grateful for the chance to observe but not participate, and resting on a hardback chair next to the frozen birds.

'If one is already imprisoned for an illegal, but not immoral, act, one may well be wearing a prison suit. This makes jujutsu so very much easier than when wearing a corset with stays. Do wear a drop-waist frock, girls, if you are intending to take military action. I tell all my warriors this. And short hair is preferable. As many Suffragettes who have been arrested are aware, long hair makes us vulnerable. It can be grabbed and held in a way that cropped hair cannot.'

A sliver of memory came to Grace, of Madoc with a fistful of her hair, holding her rigid, her face pressed into the brown wallpaper. If she could have kicked backward, or elbowed back . . . but she had stood there meek as a lamb. Regret washed through her. She was still shocked that Madoc had appeared at the Ritz last week, appalled that he had found her. She had never wanted to see him again. And if she ever saw Madoc again . . . ?

'Ladies, place one foot forward, one foot back, hands up, head down, always ready for your opponent. If a police constable pushes you, you will be able to balance and he can't knock you over.' The women positioned themselves as Mrs Garrud directed.

'Miss Rice, ring the servant's bell on the wall by the ottoman, please. My maid will bring you a pot of tea and a slice of cake. She can be rather slatternly, I'm ashamed to say, but she comes upstairs eventually. Mary, demonstrate *tomoenage* — the stomach throw — on me please, if you would.'

Mary Richardson put her legs wide apart to an

85

unladylike degree. She focused; her birthmark turned a more intense cerise and made a deep seepage on her temple and cheek. Then she grabbed Mrs Garrud's collar, put her foot on the teacher's stomach, lay down on her back and threw the instructor over her head. It took only a moment. The crystals of the chandelier swung and Mrs Garrud stood up, unperturbed. Grace had no idea an adult woman could be so agile. She had thought flexibility and agility were passing phases owned and enjoyed by small children and adult acrobats.

'Ladies, practise the stomach throw in pairs, please. Remember, it takes knowledge, rather than strength. Even if we are, as Lady Penelope is, a painter, or like Mabel, a milliner, we can all achieve this move.'

Grace watched the women. If she could have chopped the air like these women were and hit out against Madoc and kicked her leg in that free, strong way into his well-fed, well-satisfied stomach . . . If she could have darted left and right, sure of each manoeuvre, and known the Art of War, as these women were taught it, she could have stood against the brown wallpaper in the landing at home and swerved and kicked and ultimately escaped. Madoc might have come back at her, but their parents would have been horrified by their son hitting their daughter. Grace would have been the exonerated victim rather than the whorish one who must now run and hide, while Madoc basked in the golden glow of his metal military buttons and his silver sergeant's stripes.

'Give the cake to Miss Rice, please,' Mrs Garrud told the maid. 'Hurry, we haven't got all day.' The maid stomped sullenly across the Arabian carpet, placing the silver tea tray on a cherrywood occasional table. Grace folded her hands, one over the other, so the maid wouldn't see that she had maids' hands too, and was a fraud in the house of the waited-upon.

While the maid poured her tea from the silver teapot, Grace watched Lady Lytton almost gracefully hold a woman in a head-lock and the other ladies leaping, throwing and landing, while the glass cabinet of dead birds quivered. The kingfisher, tied less securely to its golden branch, shook as if it might be alive.

'Goodness!' exclaimed Mrs Garrud, looking at the rattling piece of furniture.

These women could defend themselves, Grace thought.

'Do have at least a morsel of cake,' Mrs Garrud said to her. 'And relax, ladies. Jujutsu is not unlike ballet, only instead of trying to turn women into swans — a hugely pointless pursuit — it can turn women into warriors. And to build a better country, we *need* to be warriors. Is that not right, girls?' There was a round of applause from the ladies and Mary called, 'Bravo!'

These weren't merely words spoken in a meeting hall, or an X on a ballot sheet, Grace realised: this was the ability to kick back. This, more than anything, was the power she had wanted and hadn't known existed and couldn't have now: her body was too burdened to fight. But Grace was beginning to understand that women could have power — and not only like her mother, through the power of cruel words — but in her body and her mind, and maybe, if she could vote, in her town and her country.

'You haven't had one piece of pineapple upside-down cake, Grace. And you look so rapt. May I ask what you are thinking?' Lady Lytton asked kindly. Grace demurred and picked up a book lying nearby.

'I want you to practise these moves in your drawing rooms or lodgings every day for a quarter of an hour,' Mrs Garrud advised her pupils. 'The class is dismissed until next Wednesday. And let us remember as we go about our work, the Suffragette virtues of dignity, purity and hope.'

Grace noticed how the women stood taller and prouder as they dressed themselves after the lesson, as if they had more dimensions, their cheeks more colour, from learning to defend themselves. In Narberth, did women fight? These women in London were free in their bodies, not imprisoned by them. If she had stayed in Narberth she wouldn't have known about jujutsu. How contrary that she should find herself in this drawing room at a demonstration of how women could defend themselves, when she was less able to twist and jump and turn than ever before. When the battle was over and the victory won at her expense.

7

To Be More To Her
Than He Was

Under the gate, catch your sheep, bring it back, off jumps Jack. Flora Myffanwy remembered the knitting rhyme she had learned at school. She spread the stitches along the needle and counted them. It was a dark winter's day; the sunlight came thinly through the kitchen window but the fire in the hearth was flickering. The light in the room was beautiful. Suddenly she remembered she was expecting: each day, throughout the day, she had bright moments of remembering she was expecting a baby, and, as the days went by, the life inside her grew more precious and defined to her.

She knitted a row of garter stitch and looked around the scullery, noticing the smudges on the window, the spanners on the shelf, the knick-knacks in jam jars. It was clear to her that Wilfred and his da didn't know to cook, clean and keep house. It was said that cleanliness was next to Godliness, but Flora wasn't sure about that; she thought gentleness was next to Godliness, and cleanliness was next to respectability. Wilfred and his da had lived happily and warmly in their chaotic and perhaps none-too-clean kitchen, providing as much comfort as they

89

could for themselves, and making their slightly wobbly wattle and daub house into a home. And, recently, also a paint and wallpaper shop.

She purled twenty stitches: the needles Wilfred had made her were beautifully crafted in white oak and exceptionally smooth. It was true to say that when she had married Wilfred in the summer and first came to live at 11, Market Street she had been taken aback by the snail trails on the walls and the unaired rooms that smelled like old leather. There were odd tools on the floor and a spade in the kitchen sink. Wilfred had tidied the house especially, to the very best of his ability, for her arrival. She smiled, remembering Wilfred as he had shown her around, bashfully acknowledging that his earnest attempts were woefully short of anything that could be called acceptable housekeeping. Flora knew Wilfred had needed a wife.

Flora unwound more of the ball of string she was knitting with and laid the loose string across her lap. If she had married Albert . . . In her mind's eye she saw Albert run his hands through his hair and throw back his head, laughing. When the telegram came stating that Albert had died, Flora had been glad that they had made love, that they knew that of each other, and she had the memory of Albert experiencing that pleasure. She was still comforted by the thought they had loved fully together; and even if that intimacy had been so truncated, it remained their secret. When she was intimate with Wilfred she couldn't help feeling he seemed distracted, almost as if he was thinking about something else. But what else could he be thinking of?

She put her knitting down on the kitchen table for a moment. For these first months of her marriage, through the late summer, autumn and now winter, Flora had sat quietly like a guest, not knowing where her place was in this house she lived in. Nor had she made the kitchen her own. The house in Market Street felt unfamiliar compared to White Hook, the house she'd grown up in and still thought of as home. She felt like a visitor here, and wondered if this house would ever feel like her home.

She counted how many rows of the dishcloth she had knitted and untied a knot in the string. Flora thought how Wilfred and his da went out of their way to make her comfortable, brewing her cups of hot tea in the one china teacup with its chipped blue rim, and bringing her the dilapidated cushion if she sat in the armchair. She wondered if they wore more clothes around the house these days than they were used to — they weren't ones to stand on ceremony with each other — especially in the morning, thinking they must wear trousers, shirt and tie to eat breakfast in, a habit that showed signs of being new and strange to them. And every Sunday evening, after tea, Wilfred would say: 'My da has gone for a walk to Canesten Wood and won't be back for three hours, and I will be in the workshop and will not be coming inside the house until past eight o'clock, if you would like to take a bath in front of the hearth. You can have the water first. I know the importance of balneological habits.' And so Flora had bathed

quickly and surreptitiously, washing her hair
swiftly, rinsing it in tea to give it shine, then
stepping nimbly out of the zinc bath and
wrapping herself in the unbleached linen towel
she had brought from home, not because she
was ashamed or shy — she wasn't — but because
Wilfred and his da wouldn't have known what to
say or do if they had walked in and encroached
on her privacy. They lived in the house, the three
of them, but they didn't yet know how to live
together.

★   ★   ★

Wilfred stood in the Mozart Bakery waiting to
be served, savouring the warmth and the fresh
smell of bread. He gazed at the lumps of dough
on the shelf behind the counter, like a row of
bald, unmarked heads waiting to expand. Wilfred
had always been captivated by the Mozart
Bakery, especially when he was a boy and had
often missed having a mother, and when the
bakery had seemed to him like the land of milk
and honey.

This morning, customers were crowding
around the counter waiting for loaves, hot from
the oven. And there was a glass shelf laden with
rock cakes, lardy cakes, Chester cakes and
custard slices. And pastel-coloured cream cakes,
some with glacé cherries on the top, for very
special occasions. His wedding had been a very
special occasion though they hadn't celebrated
with cream cakes. Instead they had had a block
of boiled fruitcake that his Auntie Blodwen had

insisted on cooking, though each slice lay in one's stomach like a brick.

Thoughts of wedding cake unexpectedly reminded him of Grace. He hoped she was well and wondered where she was. She must have caught the train to Swansea, but not Cardiff, that was too far away and almost outside Wales. He hoped she was eating well and in good health. He had spotted that dreadful brother of hers, Madoc, in the Post Office the other day, back on leave.

'Morning, Wilfred,' said Mrs Willie the Post.

'Morning,' Wilfred replied, lifting his hat.

'I've come for an iced bun,' Mrs Willie the Post confided in a whisper. 'I've been on forty-five diets and none of them have worked.'

'After you, Mrs Probert,' Wilfred offered, seeing Mrs Probert and letting her stand in front of him in the queue.

'Thank you,' Mrs Probert replied in barely a whisper, keeping her head down, looking at the slate floor. She's a bag of nerves, Wilfred thought to himself. He noticed the dark arc around her eye, the bleary puffiness underneath it, and the scabs of dead black blood.

'I walked into the table,' Mrs Probert mumbled.

'Oh! There's nasty,' replied Wilfred. 'Have you seen Nurse Henton?'

'No, it's — '

'What can I do for you, Mrs Probert?' Mrs Cadwallader the baker called musically from behind the counter.

'Small cob loaf, please.'

Mrs Cadwallader had appeared not to notice

Mrs Probert's eye; she diplomatically served her in the usual matter-of-fact way. Mrs Cadwallader was a capable woman: she pounded the dough and sliced the bread with strength and confidence, all the while singing arias from operas. She was unlike Mrs Probert, who was slight, trembling, delicate, almost like a fragile bird whose bones could shatter. But women were like that. Wilfred had thought about this: men were like vegetables — big, strong, usually green — and by green he meant they were all the same colour, all quite similar. There wasn't much difference between men. But women were like fruit and came in all different and surprising sizes and shapes: soft fragrant strawberries, dark, velvety figs, squishy little blackberries, or strong round apples. Some were juicy plums, others big, bright oranges. Flora was like a beautiful ripe peach. The most delicious and . . . Wilfred struggled for words . . . the most beautifulest peach in Narberth, the First Prize-winner of the fruit and vegetable competition in the Bethesda Chapel summer fête. Now, Mrs Cadwallader was like a conference pear — full and curvaceous. But with men, if one was like a potato, his brother would be like a turnip and the other brother like a swede. There wasn't much difference.

'What are you having, Wilfred?' Mrs Cadwallader asked.

'Vegetable pastie, please.'

★　★　★

'There's busy you are knitting, dear,' said Wilfred, coming into the kitchen, followed by his da, and putting a greaseproof paper bag on the table. 'I've bought a pastie for a bite to eat. But come outside first and look at this cloud.' Flora followed Wilfred out into the cold back yard, where he pointed to the sky: 'That cloud looks like Jesus,' Wilfred stated. 'That one there, with the beard.'

'That one there?' Flora asked, looking at the jumble of clouds above them.

'No, that one there. Don't you think it looks like him, with a beard and a long white cloak?'

'It looks a little like a table.'

'And there was I, thinking it looked like Jesus . . . Come inside, my dear,' Wilfred said after a moment. 'I don't want you catching cold.'

'I think . . . ' broached Flora Myffanwy, sitting back down in the kitchen.

'Yes, dear?' said Wilfred eagerly.

'I would like to do all the baking here, instead of buying bread and pasties at the bakery.'

Wilfred da's looked down diplomatically at his shoes: there were obstacles to overcome.

'Certainly, dear,' said Wilfred, wondering how on earth anyone could bake properly in their scully but that was the thing he liked best about Flora Myffanwy: she was always saying unexpected things.

'I thought,' continued Flora in her quiet, dignified way, 'that I might clean the kitchen first.'

Wilfred and his da looked at her, astonished. The kitchen was as black as balls. Wilfred

95

couldn't imagine it properly clean, yet Flora seemed willing — and even more importantly, able, to bring order and cleanliness to 11, Market Street. This lovely elegant lady whom he was so proud to call his wife was of her own volition offering to clear the somewhat chaotic kitchen. What had he done to deserve this? He thought with guilt of Grace, who had tried so hard to please him when she was his wife. Grace, for whom he had cared so little. A fragment of memory came to him of how she touched him one night and how he had almost — *almost* — consummated the marriage.

'I could buy you an apron!' blurted Wilfred in an expression of gratitude to Flora as well as relief that he had not had conjugal relations with Grace, had been spared to have the life he now had. 'And a dustpan and brush.'

'Thank you,' Flora said gently.

'The dustpan and brush we have is not adequate,' Wilfred stated. 'On the admittedly rare occasions when I've used it, it's shed bristles and I have made more mess than I've tidied.' Wilfred smiled, then remembered that the dustpan had been brought to the house by his mother on her marriage, which was why it had not been replaced in the twenty-nine years since her death. His da could no more part with her rusted dustpan and brush with its struggle of bristles than he could part with his memories of her.

'Although we won't replace it,' said Wilfred quickly out of consideration for his da's feelings. 'We will buy a second dustpan and brush as well, so we have two. Is there anything else you need, dear? If there is, go straight to Mrs Annie Evans at the Conduit Stores and put it on the tab. Do you need . . . ?' But he was unable to think of cleaning tools his wife might require. 'The things that a housewife might need, you must get, dear. I know! How about a Whirlwind Suction Sweeper?' he suggested, not caring that the cost of such a modern machine was the same price as two funerals, eager to do anything that would help Flora make this house her home.

'I'll make a start soon,' said Flora in her clear way.

'You start whenever you want, dear, and it will be more than I deserve to have a clean scullery, but don't exert yourself now, not at all. You have to lie down the very moment you feel tired. You are not to be straining yourself. Nor to be lifting tins of paint or serving customers in the paint and wallpaper shop. Nothing is more important than you resting.'

Flora smiled. No, Wilfred thought, nothing was more important than Flora Myffanwy resting.

'Now Da, let me share this hot pastie with — That's the doorbell! Could be a customer — touch wood.'

Wilfred jumped up and walked purposefully through the hall and into the front room, which had been changed, with high hopes, into a somewhat sparse but proudly arranged paint and wallpaper shop.

'Mrs Newton-Lewis, good day to you.' Mrs Newton-Lewis had the cleanest doorstep in Narberth and subscribed to French magazines about house decoration. And Wilfred knew for a fact that she liked Paisley wallpaper.

'There's tidy you've made the front room. What did you do with your mother's best furniture?' Mrs Newton-Lewis asked.

'It's in the back room.'

'There's crowded it must be.' Wilfred's da had also pointed this out.

'Well, Wilfred, let me see . . . ' Mrs Newton-Lewis looked around the almost-bare shop with purpose. Mrs Estella Newton-Lewis was his first customer in five days: many curious people had bustled through in the last few months, but so far he had only sold the odd pot of paint. There was a poverty creeping throughout Pembrokeshire. He had heard that the miners at Stepaside were paid so meagrely these days, they had to scavenge for coal in the cliffs to heat their cottages. As yet, no one had bought very much but, as Mr Auden had taught him, life was one quarter enjoyable and three quarters difficult. Perhaps a paint and wallpaper business worked on similar proportions.

'I'd like my withdrawing room wallpapered,' Mrs Newton-Lewis declared. This was very encouraging. She browsed through the enormous Arthur Sanderson & Sons wallpaper book which the travelling wallpaper salesman had given Wilfred.

'I want to decorate the walls and the ceiling,' she continued. 'Can you do that for me?' Wilfred didn't have a clue how to wallpaper a ceiling; surely the wallpaper just fell off?

'Certainly, Mrs Newton-Lewis,' he replied hopefully. Wallpaper was always peeling off walls, never

98

mind ceilings. Perhaps there was some way he could nail it on.

'I knew as much,' Mrs Newton-Lewis declared. 'I said to Mrs Annie Evans, 'That Wilfred Price has no end of skills up his sleeve: undertaker,' I said, 'decorator.' I said, 'I'll buy my wallpaper here in Narberth instead of going to Ocky White's in Haverfordwest and Wilfred will be able to do the decorating as well'.'

'Thank you very much, Mrs Newton-Lewis.' When Wilfred opened the shop he'd put up a shelf for paint on the back wall, built a counter and bought a till. He'd expected he might occasionally be asked to paint the odd door or wall, but he hadn't thought of himself as a decorator.

'You'll need to somehow move my antique Welsh dresser to paper behind it. And I'd like it done by the day after tomorrow as my two sisters are coming from Llanddewi Velfrey. Can you finish it by then?'

'Oh, yes, indeed,' said Wilfred, praying that no one would die in the next few days.

'I considered having a Paisley in a fuchsia and yellow, but I have changed my mind. I am thinking of the *Tulip and Willow* by William Morris.' She turned a large page in the wallpaper book. 'Or perhaps the *Cornucopia?*'

'We have plenty of rolls in stock of this one in bice-blue and biliverdin,' said Wilfred, unsure if he'd used his new *B* words correctly, and showing Mrs Newton-Lewis a large sunflower print with a blue background.

'There's lovely. There's posh. Yes, I'll take it.

99

Yes.' Mrs Newton-Lewis smoothed the matt wallpaper appreciatively. 'I expect you learned to decorate when you were an apprentice.'

Wilfred had learned nothing of the sort during his four-year apprenticeship with Mr Ogmore Auden of *O. Auden, Wheelwrights & Cabinet Makers of Whitland*.

'Are you thinking of painting the skirting-boards?' he asked, by way of a diversion.

'Thank you for reminding me. I like a clean, fresh skirting-board. I was thinking of a Van Dyke Brown. And how many rolls of wallpaper will I need, Wilfred?'

'I'll work that out for you, Mrs Newton-Lewis.'

'I would say ten.'

'Yes, I agree,' said Wilfred with no basis at all for agreement.

'Do you gloss-paint front doors? If you do, I can tell the ladies in Narberth Lest We Forget Society, while we are knitting for those poor soldiers so afflicted by the War.' Mrs Newton-Lewis knew everyone, saw everything and told everybody. 'And I expect you lime-wash the outside of houses as well. Do you do that, Wilfred?'

'These things are possible,' replied Wilfred non-committally.

'I know Mrs Roberts wants the whole house decorated.'

Mrs Roberts lived in the big house at the top of the High Street. Wilfred swallowed.

'I'll tell her at chapel all about your book of wallpapers, and that you know how to decorate properly. I suggested to her to paint the outside russet or a cinnabar, so I expect you'll have to dye the lime-wash with rowan berries.'

He was an undertaker, not a painter. Honey hell — he was radical wrong if he thought he knew how to decorate! Mind, Wilfred thought to himself, it was work and it was money and would help replace his savings. And he didn't want to be a lazy Herbert. There could be no vanity to it — he was going to be a father and he must provide for his family.

So he replied: 'You tell the lovely ladies of the Narberth Lest We Forget Society, Mrs Newton-Lewis, and I'll be glad for the work.'

★ ★ ★

Several weeks later, Flora walked down the frost-bitten lane past St Andrew's Church, where the blackberries grew in a tangle, searching for a view of the valley to photograph. She wanted to take photographs of the hills around Narberth before the baby was born, while she still had time on her hands, and because today she wanted to take her mind from what was worrying her. She would have liked some company. Wilfred was always ready to talk to her, and he showed her so much affection that Flora wondered if sometimes he held back from fear that he would overwhelm her with his ardour — but today he was visiting a miner in Providence Hill who claimed he'd seen the Grim Reaper and wanted to arrange his funeral.

Flora spotted a woman ahead walking

nervously, almost scared to put her feet on the frozen earth. They met at the stile and the woman waited, offering a chapped white hand as Flora climbed carefully over. As the woman looked up at her, their eyes met. Flora saw — or rather the woman showed her, with a look almost of defiance — her cheek and eye, witness to the violence and force that had created the bruised colours.

The two women walked alongside the drystone wall, stepping over hummocks of frosted grass. The field was dotted with Welsh Black cows.

'You're Wilfred Price's wife, aren't you?' the woman said.

Flora nodded.

'I'm Phyllis Probert.'

Wilfred had mentioned Mr Probert to Flora and she knew he worked in the Dragon Inn. Flora wanted to reach out to this woman, to make a friend in Narberth, but didn't quite know how. She was aware that the other women in Narberth treated her with some distance and a little suspicion. She wasn't from Narberth or even Templeton, she was from Pleasant Valley in Stepaside and from a different family with different ancestors, and they knew instinctively that she wasn't one of them. She had married their much-respected undertaker who would have been a catch among the Narberth ladies, with his good looks, integrity and his warm, friendly jokes. He had a good business and he didn't drink. And he didn't hit her. Wilfred had once been, no doubt, the pinnacle of many women's romantic dreams in Narberth — all of

102

them, she imagined, dashed when she emerged, as if out of nowhere, as his wife.

The two women followed the path towards the next field.

'Is it due around the spring?' Mrs Probert asked. 'That's when Lady Elizabeth Bowes-Lyon is having her baby.'

'Yes.' Flora wrapped her scarf around her neck. 'Sometimes that feels a long way away, and sometimes it feels soon,' she admitted, hinting at what was on her mind and beginning to concern her. Flora had talked very little about the baby to anyone except Wilfred. And every time she mentioned the baby to him, he immediately talked about the paint and wallpaper shop. The wind blew and Flora brushed her hair from her face.

'It's your first, isn't it?' the woman said to Flora. 'That's why you're scared.'

Flora noticed that the woman's other eye was stretched with very fine lines and seemed to move slowly, almost tiredly. The woman said something, almost shy to reveal an aspect of herself in return.

'Pardon?' Flora couldn't hear her words above the wind, but understood that the woman was pulled taut with violence and poverty. She and Wilfred had a smoother life: it seemed they had enough money — certainly every Wednesday when she bicycled to visit White Hook, he gave her a one-pound note to give to her mother. Although Wilfred didn't tell her the details, she didn't think they were poor, but if they were, she imagined Wilfred would keep it from her to spare her the worry.

'I walk around Narberth every day,' Mrs Probert repeated, 'when Mr Probert is at the Dragon Inn.'

'It's a beautiful walk, even in the winter,' Flora stated. They walked silently together, unable to talk easily above the blustering of the wind, until they reached the further field.

'I'm going to stay here and take a photograph of the valley,' Flora said.

'I'm going to keep walking,' Mrs Probert replied quietly, but with determination. 'I want to be strong enough to walk around Narberth three times: I have a plan.' She didn't explain any further.

Flora smiled, intrigued, saying, 'Then perhaps we will meet around Narberth again.'

'I expect we will.'

'If you would like to come for a cup of tea one afternoon at eleven, Market Street?' Flora Myffanwy offered. She had been lonely in Narberth and wanted for female company. This woman's life was different in some ways from her own, since Mr Probert worked in a public house, while Wilfred had his own business, and that might mean it would be unusual for Mrs Probert to pay a visit. But they had shared confidences, and that was the essence of female friendship: trust in which one could reveal oneself. She liked this bird-like woman with her bad nerves and her flintiness. And the house would soon be looking clean enough to receive visitors.

Mrs Probert thanked her, pulling her thin, loose coat around her.

'Wait,' Flora said on an impulse. 'Would you

like this?' She put her hand in her handbag and brought out a small gold-coloured tube.

'Lipstick?' Mrs Probert asked. 'I have no need of lipstick.' Flora saw she was ashamed of her face.

'Take it; I want you to have it.'

Mrs Probert blushed, accepting the gift.

★   ★   ★

The trees along the dawn-lit lanes were leafless and the air pristine with cold as Wilfred drove them to Wiseman's Bridge. They had taken to going for a drive every Saturday morning of their married life. That morning, Flora had woken before first light, unable to sleep. Wilfred had asked if she would rouse him, and she waited until twenty past six to put her hand on the strong, relaxed muscles of his upper arm and whisper his name. He woke quickly — like a man who had much to live for — and they had both washed by splashing cold water from the bowl they filled from the jug. Flora put on her dark green wool dress, on which she had let out the waist, her cardigan and wool coat, Wilfred wore his Oxford bags, a red tie, his tweed jacket and an overcoat, and they left before breakfasting so as to return in time for Wilfred to open the wallpaper shop at ten o'clock, though customers were few and far between.

Flora looked out of the automobile window and put her hands further into her muff. The bare shells of cow parsley, large as a child's head, swept against the side of the hearse. She

105

remembered how green the land had been in the summer. Now the hedgerows were lined with fractured sticks of bracken, but the land still held its beauty despite the change of season. There was something she should tell Wilfred, but she didn't yet know how to say it.

'You're looking fetching today, and very fresh-faced, my dear,' Wilfred commented, taking her hand. 'You're not wearing your lipstick.'

'I gave it to Mrs Probert.'

'There's kind of you. That Mr Probert — *ach-y-fi*. He's too spifflicated on beer for my liking.'

'You're not wearing your undertaker's suit,' Flora replied, attempting to make the conversation more comfortable.

'Indeed I'm not. But I'm still an undertaker,' he stated. Wilfred rubbed the black stubble on his chin the way he did when he was thinking. She glanced at Wilfred as he drove, wondering about him. Being married to Wilfred meant watching him do that several times a day for the rest of her life. As well as seeing that resigned, slightly sad and wistful smile he had when he didn't know the answer. And falling asleep to the smell of his hair oil. It meant dead bodies in the workshop waiting to be buried. And it meant new life. It meant that too, she hoped. He was becoming more familiar to her, much less of a stranger, though she had still only known him less than a year. She felt curious about him.

'I watch you about at your work, but I still don't know very much about what you do,' she admitted. Wilfred was so alive, with his flushed face, purposeful movements, strong body and striding walk, she didn't think of him surrounded by the dead. He had buried her father — that was how they had met, after all — but she had only seen him driving the hearse and directing the funeral. Wilfred, she now realised, had made her father's death elegant and ordered, and it had occurred to her recently that death — what the undertaker saw — wasn't necessarily always neat.

'People in Narberth die,' Wilfred answered, changing gear. 'I make their coffin. Sometimes I bring them to my workshop where I look after them. Then I drive them to chapel, carry them to their grave and I speak kindly to their devastated loved ones. And then, my dear, the bald fact of the matter is I charge them five pounds.'

Silvery seagulls flew above them in the empty sky.

'I'm grateful for the business,' he added. 'And for the decorating work from Mrs Newton-Lewis.'

Flora Myffanwy touched her wedding ring. She understood. When her father had died, Flora and her mother had little income to speak of. A man needed a job so his family would have enough money, especially in times such as these. A man did what he needed to do to care for his family.

'I must consider my da, and now you, of course, my dear,' Wilfred said, echoing her thoughts and placing his hand over hers, 'before I can think of whether I want to have a dead person sitting on a mahogany chair in the boiling heat under the glass roof of the workshop.'

Flora nodded: the unspoken had been spoken.

'Before I met you,' she said, her voice slightly tinged with anxiety, 'all I knew about death was the shiny hearse, the black clothes and the devastation.'

'That's enough for any human being,' Wilfred replied.

Fear came over Flora. She was holding something to herself that she didn't understand but couldn't ignore. She looked out of the window towards the dark, striated cliff-faces that framed Wiseman's Bridge, wanting to distract herself from her thoughts.

'Wilfred, would you like me to help in the business?'

'No, Flora Myffanwy,' Wilfred said with certainty. 'It's not a business for a woman. When one is an undertaker, such as I am, one is surrounded by people who feel anything but joy and happiness. That is not for you, Flora. Take photographs with your camera. Be as you are, and be my wife.'

★ ★ ★

They drove in silence down the hill past the cottage in the cove where they had first met. Flora remembered how she had tidied and cleaned the derelict house, putting a vase of flowers on the chair with three legs, and waiting in anticipation for Wilfred to arrive on Saturday afternoons.

In the distance the mumbling waves made white curves along the bay and the air was full of the freshness of the sea.

'Right, my dear,' declared Wilfred, pulling over on the road. 'Let me give you a driving lesson. You'll only need the one. I know you told me you wanted to learn to drive, and you won't be able to bicycle to your mother's for much longer.'

Flora wanted to drive, although she realised she had come to like her place in the motor car, in the front, next to Wilfred; it was rather like her place in his life — going forward together. But she liked to be independent, too.

Wilfred stepped out of the hearse and opened the passenger door for Flora.

'Come and sit in the driver's seat. Is there enough space between you and the steering wheel?'

'Yes,' said Flora, smoothing her coat over her rounded stomach, glad to have something to do and focus on.

'There's no need for you to look anxious, dear. Being bimanous makes driving much easier. The controls are the accelerator, brakes, clutch, or A. B. C., as I like to think of it. It is alphabetised. The engine's ticking so press your foot down on the accelerator pedal and, that's right, move away from the hedgerow — well done, my dear,' encouraged Wilfred, one hand guiding the steering wheel. 'The whole point of driving is not to hit anything,' he stated. 'Mr Auden told me that and it seems true enough.'

'How do I change gear?' Flora asked, looking down at the gear-stick.

'Don't worry about that, I'll do it for you.'

109

The car edged forward then began to pick up speed. Driving was easier than Flora expected and she liked the feeling of power and speed she sensed the motor car could give her.

'Well done. The hearse is nifty,' Wilfred explained as Flora drove carefully along the road, 'not that it ever needs to be, of course. But in the unlikely event of my being late for a funeral,' he continued, 'the Super Ford hearse is capable of speeds of thirty miles per hour — a great pace. Of course, I have never gone thirty miles per hour. Fifteen for when there is a body in the back, twenty miles per hour without a corpse. But did you know the Packard Eight Coupé automobile goes at almost aircraft speed in the open? I read it in an advertisement in *The Light Car and Cyclecar Magazine*.'

Flora felt a sense of exhilaration as the car gathered momentum: she liked driving and was taking to it immediately. It was like cycling, only freer.

'Now, let's do a spot of reversing,' Wilfred suggested. 'Then you can pass your driving test. Police Constable Jones will watch you drive forward and backwards six yards so he knows you're safe on the roads and will give you a driving licence.'

Flora reversed backwards confidently, looking over her shoulder.

'Wonderful! The eel's eyebrows,' Wilfred remarked. 'I'll ask Constable Jones to watch you drive tomorrow' — Wilfred bibbed the horn — 'then the world will be your oyster!'

After the driving lesson, Flora, under Wilfred's instructions, parked the car and they clambered down the smooth brown boulders into the cove. He surveyed the cove and was exact in his search.

'I'm looking for a rock that is at the right slant.' He took a large step across the gap between two boulders, looked down, and hummed. Then he remembered his wife standing behind him.

'Oh, my dear.' He walked back and offered his hand. 'This rock is the ideal angle.' He unbuckled the Welsh blanket from its leather holder, spread it out and lay down, despite the cold.

'This is the life, dear. I'm just watching those bilateral seagulls,' he announced, keen to use his new *B* word. After a moment, he sat up again. 'I think I'll put my bathers on,' he said, picking up a small towel. Then followed what he felt was an enormously inelegant palaver involving the small towel, trousers and eventually a sleeveless woollen one-piece his Auntie Blodwen had knitted for him.

'I'll be over there, having a swim.'

Flora smiled, wrapped the red blanket around her and then took out her Box Brownie camera, the ball bearings in the shutter rattling.

'I'll take care,' he reassured her, remembering how, before they were married he'd taken Flora out at low tide to see the petrified forest and how she had nearly drowned when the tide had come in unexpectedly.

Wilfred jumped athletically from the rocks onto the hard sand, running confidently — and self-consciously — towards the murmuring sea. If he was going to brave the water, he'd better look comfortable about it. It would be cold. He could still go back and sit on the rock. But he didn't want to appear so lily-livered that Flora might think he couldn't fart in a colander. He turned to see the figure of Flora on the rocks. He waved. His wife would want an athlete, a man in fine fettle, fit as a fiddle, a man who could master the elements. He sprinted towards the sea in the hope that, at such a distance, Flora wouldn't notice the slight wobble of his stomach.

Wilfred bounded over a band of razor shells and seaweed that crushed and prickled against his feet, then through the shallowest waves. Honey hell, it was cold! White spray frothed up about him and he breathed in sharply. A wave lolled and slapped his chest. It was astonishingly cold. There were no words in the *A* and *B* section of the dictionary to describe it.

He glanced back to see if Flora was watching. She was. She was taking a photograph. He dived into the sea and swam a brisk breaststroke in the direction of Laugharne, many miles away. He bobbed over the waves as they came towards him like rolling hills of water, then he broke into a crawl and very much hoped Flora was watching him now. It was important to prove oneself to be a man of vigour and energy — and to be noticed as such by one's own wife. He flipped into a backstroke. Perhaps he was reminding his wife of that chap, Johnny Weissmuller, who'd won three Gold Medals in the Olympic Games in Paris last year.

Well, he thought, as he cut the water with the fingers of his right hand in an elegant over-arm motion, Flora Myffanwy must *surely* be impressed by this. The water was agonisingly cold and there was no one else in the sea, only a few Jack-the-lads at the sea's edge, skimming stones. And Wilfred needed her to be impressed, especially as he struggled so much during the intimate moments of their marriage to keep his thoughts on the prime minister, something that deeply dented his sense of himself as a man. True it was that his wife was beautiful, and such womanliness would test even the willpower of a prophet. But Wilfred had to do better on a Saturday night: it wasn't good enough to spend the whole time thinking about Stanley Baldwin. Good grief! He probably thought about Stanley Baldwin more than the most ardent Conservative supporter. What with him picturing the prime minister, and Flora lying there calmly, as was her wont — perhaps a little more calmly and more disengaged than he would like, a spot of rugged swimming in the wild Welsh winter sea — indeed, the sea that had almost killed them on that fateful day before they were married — was bound to be impressive.

He was married to Flora, but he wanted to be more to her than he was. He wanted to take away the sadness that pulled at her — the grief for her father was what he knew it to be — the longing in her eyes for a fuller, more promising world. Wilfred began swimming towards the shore. He must be within himself more of a man for this woman — his wife — in order to be worthy of her.

Once back on the rock, dressed, shivering and chilled to the bone, he ate a thick piece of cold omelette that Flora had made at home and waited while she photographed some scallop shells she had found and arranged on the sand. He hoped it was the time for her to say what she always said on a Saturday morning.

'Shall you tell me to tell you something?' Wilfred prompted Flora, waiting for her gentle invitation. He knew what to expect now, and this week, for the first time, he had thought about it in the workshop while sawing through beech-wood and throwing golden dust into the air that rose as if it were full of yeast. He could explain how he had been wondering if he had been dead for thousands of years before he was born, or talk about when Mrs Christabel Pankhurst had spoken in Narberth High Street. Should he say more about his marriage to Grace? They had spoken about it only once and there were things he should perhaps reveal to her that were weighing on his mind, but he didn't want to spoil their outing. Instead he would tell her the story of when he was a schoolboy and a travelling harpist who had won the Eisteddfod played Johann Sebastian Bach in Market Square and —

'Can I tell you something?' Flora asked. 'Shall I be the one to tell you something?'

'Oh. Yes, my dear. Certainly.'

'Something is wrong,' Flora said unexpectedly, and as quietly as if she was praying. Wilfred looked at her. She had that unbridled look in her brown eyes. Her eyes saw deeply and clearly and there was no lie in her. This is what made Wilfred love her and made him almost — despite her being his wife — frightened by her. So much truth held enormous power. Sometimes he looked at her and felt like a puppy looking at a cathedral.

'My dear?'

'I feel as if I'm dying.'

'But you can't be dying, dear. You are only twenty-eight. And you're expecting. You look the picture of health.' Wilfred put his hand to her cheek. 'Red cheeks, shiny brown hair: bright-eyed and bushy-tailed you are, Flora, my dear. No, no, no. Now, there's nothing for you to worry about. You're in the pink. And the wind has given you a colour today.' Wilfred put his hand to his collar and moved his tie knot from left to right, and a fear colder than the sea rippled up inside him. 'No, dear. I know what the dying look like from those who come to see me in their last days to pay their funeral bill in advance, and you don't look like one of them.'

8

Newfangled Things

'Malcolm,' announced Wilfred.

'Malcolm?' asked Flora.

'Yes, dear. I was thinking of Malcolm. For a name.' He helped Flora onto her bicycle so that she could cycle to visit her mother. 'One more quick lesson in the hearse,' he added, 'and then you'll be able to motor to your mother's.'

'What made you think of Malcolm?'

'Well, it's such a modern name, so very dynamic. It reminds me of all these newfangled things like the bread-toaster machine, Wembley Stadium, vitamin pills, even televisual transmissions. I could imagine a boy called Malcolm making his own motor car from a kit, or a wireless,' Wilfred put his hands on his hips, 'or even his own aeroplane, like Bill Frost, the fly-boy from Saundersfoot. Malcolm is a name for a man living in modern times, one born in 1926, don't you think, dear?' He lifted Flora's bag for her, slipped a folded pound note into it for her mother and put the bag in the basket on the handlebars.

'Wouldn't you like something Welsh, like Ieuan or Aubrey?' Flora suggested, putting her foot on the pedal. 'Or we could call him Wilfred.'

'After me? Another Wilfred Price?'

'Or perhaps Malcolm Wilfred Price.'

'You can choose,' Wilfred offered. 'That is only right.'

'Wilfred,' Flora Myffanwy said, about to set off on her bicycle, 'we will decide together.'

As he watched Flora bicycle away, making an effort to pedal, Grace came to his mind. He understood now, from watching Flora, that Grace had been more vulnerable than he had comprehended. Where had she gone? Was she well? He turned, unable to answer the questions that weighed more heavily on his conscience, and went into his workshop. He had work to do. He must make a pillow for Mr Carr from Cold Blow this afternoon.

Wilfred sat down on a stool in his workshop and unwrapped from a starched tea towel the pastie Flora had made for him. He put his ankle on his knee and bit through the crust arcing around his pastie and into the mush of vegetables and potato paste. By damn, it was tasty. That was the thing he liked best about Flora, she was wonderful at making vegetable pasties.

Wilfred looked across at Mr Carr, who was lying in his coffin, waiting.

'Just finish my pastie, Mr Carr, and I'll be with you now in a minute.'

Mr Carr's family was upset at his death, but not particularly so. There was nothing like a funeral for revealing how loved someone was. When he was an apprentice he'd helped Mr Auden bury a man who worked in the Tax Office in Carmarthen. 'He will not be missed,' Mr Auden had said.

'Right, Mr Carr, I'll start making a pillow for

you,' Wilfred announced, setting to work. 'A pillow will make you look a bit less red and drain that blood from your face. I always use shredded newspaper in a white cotton slip for the pillow. It's cheap as chips.'

He found some scissors amidst the tools on the workbench and picked up some old copies of *Narberth News*. Wilfred knew that when the deceased had been cherished, the days between a death and a funeral were a time of shock. And busy-ness. Visitors calling in on the bereaved, conversations demanded, sometimes even needing to make a telephone call, death notices to send, the black crêpe clothes to be washed and pressed, the drapes to be drawn, the furniture to be covered.

Wilfred stuffed some shredded newspaper into the pillowslip, then brushed some dust and paper from his thighs. People in shock said, 'I can't believe it.' Wilfred frequently heard his customers telling him, 'I can't believe it for the life of me.' That's what they said. 'Only yesterday he was sitting there, right as rain, talking away, reading the *Narberth & Whitland Observer* and today he's . . . ' and then came one of those gentle words the shocked used in their grief to describe death: 'asleep', 'with the good Lord', or 'in greener pastures'. Sometimes they said, 'The bugger was in a bad way, but we didn't think it would come to this.' Even if the person had been at death's door, rattling away for weeks, the bereaved were still shocked. No one, it seemed, believed in the mortality of their loved ones, not even when their loved ones were dead. So shock

118

was useful. Shock stopped the bereaved from understanding that the deceased had not actually fallen asleep, as a lot of them liked to believe — if only it were that simple — but was dead. Otherwise, Wilfred would be rushed off his feet. Say a farmer died, his wife might pop her clogs the moment she heard, then the son would do something silly, and the daughter would have a heart attack. That would be three more funerals. And so it would go on. While shock was a dreadful stress on the kidneys, and could make people do peculiar things and even lose their mind, it was because of shock that Wilfred wasn't overrun with work. People had a lot to be thankful for to shock: it gave the bereaved a week or so of grace. And there was no one who died in Narberth who hadn't been buried by people in shock.

★　★　★

'Made a nice pillow for Mr Carr,' Wilfred announced, coming into the kitchen from the workshop late that night. 'He's more comfortable now.'

'That Stanley Baldwin — no use to man nor beast,' replied Wilfred's da, folding the *Daily Graphic* in half and dropping it on the table with a flat plop. 'What's he ever done for anyone? That's what I'd like to know. Tell me, Wilfred, what's that Stanley Baldwin done for anyone?'

'Well . . . ' said Wilfred, picking up the paper and putting it to the side.

'It says there — look!' said his da, pointing at

the headline. *MINERS' WAGE DEADLOCK*. His da sighed with resignation and lifted his hands as if dealing with a madman. 'If you can tell me one thing that Mr Stanley Baldwin has done for this country, I'll eat my hat,' and with that his da stood up, confident in his own judgement.

'What are you reading, Wilfred?' his da then asked, putting on his greatcoat and tying some twill round his waist.

Wilfred crossed his legs and sighed. 'Very important book, like.'

'Not that ruddy dictionary,' his da protested. 'Where's my spade . . . ?' He looked around, unable to find it.

'Flora has taken it out of the sink and put it inside the workshop.'

'The workshop?' repeated Wilfred's da, puzzled. 'I'm digging down by James James's grave tonight. The soil is soft there.'

'Like James James,' said Wilfred, looking out of the window at the starless sky and thinking about going to bed. 'Dark it is, tonight. Back before dawn, Da?'

'Ai, back at four.'

'Keep your kidneys warm, now,' said Wilfred, in an inversion of their father and son relationship: something that was happening more these days. His da was not old, Wilfred thought to himself, was not infirm, was not . . . something Wilfred didn't want to put into words yet. 'Keep your greatcoat on. And done up,' he added redundantly.

Suddenly there was a sharp bang on the front door.

'Price! Where are you?' There was a kick as the front door burst open. 'You dirty bugger. *PRICE!*'

Wilfred glanced at his da, who was holding onto the back of a chair, his eyes wide with alarm.

'Price. *Come here.*' There was the sound of heavy boots on the hall flagstones, the hobnails in the boot-soles catching against the stones. '*Pr-ice!*' the voice bellowed. There was a thump on the front-room door, then the boom of a hip and shoulder forced against the wood.

Where was Flora Myffanwy? Wilfred thought in a flash. Upstairs. She had gone to bed earlier on. His father was next to him, transfixed, unbelieving. There was another boom as the door was pushed and buckled, then the panicky sound of paint tins responding.

'Get back, Da. Who is it?' Wilfred called, walking towards the hall. He went through the door to the paint and wallpaper shop and a man lunged at him. The two men spun in a clinch across the shop into the back wall, hitting a framed tapestry. It slipped to the side of the nail, hung for a moment and then the glass fell out and smashed.

The man grabbed Wilfred's shoulders and slammed him against the wall. Wilfred's head hit the bricks with force though he held his neck taut. The man lifted his fist over his head to strike Wilfred, spitting and swearing beerily with the effort of his anger. Wilfred dodged, charged into him, tried to wrestle him to the floor. But the man — it was Probert from the Dragon Inn

— was beefier than Wilfred, and nastier, and stood his ground so that instead, they hit the paint shelf. Tins fell heavily and there was the pop of a lid coming off.

Wilfred needed something for a weapon but could only see paintbrushes. He glimpsed his da hiding at the door: a frail, frightened older gentleman who was small next to this flaming, snorting man who had burst so violently into the peace of his family home. Wilfred saw red. He grabbed the man's overalls, shoved him backwards then forwards, leaned down and brought the man's face down onto the crown of his head. Probert stumbled back heavily towards the shop window, blood spluttering from his nostrils. Pots of miniature roses Flora had placed in the windowsill toppled over, the earth spilling on the floor.

The man let out a guttural bellow and charged towards Wilfred. He struck his palm under Wilfred's chin; Wilfred's head whip-lashed back with a snap. Probert clamped his whole hand over Wilfred's face, his stubby fingers dragging down Wilfred's eyelids. With all the might Wilfred could muster he punched him hard and fast in the stomach. *Umph* — the air pumped out of Probert with a deep, almost animal sound. Wilfred took his fist back past his hip and slammed it into the man's stomach again. The man was winded for a long moment, air seeming neither to enter nor leave him. He collapsed to his knees. Wilfred looked down dizzily at the man who was doubled over at his feet, gasping for air and coughing.

122

The man rubbed his eyes. 'You gave my wife lipstick, Wilfred Price,' he panted. 'You made a whore of her.' He spat. 'Now she's too proud to take a beating silent. You deal with the dead. Leave the living alone.'

Lipstick? Wilfred didn't understand. He looked down at the man and felt contempt. He wanted to kick him. The bully, he thought. Then he remembered.

'My *wife*, Probert. It was my wife who gave your poor wife a lipstick because that's what she deserves — some friendship and some kindness. God knows she gets scant enough kindness from you. Now get out of my house. Go on. And don't come back here again.'

'I'm going. But you'll be sorry.' Probert stood up, swaying from side to side, his hands on his thighs, his head down.

'It's good to see you bowed, Probert,' Wilfred said. Probert shuffled out of the door, holding his hand to the architrave to balance himself — the same door he had so recently been rageful enough to try and break through. Probert stumbled up the road in the dark, stiff-legged and panting audibly.

Wilfred put his arm around his da's shoulder and his da patted him on the back. 'Well done, son.'

'I thought of you and Flora and I thought of his poor scrap of a wife and I knew I was going to have him,' Wilfred said, more confident in the telling than he had felt in the moment. He was shocked at the speed of the intrusion, and the violence of the attack. He noticed that some

123

buttons on his shirt were ripped and a line of thick blood was running from his nose. The soles of his shoes were covered in paint.

'You punched him good and hard; I didn't know you had it in you.'

'Oh, I had it in me, Da.' Wilfred put his hands on his hips and felt the power and strength in his body. He wiped some blood from his nose. 'I'm like a bloodnosed beetle,' he added, attempting a joke.

'I thought he was going to bite you. *Ach-y-fi.* He's as stubborn as a pig of iron,' his da stated.

'There's not much I'd put past that man,' Wilfred said, 'not if he hits a woman.'

★ ★ ★

Wilfred walked through to the paint and wallpaper shop and looked around. A tin of Rudman's Old Gold had fallen open and spilled. There were golden footsteps all over the floorboards so that the floor looked like a follow-the-footsteps diagram for a frantic Foxtrot or a Quickstep. The shelf was broken, the round table lay on its side, and the Arthur Sanderson & Sons catalogue had a gold footprint over the words *Purveyors of Wallpapers and Paints to King George V.* Many things in his shop had fallen apart, were split, cracked and broken. He picked up the table and set it on its feet, then righted the tin of open paint.

On the wall, the tapestry his mother had made before he was born was hanging askew with a jaggedy crack in the remaining glass. He took it

124

from the nail: *Yy Arglwydd yw fy mugail.*
Blessed Are the Pure in Heart. He must put
some new glass in the frame to protect his
mother's careful handiwork from wear and tear.

Probert had broken in like a dark angel and
wrestled so suddenly and violently with him, it
was like a dream. Wilfred had never fought
before, although he had once hit a boy at school
who had pointed out, honestly but unnecessarily,
that he didn't have a mam. 'Wilfred Price got no
mam,' the boy chanted. Wilfred, unexpectedly,
had punched him squarely in the stomach,
winding him, and the boy had never said it
again. At the time Wilfred had surprised himself
with his response, but it was not surprising to
him now. It was an intolerable burden for a small
child to live without a mother, and he felt her
absence bitterly. Everyone should have a mother,
Wilfred thought. Everyone should have someone
who only sees their innocence.

Wilfred picked up a dented paint tin and read
the label:

> *To beautify unsightly walls.*
> *To cover soiled wallpapers.*

Wilfred sighed. His shop had had few customers.
He had wallpapered Mrs Newton-Lewis's
drawing-room and earned a small amount of
money, but not nearly enough to replace his
savings, the cost of the paint and wallpaper, and
to provide for a child in the way a good father
should.

The two china dogs Flora had put above the

125

fireplace were still intact. She had bought them to photograph alongside some flowers for a still life — and because she liked them. Only a married man would be in possession of china dog ornaments, he thought to himself. He straightened the dogs and moved them closer together.

On the floor, there were splashes of blood, dark red like thick wine. He wasn't sure whose blood it was. He fetched the new dish-cloth that Flora had knitted and began wiping up the stain with circular movements until it was washed away.

Wilfred limped back to the kitchen, his hipbone hurting from wrestling with Probert, and held the dishcloth under the cold water, which ran red as cochineal, then a diluted pink. He wrung out the cloth tightly. It was quiet now. His da, in his constant, calm way, must have gone to the graveyard to dig throughout the night, still caring for the dead and their final resting-place, regardless. Wilfred turned off the running tap and decided that he would start again with the shop. Like his da, he would persevere, and persevere intelligently.

Wilfred thought he should go to bed and leave the mess in the shop. It was late. He gazed out at the star-less sky. *Unto each day let only that evil be done.* Mr Auden had always said that at the end of a difficult day. Wilfred decided that he would get up at the crack of dawn and tidy. A good sleep would do wonders. He locked the back door with the key, something he had not done before. Seeing his da earlier almost hiding behind the door, he was struck again, how his father was at the edge of ageing. And why had Flora said to him when they were at the cove, 'I feel as if I am dying'? Wilfred experienced a coldness in his throat and his stomach. Flora wasn't one for drama or effect. She wasn't one to have tantrums and hysterics. She was calm; sometimes almost distant in her serenity, like a queen he couldn't reach.

Realising his da would be returning in the early morning, Wilfred unlocked the back door and went to bed. He curled around Flora Myffanwy, held her warm body and, comforted and reassured by her presence, explained the noise she had heard and had been hiding from upstairs. They lay on their sides facing each other while he told her about Probert, and the state of the shop.

'I gave Mrs Probert my lipstick,' Flora told him, 'because I thought it might help her feel more feminine.' Wilfred stroked her mass of brown hair, which fell in bright, curving coils that shone in the candlelight. He had seen people gaze at Flora, thinking about her beauty rather than listening to her gentle voice or her soft way of phrasing words. And there was an ancientness to her that made her mysterious. Wilfred didn't understand her ancientness. He just recognised it; and knew he was made from a commoner cloth.

'Come here.' He liked saying that. It was what he said at night — he liked to say the same thing to her, to create a rhythm and ways of being, *their* ways of being. She was his wife and she was alive. He held her tightly as she fell asleep and wrapped his leg around her so that no one could take her, so that death couldn't take her.

★ ★ ★

Flora Myffanwy was in a hospital bed in a dimmed room.

'You are having the baby,' a nurse said, all bristle and bustle.

'But it's too early.' Then the baby was born. 'That was so easy,' she said jubilantly to the nurse, but the nurse had left. She didn't know birth was so simple. The child had slipped from her painlessly; there had been no wrestling of two bodies, seams splitting, fighting to separate.

Then in front of her was a child, straight-backed like herself, with the same deep brown eyes. The child's hair was plaited in two plaits to her shoulders. She wore a dark brown dress with three small flowers embroidered on her flat chest. She was standing at the foot of Flora Myffanwy's bed. At the head of Flora's bed there was an open door from which the light came. The child looked at her. She had the simplicity of a child and the power of dignity.

Flora knew that the child was showing herself to her; that she was letting Flora see her. The child was unafraid and unattached. This was to be the only time in Flora Myffanwy's life that she would see her daughter. Her daughter was here now and would not come again.

'My name is Martha,' the child said. And then she was gone.

Flora woke abruptly, immediately awake. She got out of bed. 'Oh!' There was a thick red glut of blood on her inner thigh and her palms were slick with it now. She didn't know what to do with her bloodied hand. She stood with her legs apart, her hand held upwards in the air. It was a brilliant day. The sky through the bedroom window was a vivid blue and she could see the granite corner of the courthouse in exact definition against the absolutely blue, unmarked sky.

At the washstand she washed herself and within a moment the pool of water was red, as if swirled with red paint. A blood bath, she thought to herself. It got redder each time she dipped her hand in the water. She didn't know what to do. She was alone in the bedroom and aware of her aloneness. Should she shout for Wilfred? Should she lie down, should she hold on, breathe in? Never let go? There is a lot of blood, was the only thing she could think.

'Wilfred?' she whispered into the empty room. 'Wilfred?'

* * *

The nurse — Flora didn't know her — had come. Flora was sitting on newspaper in bed in their small bedroom. She heard the nurse saying, 'Listen, Mrs Price, are you in pain?'

Flora shook her head. The nurse put new pages of the *Daily Express* on the sheet under Flora. It crinkled gently. Flora looked down. The newspaper was soaked with blood. Flora

Myffanwy had not seen so much blood before, not from a person, not from herself.

Flora watched a long transparent line of saliva drop slowly, inexorable, down until it fell past her open knees and dangled over the bright red flood that had seeped and soaked into the many leaves of the newspaper beneath her. She closed her eyes and the line of dribble wavered and fell into the blood.

Flora heard herself breathe inwards loudly. She closed her eyes and, as if at a distance, heard herself make a dreadful sound such as only the grieving make in the freshest moments of their grief. This primeval sound left her and its awfulness seemed to fall over Narberth. There was a profound and reverential silence, as if many souls had heard and many souls had listened. It was a sound without words or shape that anyone in Narberth would understand.

9

Swarming

'Maid! Call for help!' a guest at the Ritz demanded, leaning out of her room, her dressing-gown held around her. 'Get a constable.'

'Yes, ma'am,' Hilda responded, obediently but alarmed.

'Or a porter. There are bees.'

'Yes, ma'am.' Hilda shoved her trolley to the side, almost breaking into a run to fetch the house-keeper. But Grace stayed.

'Do you have a nest in your room?' Grace asked. The woman nodded, considering Grace too unimportant to answer with more than a gesture.

'You won't need a policeman, ma'am,' Grace continued, feeling a quiet confidence. 'I know about bees.'

'And what do you know about bees?' The guest had come outside the room and was looking in the direction in which Hilda had disappeared.

'I used to keep them,' Grace said, remembering her hive made of a wicker coil and the grassy smell of burning leaves in the smoker.

The woman looked at her, her perception of the maid shaken.

'I kept bees, I made honey.'

The woman sighed, reluctant to allow in a

maid expertise beyond cleaning. She held the door open for Grace, with a look suggesting Grace was foolish to subject herself to the rage of wild beasts.

Grace entered the lavish suite. She couldn't immediately see any bees; she checked the vase of white alum lilies but there was nothing. The French windows were open: the bees must have left.

Grace turned to leave the suite when she saw a chair on the balcony: around its back was a lump of bristling bees seething and crawling over each other. They had swarmed, perhaps coming from the plane trees in Green Park behind the hotel. Half the hive would have left, taking their old queen with them, who would now be in the centre of the mass. They were resting, would rest here for two or three days — not that the Ritz would allow bees — while the scout bees went ahead and searched for a new home in a tree hollow.

Grace moved nearer — the bees were unperturbed. Her arms were bare, her face uncovered but she wasn't afraid. It was months since she had been near bees and she had missed their productivity and selflessness, how each one busied itself for the good of the hive, working ceaselessly over the brief span of their lives. They were beautiful and useful.

The housekeeper entered with a tablecloth draped over her head.

'You could be stung to death, girl,' she warned, waving a broom in the air.

'It's best not to do that, it can frighten them.'

Grace stood by the chair where the bees had made a cruciform with their brown bodies. 'I am a beekeeper,' Grace said. It felt a long time since she had heard herself define herself and say 'I am . . . ' but it was true, she *was* a beekeeper. And she was like a lost bee without a hive. Sometimes Grace had wondered, as she donned her brother's beekeeping hat and gloves, if the bees had chosen her to be a beekeeper rather than the other way round.

The housekeeper was too frightened of the insects to use her authority and turn Grace back from a beekeeper to a maid. She dropped the tablecloth and ran out, her hands in front of her.

Grace bent down to see the energy of the hive. Before they swarmed, the bees would have fed deeply on honey and nectar to build up their strength. They were full and satisfied. It would be days before they were busy and forward-moving again. There was nothing to be afraid of; bees and people had worked together since the Babylonians.

Grace went to the door of the suite, where the butler, the housekeeper, the guest and Hilda were gathered waiting for her. They flinched backwards when Grace opened the door.

'May I be informed of what is happening?' the guest demanded of the butler. The butler looked at Grace.

'I need a basket or a cardboard box and a cloth — that tablecloth will do.'

'Hurry! A cardboard box. You heard!' the housekeeper ordered Hilda, then she shame-facedly handed the tablecloth to Grace.

133

'What are you going to do, girl?' the guest asked, looking in her tasselled bag while she spoke. 'Oh, don't tell me,' the woman continued, thoroughly and finally disregarding Grace, angry with a maid who could speak and inform.

Once Hilda returned with the box, Grace went back into the suite and knelt by the chair. The other women stood at the doorway watching warily, looking ready to scream and flee. Grace, with the reassurance of familiarity, penetrated her hands into the hive. The bees swarmed to her bare skin and walked over her fingers and palms. She took a handful of bees and laid them in the box, where they sat contained in one ball. She picked up another ball of bees, which hung down in a deep arch as she moved her hands into the box. The bees didn't split and become ten thousand individuals; they stayed as one, as if magnetised together. Grace thought again how, as long as bees made honey, the land would be abundant with food and flowers. The bees, she felt, were the first friends she had found in London that she understood and was familiar with: it was as if they embraced her and held her hand.

When the bees were ensconced in the cardboard box, Grace tied the tablecloth around the box, knotted it and left the room, carrying the makeshift hive.

'Duchess, what an inconvenience for you. The matter is in hand,' the butler fawned. 'Girl?' he said, turning to Grace.

'They need to be taken to the countryside.'

'Take them to my office, girl. For the time

being, put that box in the cupboard behind my desk, and lock the door. Hurry, girl. My sincerest apologies, Duchess: an unforeseen incident.'

'Yes,' the duchess said, dismissing the butler as she had dismissed the maid, waving her hand, entering her suite and closing the door.

★ ★ ★

Grace only had an hour of her half-day off before she had to return to the Ritz. The incident with the bees had taken most of the afternoon in the end, so there wasn't time to go to the Suffragettes' meeting and she had missed the jujutsu class. She wanted something to do rather than sit in the stuffy dormitory with the prying eyes of the other maids on her, nor did she want to be in, in case her brother came, so she went for a walk.

As she trudged along Piccadilly, she walked past elegant women amid the dirt and the smoke. Here, in the dirtiest place she had ever been, were the most beautiful people she had ever seen; women draped in mink furs, their kohl-darkened eyes tilted arrogantly towards the weak sun, as if mesmerised by the smog that overlay the city like an unwashed blanket. Grace felt ambivalent about London. Ambivalent — that was a word she had learned from Wilfred. She remembered affectionately that he had been reading a tatty dictionary. She wondered how Wilfred was, imagined his life must be much the same, settled again, after what had happened.

She saw the Royal Academy ahead. Should she

go in? Her clothes were shabby. She had not been inside an art gallery before, but she felt emboldened by her beekeeping and, along with watching Mrs Garrud practising jujutsu, Grace had become less numb and afraid, able to venture out of herself a little more. She walked through an imposing wrought-iron gate into a square fronted by a building that looked like a palace for art. There was a statue of an artist, easel in hand, paintbrush poised as if petrified in an ecstasy of art. Grace followed the queue and paid for a ticket, standing quietly among the confident conversations around her. She was surrounded by older ladies in expensive coats, their mature faces resting in the expression they had favoured over a lifetime, be that pleasant gentleness or a scathing scorn. Their faces were set now, as if portraits.

Once inside the gallery and on the first floor, Grace walked past a great gilded mirror but ignored her reflection — she cleaned mirrors like that in the Ritz — then through an arch with two cherubs languishing on the architrave and into a square room hung with paintings, mostly of military men. On the ceiling were flabby horses, angels and perhaps God, overseeing the mastery of art. She noticed even the skirting board was gilded. The room was deeply quiet. Her shoes clacked on the floor — it felt forbidden to break the silence, like pushing a finger against the white fondant icing of a cake until it cracked. A guard sat below a painting like a stubby bulldog. Grace paused in front of a portrait of a girl with flowers: *Miss Anna Alma-Tadema*. 'Miss', that simple, poor title which a girl hoped she would shed in her womanhood, as if it were a milk tooth, loosened then replaced by a stronger edge.

A sullen woman with a rather spoiled-looking expression passed by with her authoritative but appeasing husband wearing top hat and tails, and Grace was reminded of her parents. Although her father thought for himself in his work, at home he always did as her mother demanded, acquiescing to her. When Grace had left Narberth, her mother hadn't stopped her, so her father didn't either. He was a doctor and important in the town, but weak at home. She missed her father, but she could not respect his weakness. Grace did not miss her mother. She had known her mother was nasty — she was constantly snappy — but not that she was cruel; cruel enough to let Grace, her daughter, leave home when she needed care most.

One painting stood out from the others studded around the room. It was of a man without status or title, without medals or a military uniform. He was an older man who had seen life and seemed saddened, but his gaze was direct. His hands were folded self-effacingly on his lap — hands that wouldn't invade. He looked as if he might not have long to live and was retiring and receding from the world — all power, all vigour spent. Yet he was more real than the other faces, with less façade. The painting was only oil swished onto a taut canvas, but there was a humanity to this portrait. It was as if his puffy face had been hammered by pain and experiences so that his aspect was full of acceptance, although a shade more and it might be depressed.

Grace sat down heavily on the hard bench opposite the man; the day had been long and eventful already and she was weary. She rested in his presence. Had she seen a face with that much acceptance and modesty in London? Across centuries his acceptance soothed her: what he knew of the world reassured her. That he could paint himself without pomp showed her there was another way in the world from the gilded decoration of the Ritz, the bored opulence of the ladies who slept there, the futile striding and the empty purposefulness of men who didn't need to work for money, and the children being educated with finesse for lives of little purpose. But then Grace's work these last few months had little meaning for her. She was only a pair of hands.

The card said *Self-portrait of the Artist Aged 63*, on loan from the National Gallery. So this was Rembrandt. Was he great, Grace wondered, for his skill with a brush or because his humility made him so? Somewhere in her broken sprit, she felt a balm. There was a confusion of whiskers and wrinkles about his mouth, and his dark eyes were half-hidden amid the blotched, saggy skin. The column of his neck was lost to pudginess and he had a potato-nose — he had not lied about himself. He didn't look Welsh, nor did he look English — but he looked human. She had waited a long time in this city to find someone who was this human and who had nothing they wanted her to be.

'Come on, slowcoach,' Hilda said. 'You're dragging your feet today.'

Grace felt exhausted but took a quick step and put her hands on the chambermaid's trolley alongside Hilda.

'We're both tired this morning,' Hilda yawned. 'All that excitement over the bees yesterday, and I expect you painted the town red on your afternoon off.' She nudged Grace cheekily. 'Were you doing the Tutankhamun Shimmy?' Hilda wriggled her hips from side to side. 'Twenty-seven more rooms to service. Twenty-seven beds to strip, fifty-four mirrors to polish, occasional tables to wax, brass lights to clean, shower-baths to scrub, umpteen yards of skirting-boards to dust. You ever had a shower-bath?'

'No.'

'Me neither. We have a tin bath in the back yard.' Hilda liked to talk, Grace noticed. She chattered and filled the silence that Grace's numbness created. Hilda had told her that she was a Christian — 'a Christian is always a servant!' she'd explained — and that every time she finished making a bed, she touched the pillows and silently blessed each one and the head that would sleep on it.

'But my brother,' Hilda continued, 'always skinny-dips in the Thames. I say I'm clean and he's stupid. Bet your brother isn't as stupid as my brother.' She knocked on the door to the Ballantyre Suite and waited meekly.

'Enter.'

A lady sat with her back to them, in the curve of a dressing-table, a myriad glass bottles before her prisming the light. She had a pink powder puff in her hand and was dabbing her décolletage while considering a half-finished watercolour painting in front of her. A silk kimono was hanging loosely around her and rested lightly on the carpet, cranes leaping upwards from the hem. When she turned, Grace recognised the elegant profile of Lady Lytton.

'Good morning, ma'am,' Hilda said, and bobbed into an obsequious curtsey.

Lady Lytton smiled then turned back to her toilette, selecting a sapphire necklace from a velvet-lined box, coiling the jewellery round her neck and stretching elegantly as she hooked the clasps. She smiled at Grace and Hilda's reflection anodynely and, if she recognised Grace, she didn't reveal it.

'Get in the bathroom!' Hilda whispered, pulling Grace's cuff. Once inside, door shut, they scooped up the scattered bath towels and rolled them into a fluffy bundle for the laundry. Grace buffed the enormous silvery mirror, reaching to its outer edges, while Hilda straightened the shower curtain, Welsh-combing the white silk with her fingers. She dried the steel flower that was the shower-head, then jerked out the bathplug so the bathwater slurped into the bowels of the city.

When they emerged from the bathroom, Lady Lytton turned fractionally and lifted a pink teacup to her lips, holding its gold handle delicately.

'You may go,' she stated, addressing their reflections in her cool, smooth voice, then picking up a paint set and looking at the small, vibrant squares of colour.

'The bed, ma'am?' Hilda asked anxiously.

'This maid will finish it.' Lady Lytton indicated Grace. Grace saw Hilda disguise her surprise. Hilda took the order like one who only knew how to obey and not to reply. She nodded obediently and left, taking her maid's trolley with her.

'Grace!' Lady Lytton exclaimed, turning round fully. 'I haven't seen you at Mrs Garrud's classes,' she said with concern. 'And you didn't come to the last few Suffragette meetings.' Her enthusiasm revealed her youth, despite the lacquer and polish that money bestowed upon her. 'When I failed to see you here, I thought you might have lost your employment.'

A wave of tension came over Lady Lytton's beautiful, painted countenance. 'Are you well? I wondered what had happened to you.' She took a long look at Grace and bit the corner of her lip. 'I thought I might not see you again.' Suddenly she put her hand to her eyes and let out a strangled sob. 'I see you and I see my sister.'

Grace watched quietly, unmoved, standing in front of, and apart from, the other woman who was crying, her face creased with deep pressure, lost in herself. Grace looked at this woman who had had a sister whom she'd lost and Grace thought of her brother and how she hated him and wanted him dead.

'I would do anything to see her again,' Lady Lytton confessed, her voice cracking into a high pitch on the word 'anything'. 'She was only

141

twenty-eight. You look so much like her. You even frown like her.' She dabbed her red eyes elegantly and pulled her kimono around herself with trembling fingers. 'And when I saw you and you looked so much like her, and I began to wonder if you were *enceinte* . . . '

Shock went through Grace.

'I thought you couldn't tell,' Grace said coldly. 'I thought it was hidden.'

'It's hidden if it's not acknowledged,' Lady Lytton replied. 'It was the same with my sister. She had an abortion — or tried to. You won't do anything silly,' she asked pleadingly. 'Will you, Grace?'

It had occurred to Grace. But her father was the only person in Narberth who would have known how to do it. She had tried with a knitting needle, but it hadn't worked. If it had, it would have ended her problems; she would still have had to leave home but she would have had a future, a life, her own life, instead of this constant sliding down a slippery black hole, like Alice in Wonderland, all the while getting bigger and bigger. Could she still get one now? This was London. But it was surely too late.

A silence fell. It seemed Lady Lytton grasped that she had sewn an idea in Grace's mind; contaminated another woman's thoughts with a desperate measure.

'It's too late for you now,' Lady Lytton stated.

'Is it?'

'Yes.'

But Grace saw that Lady Lytton didn't know for certain. Her father was a doctor: he always knew what he was speaking about when it came to operations and surgery, and he never spoke in that breathy way.

'It isn't,' Grace said, after a moment, hope rising in her.

'Don't be foolish, Grace. Think of yourself. Think how your sister would feel if something happened to you. Do you have a sister?'

'No.'

'Then think of your mother. And your father. Or your brother.'

Grace didn't reply.

Lady Lytton still held the powder puff, now crushed in her fingers. 'I shouldn't have said anything,' she said suddenly. 'How foolish of me.'

'Am I dismissed?' Grace asked.

'No!' Lady Lytton inhaled, self-consciously trying to gather herself, and, Grace thought, if Lady Lytton hadn't been so well brought up she might have raised her voice. Some kohl was smudged along Lady Lytton's cheek when she had dabbed her eyes. She turned back to the mirror and began patting the marks with a ball of cotton wool, then she wiped the cotton wool across her cheekbones, smoothing her skin. When she had finished, she took a sip of tea, then half-turned.

'You may leave the bed unmade. Here is my name card, with my address. You are dismissed,' she ordered, unfastening the strap of her gold wristwatch and holding it out for Grace to take. 'Thank you, Grace. That will be all.'

* * *

Grace left the Ballantyre Suite, hurriedly pushing the gold watch inside her brassière, where the metal clasp dug into her hard breasts. Lady Lytton was the third person to give her money — Wilfred immediately after their divorce, her father as she left Narberth, and now Lady Lytton. She needed money, but what she wanted most of all, she thought with exhaustion, was a home, a refuge, someone and somewhere to support her, rather than having to survive on her own. Of what use was a gold watch to her? What would she do with it?

She ran her hand over her breast; the watch made an odd metal lump so she shoved it down further and it disappeared into her contours, then she rushed down the corridor looking at the crystal doorknobs, searching for a *MAID CLEANING* sign. When Grace found the sign, she knocked on the door and Hilda came out and looked at her suspiciously.

'What did she want?' Hilda demanded.

'To finish tidying the beds.'

'And she wanted you to do that on your own? Is there something wrong with me, then?'

'No.' Grace could see that Hilda's sense of importance as the more senior chambermaid had been dented.

'Right. Start cleaning. You make the beds. Let's see if you've still got a problem with hospital corners.' Even though she was aggrieved, Hilda talked: only now her talk expressed her hurt. 'I can do beds as good as any of them,' she boasted. 'What's the matter with you?' she asked Grace chippily. 'Lost your tongue?'

'No,' Grace mumbled, aware of the bullying

tone that Hilda had adopted. But Hilda was right: she had lost her tongue. She'd lost her tongue the moment she had been forced by her brother and hadn't found it since. He had silenced her. She talked when she had to, replied when questioned, said what needed to be said as briefly as possible, but that was all. Her tongue lay heavy and useless in her mouth; like something she owned but no longer used. She had lost her tongue and got a child.

'You ought to talk more. It's boring for me. You're not the only one in the room. It's warm in here, isn't it?' Hilda said, parodying conversation and goading Grace to speak.

'Yes.'

'Oh, I give up with you,' Hilda said, throwing the starched sheet over the mattress, then flinging the feather pillows onto the bed.

Grace knew now to move away from people who were gathering themselves up to be violent in one way or another.

'If you'll excuse me,' Grace said, 'I'm going to lie down in the dormitory. I'm feeling unwell.'

'Well! That's a cheek,' exclaimed Hilda, working herself up into a steam and clearly with much more to say, but Grace had put her duster on the trolley and was walking away.

'You could lose your job for this!' Hilda called after her.

★   ★   ★

Relieved to be back in the dormitory and away from Hilda, Grace picked up a postcard that was

145

waiting for her on her bed. She knew who it was from. It was a picture of Chelsea Barracks. She turned it over and glanced at it. No, Grace didn't want to meet Madoc for a cup of tea. She ripped the postcard into tiny pieces, then stood up heavily from the dormitory bed, put her hands on her waist and arched her lower back, which was aching. She pushed her stomach out — she couldn't help herself — dropped her head back and sighed.

'Grace Rice! How *dare* you leave all the work to me and come up here?' Then Hilda's mouth fell open in shock. 'Are you . . . ?' She stood, speechless, her cap hanging loosely in her hand. 'Are you having a baby?' Hilda asked. 'You're having a baby! You've been hiding it.' She gasped 'Mr Sharp will kill you.'

Grace looked at Hilda.

'Mr Sharp! The butler.'

'Oh,' Grace replied, utterly unperturbed.

'Don't you care what Mr Sharp will say?'

Grace regarded this girl in front of her who was so gauche and without understanding, whose whole life was this great cruise liner of a hotel that sailed serenely, coddling and entertaining its wealthy passengers and its employees from the storms and turbulence of their times.

'You don't understand,' Grace said.

'I do. You're having a baby. And you're not married. You'll lose your job.'

Grace, comprehending, dragged her suitcase from under the bed, then opened and emptied the two drawers in her bedside cabinet, pushing her scant and shabby belongings into her case.

She opened the zip pouch inside the suitcase lining. There was her money, wrapped up in the envelope her father had given her — it was all she had that belonged to him. And a family photograph, but she hadn't looked at it since she left Narberth. She quickly packed her case, clipped the clasps and glanced at the stark dormitory and barred window. It wasn't much: it wasn't a home but, she reasoned, it was a roof.

'Where are you going to go?'

'I don't know.'

'You don't know?' Hilda replied. 'Here, you've forgotten your stockings.' She passed them to her. 'You've sinned,' she stated, as if the thought had just struck her. 'It says in the Book of Hebrews 'for fornicators and adulterer, God will; — ''

'Have I?' Grace interrupted. She was finding words, but with a sudden sense that the feelings she had held down for so long were being unloosened and could surge up inside her.

Hilda flicked her plait over her shoulder. 'Tell me about him,' she nudged Grace. 'What's he like? What was *it* like?'

Grace didn't answer. For a brief moment, the hierarchy between them, where Hilda was the senior chambermaid and Grace the meek and silent one, fell away. Grace knew something about life that Hilda didn't.

'You're not going to tell me, are you?' There was a pause. 'I expect I'll find out one day. When I'm married.' Hilda looked at Grace's rounded stomach with awe. 'Let me help you,' she said.

Grace held back some noise or sound, a primal wail breaking within her in response to

Hilda's unexpected warmth.

Hilda yanked open and checked inside the drawers and got down on all fours to look under the bed to make sure that Grace had all her possessions.

'Is that your hair clip?'

Grace shook her head.

Hilda glanced at the door. 'You must go before the other maids come back. If Mr Sharp finds you . . . Do you want to go back home to Wales?'

'No.'

'Do you know where to go?'

Grace reached for her coat, her hands shaking as she did up the buttons. She should have thought about the future, but she had been living from moment to moment, almost asleep.

'You can't stay here,' Hilda stated. 'Do you know the kitchen backstairs, behind the ballroom?'

'No.'

'Quickly, I'll show you.' Hilda grabbed Grace's suitcase and darted to the door. She looked both ways down the empty, windowless corridor. 'There's no one here. Come on.' They hurried unceremoniously along the corridor, then down echoing staircase after staircase, their feet clattering loudly on the hard floor.

'Don't fall,' Hilda told Grace.

Grace held onto the cold, black handrail, her throat dry with exertion, trying to catch her breath.

'No wonder you were always such a slowcoach,' Hilda said, glancing back at Grace and waiting a moment for her to catch up.

At the bottom of the stairs was a big black door.

'It's locked,' Hilda said. 'We need the key — I'll ask Jack. He might know how to get one.'

Grace stood shivering with fear in the shadows while Hilda charged up the stairs to the kitchen. She had money, she should find lodgings, she must find lodgings, she must cope, she told herself. She hung onto the suitcase in her hand. At least Madoc wouldn't find her now. Hilda soon returned, trailed by a skinny boy with dirty blond hair.

'Open the door, Jack,' she told him impatiently. 'Open it, then.'

The boy put the key in the lock and held the door open for Grace, staring at her open-mouthed.

'Sorry I wasn't always kind,' Hilda said. She put her hand to her neck and pulled out a small gold cross on a chain. 'I would give you this, only my godfather gave it to me at my christening and he'd have kittens if I wasn't wearing it.' She rummaged in her apron pocket and brought out an expensive comb. 'Take this. I found it, but you can have it. It's for you.' She dropped the tortoiseshell comb into the pocket of Grace's coat. 'You can comb your hair with it.'

'I've got to get back to the kitchen,' Jack said nervously — he looked frightened. 'I'll be in trouble with Cook if she sees I've taken the key.'

So Grace turned and left the Ritz.

10

The Dog with the Waggiest Tail in Narberth, 1926

'Letter from the Tenby Gas Company, Wilfred. That will be the bill,' said Willie the Post, poking his head round the workshop door. Wilfred was measuring a plank of elm with a ruler. He jotted down its length. 'Hear you's reading *Hamlet*,' Willie the Post commented. 'We did that at school. What is it he says? 'Shall I do myself in or not, I don't know'.'

'I'm reading this.' Wilfred put down his ruler amidst the jumble of tools on his workbench and held up *The Last Days of Socrates*.

'Who's that by?'

'Plato.'

'Never heard of him. Oh — who's dead?' asked Willie, indicating the half-finished coffin resting on A-frames.

'No one yet. It's a spare,' said Wilfred, resting the elm plank against the wall.

'Now seeing you's an important man around Narberth,' Willie began, 'and I's don't like to ask, but will you judge the dog competition at the Winter Carnival? We don't want any old bugger judging it, see.'

'What's wrong with the mayor?'

'He can't see a hole through a ladder.'

'But Willie — '

'Say yes or I'll be the arse of the world with the Winter Carnival Committee. You's only have to give the rosette to the winner. No one's going to mind.'

'Mr Gerard Henry might set that ruddy Alsatian on me if I don't let him win,' Wilfred retorted, putting his pencil behind his ear.

'Well, you's better let him win, then. We were thinking that you'd give a very proper air to the dog competition. We can't have some farmer from Carmarthen judging, who'd laugh if his arse was on fire. And the Reverend Waldo Williams is on a pilgrimage to St David's to atone for his sins.'

'Aye, I suppose so,' Wilfred said resignedly, folding up the ruler and dropping it in the bib pocket of his dungarees.

'This Saturday, two o'clock at the Queen's Hall, wearing your best suit. No one will argue with you when you're dressed as an undertaker — they'd be scared you'd bury them as punishment.' Willie put the gas bill on the spare coffin. 'And how's your wife, now, these days since she lost . . . ' He looked down at his Post Office regulation shoes.

'Well enough,' Wilfred replied, hearing how tinny his answer sounded, even to himself.

★　★　★

Wilfred came into the kitchen and dropped the *Narberth & Whitland Observer* on the kitchen table.

151

'Raining today. Is the type of rain that gets you wet,' he remarked to Flora Myffanwy, who was cleaning the floor. Every day Flora woke, cleaned one thing after another, then slept early, exhausted. And then she rose the following morning and cleaned again. Number 11, Market Street was reaching hitherto unheard-of heights of cleanliness. The kitchen table, which had had a greasiness that made one's hand stick to it slightly, was now bleached wood, the grooves in the tabletop empty of detritus. The kitchen window, with its smears, splatters and fingerprints, was crystal clear, and the blue teacup squeaked in his fingers when he held it.

'Flora,' he said to his wife, who was on the floor of the kitchen, a butter-knife in her hand, frantically bevelling the grime out of the gap between the floor and the wall. Wilfred watched his wife clean the flagstones while biting, in her grief-stricken anguish with herself, on the pad of her thumb. Flora hadn't talked about the baby. Wilfred knew enough to know that when someone didn't speak about something, it was because it hurt them deeply. She was in shock — he'd seen that look in the faces of the bereaved standing at gravesides, and recognised it for the otherworldly state that it was.

'Flora?' he asked, as if he was asking the universe, as if he was looking for her in the spaces between the planets in which she was lost and floating. She hung her head.

'It is clean now, dear.'

Flora rested on her knees and put her hands on her lap. Her complexion was pale and she was skin and bone. And the floor was scrubbed so you could eat your dinner off it. Wilfred thought if dirt was something in the wrong place, then cleaning was putting things in the right place. But Flora looked at him as if she thought the whole world would never be clean, would never be bright and new again, and so she must keep on scrubbing and digging and bevelling into every nook and cranny of their small wattle and daub house until the end of her days.

★   ★   ★

'You'll be surprised to hear this,' Wilfred announced jovially, coming into the kitchen at dinner time after a long morning in the workshop. 'I'm judging the dog competition at the Winter Carnival. Willie the Post asked me earlier, and I said yes. It's important to help people, if they ask, isn't it? What's this, dear, on the lettuce?' Wilfred sat down and looked at his lunch plate.

'Heinz Salad Cream. It's new,' Flora Myffanwy replied.

'Very nice it is and all. I don't think we've had this before, have we, Da?'

'No,' said his da, looking at the frilly lettuce with a serving of salad cream sitting primly next to it.

'We used to have so many fried breakfasts; I'm surprised I don't look like slices of black pudding. It's wonderful to eat something new, isn't it, Da, like lettuce?'

'Yes,' his da agreed.

Wilfred sat back, his knife and fork in his hand

153

and beamed. 'We've never eaten so well, have we, Da? Been reading that book, *The Last Days of Socrates*,' he continued, wanting to break Flora's subdued silence, trying to make more conversation but unable to think of anything else to say. 'Very difficult, indeed. I've only read nine pages. Can't understand a word of it. That chap Socrates and his questions — enough to drive a saint mad. I bet they were relieved when he died.'

'Well, it doesn't matter, son. I'm very proud of you for giving it a go.'

'Thank you, Da,' said Wilfred, soothed by the affection in his da's voice. 'I don't think I'm going to read as far as the chapter where they bury him. It would confound a brighter man than me. But never mind. I'm a very happy undertaker from Narberth,' he said awkwardly, and beamed at his wife, attempting to show her how happy he was. 'Even old Napoleon never felt so good!' He would be happy so Flora could be happy too: happy enough to stop cleaning. Perhaps even take photographs again.

Wilfred squished the lettuce on his fork, but it kept jumping back off. This lettuce had a life of its own.

'Remarkably good lettuce. The cat's meow. The tastiest vegetable I've ever had. Isn't it delicious, Da?'

'Delicious.'

'If there's better food in Heaven, I'm in a hurry to get there.' Wilfred put a small mouthful of green leaf in his mouth. 'And you do know how to cook peas.' Wilfred smiled at his da, who was carefully lifting up his fork with a triangle of lettuce balanced precariously on it.

'I'm full to bursting — we're eating for the winter to come.'

'More salad cream?' Flora asked.

'Most definitely,' Wilfred replied, and Flora handed him the dish with the salad cream in it — Wilfred thought it might be called a salad boat. That was one of the things he loved most about Flora: she brought to his life such dignified and extraordinary things as a salad boat. And he was sure it was because he was married that he'd been asked to judge the dog competition. He couldn't imagine an unmarried undertaker being asked to take part in such an important civic event.

Out of the corner of his eye Wilfred watched his da discreetly struggling to cut a lettuce leaf, his liver-spotted hands trembling. A rim of long hairs grew from his ears — his *barbate* ears. And there was a deep cleft in the back of his neck from holding up his head all these decades. Wisps of hair on his crown, fine and gentle, like his thoughts, surrounded his head. Perhaps his da had been grieving without Wilfred noticing and had emerged even more kind and thoughtful than before, because he soothed them both with his gentle courtesy.

More than everything is family, Wilfred thought to himself. Some people had large families. Death had kept his family small. And they seemed so fragile, the three of them, in their feelings and in their bodies, gathered at the table scrubbed clean because of pain, the humble jar of salad cream sitting between them, an offering of hope for a better life, a small gesture to buoy their fragility.

Around him, Flora tidied the kitchen table and his da sat resting after the meal.

'Wonderful dinner, dear.' It was important to be a good husband, he thought to himself, to be appreciative and say nice things. 'No life without a wife! Not according to Mr Auden,' Wilfred said, folding his napkin and patting his stomach. Wilfred had thought Mr Auden meant if a man didn't get married then he had little to live for. That was true. But now he understood that it was through having a wife that life came into the world: a wife, a woman was the conduit for new life. Their child had come into the world through Flora Myffanwy. Mr Auden's advice had been deeper and wiser than he had understood it to be only a year and a half ago. But he was much younger and more inexperienced then.

★ ★ ★

'Bag of sawdust for you,' Wilfred said to Jeffrey. He ducked under the hanging carcass of a gutted cow, swung the sack of sawdust from his shoulder and put it down on the flagstones in Lloyd the Butcher.

'Thank you, Wilfred,' Jeffrey called. 'That'll be handy for the floor. Be with you now in a minute.' He turned back to the chopping board and brought the cleaver down on a piece of lamb. There were three clean, quick cracks. Jeffrey turned the cleaver on its side and slammed it flat along the meat.

156

Then he took a piece of the *Narberth & Whitland Observer*, enfolded the chops into a neat square package, slapped it between his two hands and gave it to Mrs Prout.

'Right you are. Let's head off to the Dragon Inn and put our names down first on the list,' Jeffery said to Wilfred, walking out from behind the counter, sawdust spilling from his turn-ups. 'We mustn't miss out on the tug-of-war this year. I want to see those chaps from Carmarthen flat on their backs in the mud — crying. That'll do me.' He patted his biceps.

'You've grown quite a moustache there,' Wilfred remarked, looking down on his friend who was a head shorter than him, as they wove their way around the muddy carts standing in the busy High Street.

'Aye,' Jeffrey replied, stroking the edges of his tremendously bushy red moustache and stretching upwards on the balls of his feet. 'Ladies like them.'

Wilfred wasn't sure if ladies liked moustaches. But perhaps men didn't like to be short as much as ladies didn't want to be fat.

'I spent the morning delivering pork to Mrs Coles; she will die talking.'

It was market day and the High Street was bursting with people who had come from the villages around Narberth. Market Square was heaving with sheep and lowing cattle, and a crowd had gathered around a pen where pigs were being auctioned. Jeffrey walked round a horse drinking barley water from a bucket.

'How's the wife?' he asked.

'Well enough,' Wilfred replied.

And there it was: Wilfred was having an experience with Flora that was too profound to explain to his unmarried childhood friend. These days there was a small distance between the two of them, and they both knew it. It would be easier if Jeffrey was married as well, but he enjoyed the company of ladies too much to settle down in a hurry.

'How's Clementine?' Wilfred asked, shooing a chicken from under his feet.

'Clementine?'

'I though you were courting Clementine.'

'The mind plays tricks.'

They entered the Dragon Inn. The air was muggy, smoke hung in a flat layer at head-height and the limewashed walls were stained a mustardy-brown. Wilfred had not been into the inn since Mr Probert had appeared, drunk and angry, in the wallpaper shop. A big pink pig with black trotters and a ring in his nose trotted in behind them.

'Get that ruddy pig out of here, Probert!' Jeffrey called. Probert staggered round from behind the bar, slapped the panicking, squealing pig on the rump and bullied it out of the public house.

'Put the ruddy gate on the door!' Handel Evans shouted from the table by the fireplace where he was playing Whist with the Reverend Waldo Williams. 'That pig nearly knocked the card table over and I'm all set to win five bob against the reverend here. Not that he'll pay me!' There was loud laughing and guffawing from the crowd of men gathering in the pub.

Probert dragged from the back yard a barred gate, which he locked onto the circles on the doorpost. Then Wilfred watched as Probert clumsily hauled a wooden barrel up from the cellar, through the trapdoor, dropping the barrel on the flagstones where it landed heavily and bounced heftily a few times, threatening to injure any feet or fingertips that got in its way. Probert rolled the beer barrel across the floor, the rings cracking loudly, then kicked it with his hobnailed boot towards the bar. He then went behind the bar.

'Pint of beer,' Wilfred ordered above the noise.

Mr Probert soon plonked the beer onto the stained counter, and the reddish-brown liquid slopped down the bevelled glass. Then he rubbed his hands down his hessian apron and swigged a mouthful of what smelled like parsnip wine from a tankard under the counter.

'Two shillings, Price,' he said. 'How's married life?'

'Good.'

'Nice wife you've got there.'

'Indeed.'

'Bit of a Sheba. Wouldn't mind her being my wife,' he goaded.

'Bit late now,' Wilfred replied.

'My wife walked into a table yesterday, Price,' Mr Probert said, locking eyes with Wilfred and laughing confidently. Wilfred looked at Probert and could counter it no other way: men were crueller than women.

'Told her not to go walking with your wife

again — don't want her causing any more trouble between us,' Probert said, referring to what had happened in the paint and wallpaper shop. 'You agree with that, Wilfred Price?' he asked, making it sound like a question when Wilfred knew it wasn't. Wilfred stared into his mottled beer glass with its layer of dying froth. His fists were digging into his thighs. He moved away.

Wilfred finished the dregs of his pint, which tasted bitter in his mouth, and looked across the small, beery room. It was a Bacchanalian public house, he thought to himself, remembering the *B* word he had read in the dictionary that morning, and was packed with hoary men with moustaches wearing thick tweed jackets, bellowing like bulls. There was no divide between the labouring and the professional classes in the Dragon Inn. Here, the solicitor and the lighthouse engineer, the coalminer from Wiseman's Bridge and the brewer from James Williams's Bottling Factory mixed together. There was another roar of laughter as a young farmer slapped his thigh and mimed riding a horse.

'There's that ruddy pig again. Get that pig out of my way!' Handel Evans shouted at the pig, who was now snuffling about outside, next to the door. The church organist attempted to climb over the low gate across the door. 'Move, damn pig, move!' The gathering of men jeered mercilessly at Handel Evans as he lifted his short, stiff leg to straddle the gate.

'Up she goes!' the blacksmith bawled.

'Been some time since Handel Evans got his

leg over something,' Lloyd the Butcher quipped.

'He doesn't have much chance; he's always playing with his organ!'

'I'll be having the lot of you!' Handel Evans rejoined, now standing upright on the other side of the gate, pulling his jacket down from the hem with both hands, his face puce from the exertion.

'Lads, listen you,' announced Lloyd the Butcher, stepping up onto a wooden crate. The men who had crowded into the pub gathered round, looking up at Lloyd, who was pink as a pork chop, his starched white apron stained with blood. 'If you want to be in this year's Narberth versus Carmarthen tug-of-war tournament,' he announced, pink and proud, 'and beat those salty buggers from Carmarthen who only fart to frighten themselves, shout out your good name now.' He took a notepad and a pencil from his apron pocket. 'Don't be a sitter and a looker,' he encouraged. 'Live as though you would die tomorrow!'

★ ★ ★

'Da, I was thinking . . . ' Wilfred said late that night, standing bare-chested in the kitchen and cutting a thick slice of bread, 'do you think I'm a good person?'

'What are you doing asking me that for?' Wilfred's da sliced the top off his boiled egg, revealing the circle of wet yellow within.

'Well, it's not living that matters, but living rightly,' Wilfred quoted, slathering soft butter on the bread with the bread-knife. 'Socrates says

161

that not life, but the good life, is to be valued. But how do I live a good life?' Wilfred sat down at the clean table, not bothering with a plate. 'Become a vicar?'

'They'd never have you.'

Give my money away, Wilfred nearly said, but he had already done that. 'Help old ladies across the road? Or try not to knock people over?'

'I would say, Wilfred *bach*, that not running people over is very important.'

'Not even if it was an accident, mind you? Would I be a good man if I knocked someone over by accident in the hearse? So that I had to bury them?'

There was the gentle chaff of the spoon on the eggshell. 'What did Socrates says about accidents on the road?' his da asked.

'Didn't have a motor car,' Wilfred replied. 'I'm in puzzles about it. It's difficult, isn't it?'

'It's not if no one has a motor car.' Wilfred's da scraped out the bottom of his boiled egg with a chalky sound.

You're good, Da, Wilfred said silently, reaching out and putting his hand over his da's weathered hands.

'Right. Time for bed,' Wilfred announced. 'Can't find my toothbrush for the life of me. I want to polish my pegs.'

'Flora Myffanwy had it,' his da replied, turning his cap around in his hand. 'She was cleaning with it.'

'Cleaning her teeth?' Wilfred asked, puzzled.

'No.'

'No?'

'Cleaning the wall,' said Wilfred's da reticently. 'In the scullery.'

Wilfred looked bewildered.

'Clearing the dust from the ledges on the wall,' his da admitted.

'When was this?'

'Last night.'

'But last night she went to bed at eight o'clock.'

'This was three in the morning.'

Wilfred collapsed onto the kitchen chair. She's gone mad, he thought. Flora Myffanwy had gone mad. He dropped the newspaper onto the scrubbed, gritless, dustless flagstones of the kitchen floor. I am Wilfred Price, he said to himself, trying to orientate himself, to remind himself who he was and what he was. I am an undertaker. A purveyor of superior funerals. And I have read the whole of the *A* words and some of the *B* words in the dictionary, he thought, struggling to define himself with certainty. I am in the kitchen in Narberth with my da. And I was going to be a father.

★ ★ ★

Flora Myffanwy swept the hearthstone in the bedroom again. It was clean, but the cleaning of it gave her something to do with her frantic, restless hands and somewhere to put her thoughts. Each day, as she cleaned the house, she took each utensil, each ornament, each crevice and corner, and — carefully and concentratedly — in the washing and the rubbing and the

163

polishing of the contours of each object, she made the house her own.

Flora brushed the fallen leaves and twigs from the chimneypiece onto the rusted dustpan. The child had meant so much more to her than she had realised. And she was missing her father acutely, as well. He'd been buried the day she met Wilfred and her grief for him had been suspended — locked away — by shock, courtship, marriage and pregnancy. But her sadness for her father had been joined by her grief for her child and all the grief came tumbling out, like a swollen stream in spring full of melted ice water. And somewhere in her mind, too, was the memory of the loss of Albert.

She lit a small fire in the hearth. Wilfred was collecting the body of a farmer's wife who had died in the night, and Wilfred's da had taken an early-morning walk to forage in the hedgerows around Chamomile Bank. Flora had been waiting to have the house to herself. She looked around surreptitiously and scrunched up the newspaper into a ball, tearing stories of other people's lives in half, crushing the paper and placing it in the fire. It burned quickly and easily, almost with panache.

She took the small cardigan from the chest-of-drawers. It was peach-coloured wool and she had knitted it herself, counted each stitch one by one, in a gentle exactness so that the cardigan would fit the small chest of the child when it was born. She did up the buttons, simple bone buttons, four of them. She folded the sleeves inwards and laid the cardigan on the fire. It smoked blackly. She took the white wool bootees for feet that couldn't walk, and the delicate cotton bonnet for a fragile head and put them in the fire, too. She found the nightdress that was caked thickly with blood and she placed it on the fire, that second skin of hers, and she watched it, mesmerised by her own blood burning. She sat there on her knees in the cold morning light, burning her clothes and her daughter's clothes, until they were no more.

She would not have her daughter with her: that small dignified child with her brown plaits and her brown dress and her flat chest. The child who had come to her in a dream of knowing and said to her, before she went, forever: 'My name is Martha.' The baby had grown beneath her heart and would stay in her heart.

The fire flickered confidently and with energy, growing straight and tall and licking the chimney with exuberance. It cackled and the buttons on the tiny cardigan cracked and then smoked and the cotton smouldered. Flora shifted on her knees, the hearthrug leaving its impression on the bare skin of her calves. The newspaper turned to black carbon and kept its shape. She sat watching the fire, feeling it warm and colour her cheeks, and holding her thin white hands against it, letting its heat flow through her.

This house, here, that she had stayed in like a guest, in which her daughter had lived her brief, unlived life, Flora would make her home. Her daughter had left, but Flora would stay. Wilfred was kind to her, and during these painful days when she had been cleaning and hurting, she had come to understand the quiet value and immense consolation of Wilfred's kindness. Now, she felt married to Wilfred. There was nowhere else she wanted to run to, no other man — including Albert, as vital as he had been to her — that she wanted to marry. This surprised her, but it comforted her too. It was a gentle and quiet choice; she had come to it gradually, and it gave her peace. Albert she had loved, but Wilfred was the man she was with now, wanted to be with now.

Once the minute specks of scarlet fire had chased themselves around the cardigan, the cotton and the paper, and Flora had prodded the fire until it had died into black, she swept the hearth of the fine, clean ashes and flung open the window in the bedroom. She put her winter coat over her nightdress and bicycled along Water Street, then down the grassy hill to the tree-lined lane where she placed the ashes in the stream and watched the black bits of broken buttons bob away in the clear, icy water.

★ ★ ★

'I am delighted to welcome,' announced the Master of Ceremonies, 'our very own Narberth undertaker, Mr Wilfred Price, known to all and sundry as Wilfred, and his beautiful wife, Flora Myffanwy Price, who will be awarding the prizes in the dog competition this afternoon.'

The Queen's Hall was jam-packed, and well-meaning people strained to glimpse Wilfred and Flora standing at the front with the judges.

166

Wilfred doffed his hat and felt a certain embarrassment; although the crowd looked kindly at them, there were a few whispers. It was stuffy in the Queen's Hall and it smelled of dog.

'Are you well, my dear?' he asked Flora quietly.

'Yes,' she replied, removing a dog hair that had floated on the air and stuck to her lip. Ruddy dogs, Wilfred thought to himself. There were hairs all over his best work trousers and if that ruddy Jack Russell didn't stop yapping soon . . .

'Ladies and gentlemen — and you, Willie the Post!' the Master of Ceremonies called. 'This first category is The Most Obedient Dog in Narberth Competition. Narberth's most sensible dog, ladies and gentlemen.'

A cluster of owners and their dogs began eagerly jogging in a circle in front of the judges. One small boy, not much taller than his Scottie dog, was being dragged by his pet, not that the dog appeared to know where it was supposed to be going. A poodle, highly-strung, flew at an Alsatian, which barked ferociously.

'Mrs Morgan going past the judges now, with some off-lead heelwork,' the Master of Ceremonies commentated.

'And, Mr Peters, not really a dog, but a very loved member of the family, isn't he?' the Master of Ceremonies continued.

'Indeed,' Mr Peters admitted gravely.

The judges watched, imbued with a sense of importance at the civic duties bestowed upon them. Wilfred smiled. He would attempt to enjoy the afternoon. He would follow Mr Auden's advice. 'Hold all things lightly,' his apprentice-master had said to him once, offhandedly, in the earliest and most innocent days of his apprenticeship. 'It is the only way we can be undertakers, the only way we can live amongst all this death. Because nothing is deathless.' Then Mr Auden had clapped his hands and rubbed them together, as if he was a man who had just got up from his knees and finished praying.

Wilfred, trying to look enthusiastic, watched the dogs walk in obedient circles. Then a thought occurred to him: perhaps he was being punished.

'Now, ladies and gentlemen,' the Master of Ceremonies called, attempting to bring order, 'the Dog with the Waggiest Tail. Not you, Handel Evans!' The crowd laughed.

'I'll have your guts for garters!' Handel Evans retorted and punched the air jovially. There was a kerfuffle of chairs and barks, and purposeful people bustling in front of Wilfred. Another procession of owners paraded onto the floor, proud as punch of their pets. The Scottie terrier came along again with an even smaller boy — the younger brother, Wilfred presumed — and the small child kept tickling and patting the dog to make its white tail swing, while the judges consulted back and forth, writing notes intently on clipboards and scrutinising the dogs' tails.

Wilfred watched the dogs walk in obedient circles. Then the thought occurred to him again. Maybe he was being punished. Had this loss happened to him because he had done something wrong: not been good enough, not prayed hard enough, not read the Bible and disobeyed

God without even noticing? Perhaps he should have stayed married to Grace, obeyed his holy vows, not had a pint in the Conduit while Grace went alone, abandoned, onto a train and to goodness knows where. Maybe he should have thought more about Grace and less about his overwhelming love for Flora Myffanwy.

He realised that his guilt over his carelessness towards Grace had become a very heavy weight on his mind, one which he couldn't ignore, couldn't move aside or bury away, a guilt that sat rigidly in the centre of his thoughts, rotting and leaking shame. He wanted, as it were, to bury his guilt in a nice coffin, lower it into the ground and leave it be. But now it was too late: Grace had gone and his guilt had stayed.

Wilfred nodded absentmindedly at a dog-owner walking past with a Corgi. Yes, maybe he was being punished. He had had his chance to be good, to love and honour Grace and her child, to sacrifice himself to care for an honest, kind woman with a burden. He could have helped her, stayed with her, at least tried to love her, instead of lying in their marriage bed hating her. But he hadn't, he had wanted his own way and the wife he yearned for, Flora Myffanwy. He sighed. And though he had had his heart's desire in marrying Flora, he thought that perhaps she hadn't truly opened up her heart to him. So he couldn't make love, not really, to Flora, and he felt so ashamed of himself. No, he thought, with a sinking, shrinking feeling, he had not been a good man; he had not lived a good life. And now, he thought to himself, God had punished him.

'And the owner of The Dog with the Waggiest Tail in Narberth is . . . ' There was a dramatic pause while the judges whispered gravely to each other and the Master of Ceremonies waited on them for confirmation. The tension crescendoed. Finally the judges nodded solemnly in agreement.

'And the winner of The Dog with the Waggiest Tail in Narberth Winter Carnival, 1926 is . . . Bonzo and Mr Gerard Henry!'

Mr Gerard Henry didn't smile but closed his eyes in proud acknowledgement of his achievement, then strode up to Wilfred to be presented with the modest silver-plated cup he so richly deserved.

'Well done, Mr Henry.'

'Thank you *very* much indeed, Mr Price,' Mr Henry replied portentously, bending down and slapping his Alsatian hard on the chest. He pumped Wilfred's hand, his jacket straining over the bulk of his biceps.

Wouldn't like to have a dog like that in the house, Wilfred thought to himself, trying to focus on the goings-on around him. Not with that tail knocking over the ornaments and smashing into things all the time.

'Wonderful,' the Master of Ceremonies declared. 'A round of applause, please. Mr Henry and Bonzo, ladies and gentlemen! And our commiserations to all you other owners. Give them a big round of applause, ladies and gentlemen.'

Wilfred watched the little boy's shoulders slump as he led away his eager Scottie dog, its tail still swishing happily, unaware of its deficiencies. The

170

child padded over to his mother, looking as if he might cry.

'Some very waggy tails there, ladies and gentlemen,' consoled the Master of Ceremonies, trying to soothe the bruised feelings of the losers. Wilfred sighed; it all seemed so pointless. Very nice to have a dog with a waggy tail, but what did it mean? What was it all for?

'And now, ladies and gentlemen, it's time for The Bonniest Baby, The Beautifulest Baby in Narberth, 1926.' A line of nervous- and defensive-looking mothers came forward, carrying babies, many with large bows in their hair — some, Wilfred thought to himself, almost engulfed in fat. A dog yelped. Wilfred was suddenly surrounded by babies, gurgling and crying. There was the chink of tea saucers and teaspoons jingling and men teasing each other mercilessly.

'Don't let him walk away. Get the silly bugger!' he heard a dog-owner urge.

'Wilfred, word in your ear, please,' motioned Handel Evans. 'I, myself, in my own opinion, if you ask me, think the Jack Russell should have won. It had the waggiest tail. No doubt about it.'

'Wilfred Price, what are you doing here?' A man grabbed his hand and patted his upper arm. 'Looking for someone to bury?'

'Wilfred, I's want you now for a photograph with Mr Gerard Henry and Bonzo,' commandeered Mr Arthur Squibs of Squibs Studios in Tenby. 'Stand right next to Bonzo, Wilfred.' Mr Squibs covered his head with the camera's dark cloth. 'Can you get that dog to keep its ruddy tail still? *Get that damn dog to stand still!*' Mr

171

Squibs shouted, his voice muffled by the cloth. 'Smile, Wilfred. You're not at a funeral now. One, two . . . three!' The flash popped, fizzed then smoked. Wilfred saw two white blobs dancing in front of his eyes.

'Are you enjoying yourself, dear?' he asked Flora.

'Yes,' she replied, but the vein bisecting her forehead was standing out and pulsating, and Wilfred knew from the last few weeks that that's what happened when Flora was trying to hold back the tears.

'Even so, we'd better be going. Let me help you with your coat, my dear.' He put his hand in the curve of her back. 'Yes, oh yes, off home now, enough excitement for one day,' he said to the people who jostled and greeted him. 'Didn't know Narberth had such dogs in it. Oh yes, they're the caterpillar's whiskers. Wonderful, wonderful, the elephant's eyebrow,' he commented as he guided Flora to the door, to their empty home devoid of dogs. Their pristine, empty, dog-less, childless home.

11

Small Enough to
Fit in a Shoebox

Grace looked around the Conway Hall and searched the faces in the packed gallery. She had not been to a meeting here for a couple of months, but had stayed in her dirty, lonely room in the Caledonian Lodging House, where Madoc wouldn't find her, not working, only reading, eating, sleeping — and waiting. She had tried to decide what to do, was thinking of a plan, and was intending to get a cardboard box but found it hard to think clearly about the time ahead. Her sense of the future was getting smaller and smaller. When she first came to London she had thought in terms of weeks, now it was reduced to a few days at a time.

The straight-backed women surrounding her in the meeting were listening intently to the speaker. The air was hot and stuffy and the hall was even fuller than last time. If there was a fire, few people would be able to get out, what with the wall-to-wall chairs, although some of the women looked like they might be willing to sacrifice themselves for the Cause, so ardently were they listening and nodding. She took the gold watch from her pocket and glanced at it; the second hand had stopped. It needed rewinding. Grace fidgeted on the chair: her corset was digging into her very uncomfortably and she kept her coat on and loose around her. She knew she would need a place to give birth very soon and had a vague idea of walking to the Princess of Wales Hospital, then leaving the baby, perhaps in the cardboard box, outside a convent, but if she tried to make her ideas anything more than vague, her mind slipped away and refused to think. Then today she had woken up and felt stirred and disturbed. Today she was frightened to be alone, and needed people.

Grace focused her mind on the meeting. There was more fervour in this meeting than the last one: a sense of conspiracy and dedication to things not yet realised that could change their lives. The Suffragettes were rapt and attentive to the articulate woman addressing them, as if she held the dream for all of them. Grace fiddled with the watch in her pocket, barely listening to the speaker.

'We are a small band but we are strong and we claim our voice,' the lady asserted in an almost masculine manner, like a modern Boudicca. 'The battle we fought so ardently before the War is not yet over: we must continue to fight, until women have an equal voice in Parliament.'

Grace was searching for Lady Lytton but was distracted by the oratory of a clear female voice. She tried to recall, before these meetings, when she had heard a woman address other women at an event, but didn't think she ever had. Women usually spoke after men had spoken, and then only to agree or to be interrupted.

'Mrs Pankhurst, ladies.'

The audience burst into a standing ovation, causing the bunting in the hall to flutter energetically. The clapping continued and Mrs Pankhurst stood in front of the women, as if acknowledging that the applause wasn't for her and that she was subordinate to the Cause. Eventually the clapping subsided and conversations broke out, and in the hubbub after the meeting, Grace saw Lady Lytton, her auburn hair catching the light.

'Lady Lytton,' she called. Lady Lytton, a sketchbook under her arm, was talking intimately with another woman. She turned gracefully and looked at Grace.

'I won't interrupt you,' Grace began. 'Your gift. I want to give it back to you.' The words fell from her and, something of her truth, her core, emerged. Grace pulled an unmarked envelope from her pocket and passed it to Lady Lytton, who simply glanced at it.

'I can't sell it,' Grace whispered as women thronged by, 'and I can't keep it; I would be taken for a thief. It belongs to you; it has your name engraved on the back. It is of no use to me.'

Lady Lytton considered her, as if studying her for a portrait. She rested her hand on Grace's worn serge coat and said quietly, if sadly, 'You are foolish if you reject friendship.' She pressed the watch back into Grace's hand. 'Take care of yourself, Grace.' Lady Lytton pulled her silver mink stole over her shoulder, turned her head and then moved away towards the door.

★ ★ ★

Grace walked out of the Conway Hall, across Theobalds Road and through the dark streets towards King's Cross and the Caledonian Road. Her back was aching; her body felt tight and the rhythm of walking eased the stiffness in her hips. Grace felt stung; Lady Lytton's words had hit home. Hilda, Lady Lytton, Wilfred in his own way, had all offered their friendship and she had dismissed their care and generosity, too numb and too lost as she was in her own pain. Even her father had given her money and asked — perhaps he had been imploring — that she write. But she had rejected them all.

As she walked slowly in the direction of her lodgings, she thought about the sharp new aspect she saw in herself: how she had pushed everyone away in what she hoped were the darkest, most uncertain moments of her life. Something dreadful had happened to her and she had been paralysed and unreachable, yet the world had still turned around her, offering her some kindness and succour. And she hadn't seen it. She looked at the gold watch clenched in her hand. *You are foolish if you reject friendship*, Lady Lytton had said. She was right and the words echoed powerfully in Grace's mind.

She trudged down a street that narrowed and turned sharply to the left. Unexpectedly, there was a pack of lupine-looking men leaning around a dirty fire in an oil drum. Some of the men were dodging here and there, moving away then prowling back into the huddle, making comments,

176

their heads to one side. One man in a smart —
almost exceptionally smart — three-piece suit stood
at a distance from the group. Two women were
leaning against a ragged brick wall. The tart, man-
nered gesture with which they crossed their ankles
gave them away. The women stopped their conversation abruptly and stared at Grace, their ringed
fingers now removed from their pockets, like
gold claws. The men stopped their conversations
too, aware of the tension that had come over the
women, aware of the direction in which they
were looking. Grace didn't belong here. It was
yet another place in which she didn't fit but had
stumbled into.

She went to turn back but the man in the suit
called out, 'You, girl. Woman.' He flung his arm
wide and towards her.

Grace pulled her coat around her, the brightness
of the smoking, carbon-speckled flames blinding
her.

'You're a pretty innocent to be walking through
here. With them, are you?' The man nodded in
the direction of the two women. The men laughed.

'Not by the look of her,' one of them sneered.
Grace felt humiliated.

'What have you got in your hand?' Grace
reluctantly opened her hand, the diamonds of
the gold watch glittering in the firelight.

He looked at her closely, this time taking her
seriously, and walked towards her. 'Where did
you get that? You in service?'

Grace fell back upon the silence and secrecy
that had enfolded her these last months, and said
nothing.

'Give it here.' The man dangled the watch by the end of the strap as if it was a tiny, rare, just-caught fish shimmering in the light and wiggling for its life. He held it high above the fire, glanced at Grace fleetingly, then dropped it.

'Ah!' Grace exclaimed, reeling forward. But she was too stout, too many yards away. The man caught the watch a fraction after he dropped it, putting his hand in the flame for a split-second, smiling with a triumphant serenity at his trickery and showmanship.

'It wouldn't have mattered,' he said, walking towards Grace. 'The white gold would only have melted eventually into a golden ball in the bottom of the can when the fire died. The diamonds would have been untouched.' He smiled and the flames lit up his oily skin. 'What's your name?'

'Mabel,' Grace mumbled.

'And I'm Jack Robinson,' he replied, looking around at the men for their rookie laughter. They laughed.

'I don't want it,' he stated, holding the gold watch out to Grace. 'Keep your Cartier Baignoire, or give it back to Lady Penelope Lytton.' The man threw the wristwatch up and caught it with one hand. He wound the diamond crown on the watch and the black hands turned. 'I live without trace. I work without trace,' he said. Grace felt her heart thumping so hard that her bones vibrated with its rhythm.

'Come back and see me again,' he raised his eyebrows teasingly, 'if you've got something to sell.' He handed back the now-ticking watch.

Grace held the watch tightly in her hand, turned and left, stumbling through one street after another towards a foggy light in the distance.

★　★　★

Grace ran as fast as she could, though running was hard and slow, and kept checking behind her but no one was following. The group wasn't interested in her, only themselves and the two women who had been hostile and wanted her to leave, but still Grace felt anxious and afraid.

She paused and noticed a vivid light ahead that seemed like a curly light bulb spelling out a word that she hadn't seen before. It said *Beigels*. She trudged up to the window of the bakery, panting, her stomach tight and hard, wanting to find safety, sit down and rest. The baker's was bright with warmth coming from it. Grace stood by the window for reassurance and the woman inside smiled and beckoned her in. Grace obeyed.

Inside, Grace stood at the very high counter, and felt like a child. She dropped the watch back in her pocket.

'When's it due?' the woman asked directly.

'I don't know exactly,' Grace admitted. She had not seen a doctor; her father would be disapproving.

'Very soon, by the looks of you.'

Grace nodded, her hands trembling. The woman retied her headscarf.

'You look lost.' She slit a hollowed bread roll with a very long knife, spread it with butter in a slip-slap motion and put on floppy slices of meat, then mustard and replaced the top, all with split-second timing and deftness of hand. 'Here, you're pale. Eat this.'

Grace lifted her coat slightly, rolled down her stocking and took a note from her stocking hem.

'It's on the house,' the woman said, dismissing the note. 'Keep it. You're going to need it.'

Grace took the bread and nodded silently.

'Stay if you want. We are open all day and all night,' the woman stated.

'All night?'

'Yes. Those are neon lights and they are always burning. We bake through the night. There is always hunger, and people who want to buy bread.'

Through an arch beyond the counter Grace could see three men kneading huge balls of dough. She felt her stomach cramp. She closed her eyes and felt something inside her open up.

'Sit down. Make yourself at home.' The woman indicated the many benches at the front of the bakery — all of them empty. Grace moved along a small, warm bench, easing herself in and resting her feet.

'You on your own?' the woman asked.

Grace nodded. 'Yes,' she said. 'Yes — I am on my own.' She sighed.

The woman held another beigel on its side and within a moment it was in two halves. She placed the two halves up on the counter, their pale insides exposed.

'No one?'

'No one I can think of.'

'Like my grandmother. She came to London in 1850 alone, but she knew how to bake, then she married and had children.'

Grace took a bite of the bread, her teeth cutting, her body rising to meet the food, welcoming it into her body.

The woman took a handful of eggs and put them in a pan of boiling water.

'She walked from Poland,' she said. 'Took her three months. She was an orphan, her country was overrun by the Cossacks and her home was burned down.'

Grace put her hand across her eyes, still listening to the woman.

'People's lives were harder then,' the woman stated, turning back to the pan of rattling eggs. She put another huge pan of water on the hob and began lifting trays of eggs to boil from under the counter. Grace sat at the bench, waves of tension coming and going over her, while the woman worked.

Grace looked at the half-eaten beigel on the plate in front of her. Instantaneously, she remembered Wilfred eating dinner in her parents' house many months ago now, and him saying to her father, 'Please could you pass the salt? Salt for the meat.' She recalled the phrase, the power of it, how strong Wilfred had seemed as — because — he was released from their marriage, free to embark on a new life. And how friendless she felt without him. She had often wondered what had happened to him — he'd told her he was in love with another woman — and what he'd done.

A man walked in and placed his ruddy-faced baby on the glass counter. The baby's mouth was

stained with food and his eyes and his hands
were searching. The man stood holding the baby,
balancing him on the glass edge.

The woman took a basket of beigels from the
shelf behind her.

'Sir?' she called.

Grace watched the woman serve several eager
customers who were arriving and standing alertly
in the line, waiting not without slight agitation. A
baker in a white apron came through carrying a
box of gherkins. There was a shout from the
bakery at the back. A wave of pain washed over
Grace, then receded. She felt she was going to be
subsumed by some form of drowning: Grace
stood.

'Is it time?' the woman said to Grace, her back
still to her. Grace nodded, her hand pressed hard
to the space between her eyebrows.

'You got anywhere to go to do this?' the
woman asked.

'No.'

'Down the back, to the storeroom,' the woman
stated. She spoke in a matter-of-fact way and
took Grace by the arm. Grace was floundering
now, and vulnerable. She was led through the
kitchen with its sounds of clashing, a flour-
covered tabletop and a stack of wooden trays
filled with unfinished circles of bread. A baker
with a tray of sliced red meat lifted it above his
head, stood and let Grace pass.

'Comfortable there?' another baker asked her
and smiled. 'Not really,' he said, answering his
own question. 'Women's business.'

Suddenly from outside in the darkness came a

great shout — a call rising up — indecipherable, sounding like a sea shanty, the voice of a reveller spiralling with strength and full of yearning. Grace felt the sound go through her, and heard a voice within her say, *I am strong enough to do this*, and the words echo around the chambers of her body.

Grace let the storeroom around her recede. At first she saw the door, the flour-patted walls, the tools of a bakery, heard voices demanding . . . but then the sights, the colours, the objects in front of her became blurs and the room lost its form, became a coloured mist, then disappeared, and the sounds became silence. The feel against her flank of tea towels warm from a stove faded, along with her sense of time, as all of her went within herself, deeper still, until she was nothing but a heartbeat and consciousness, and what was around her was nothing to what was within her. This is beyond pain, Grace thought to herself.

After what felt like — perhaps was — hours, she heard someone say, 'It's a boy.'

★　★　★

When Grace opened her eyes, the woman was sitting by her, watching over her. Grace lifted her head from the sacks that had been folded into a pillow.

'Rest a while longer,' the woman said, looking down at the child in her arms.

Grace got onto all fours and made to stand up. 'I must go,' she said.

183

'You've just had a baby.'

'No, I'm fine. I am.'

The woman put her hands on her ample hips, blocking the light from the bakery behind. Grace stood, like a weakened cow, her legs akimbo, wobbly, new, raw.

'You can't go.' The woman put her hand on Grace's arm and Grace almost collapsed next to a sack of flour. 'You have a mind of your own, don't you? The child needs to be fed and in the warm; you need some tea and food. You can't labour, then walk.'

Grace knew this wasn't true. In the past, the poor women in the farms around Narberth, burdened by pregnancy, had worked in the fields even in winter, hacking out vegetables, clawing into the frozen earth with picks, bundled against the cold in their shawls and woollen skirts. They gave birth in the fields, lying on their backs or down on all fours. And then they picked the baby up from the earth and swaddled it in a shawl tied to their fronts, rested, drank from a flask of brandy, ate a hunk of cheese and a piece of black bread. A couple of hours later, they would stand on stout limbs and labour again, at the hard winter soil. It was ever thus.

Grace took a step.

'You need a bath.'

Grace had to admit she needed a bath. There was a butchery to birth, as if the inside ruptured onto the outside, and she must wash herself.

Soon the woman had placed a tin bath in the corner of the room and was filling it, pitcher by pitcher, with hot, steaming water. Grace sat

184

leaning against hard bags of flour. The child was wrapped in a clean warm cloth at her side.

'Don't you want to hold your child?' the woman asked. She picked up the child and put him into Grace's arms. Grace took him but then placed him on the floor beside her, stood up, removed the remains of her splattered clothing and stepped carefully into the bath.

The woman began mopping the floor in the middle of the room.

'That was over mercifully quickly. And quietly,' she said, putting her hand to her brow in relief. Then: 'You're a queer one.'

Grace sat on her haunches in the bath.

'Are you going to keep the child?'

Grace turned around in the bath and faced the other way — in the opposite direction to the child. The woman rested the bloated mop against a table piled high with empty wooden trays. 'Hmm,' she said, and picked up the child.

Grace looked down at her body in the bathtub; she had not properly looked at herself naked for months. Her nipples were a freckled coffee brown. Her tummy button was blackened. But it was her body again. It had been used and returned. She wiped clots of blood from her ankle, then her forearms, and felt purged, expunged, lightened, as if a burden of sin had been removed, a memory and an experience razed and forgotten. She rested her head on her knees. She was herself again. It had been a long time.

'So do you have somewhere to go?'

'Yes.'

'Where?'

Grace rubbed at her legs.

The woman put her finger in the baby's mouth and the baby sucked toothlessly.

'Do you want your child?'

Grace stood up suddenly in the bath. She took a clean tea towel from a pile on the table and briskly rubbed herself dry. The child mewled: a small, pathetic sound.

'He's hungry. He'll need milk soon,' the woman said.

Grace dressed silently. Would she be cold and sharp as broken cut glass? And leave her child to the world? Not care? She shocked herself by the hardness she felt, but it was familiar to her too; she felt as if something of her own mother came upon her. She had watched her mother's cruelty all her life, seen its mannerisms and its sighs, its gestures and its phrases. And she could ape it, adopt it and feel it ripple into herself. So Grace took the corset and wrapped it round herself, tightening the xylophone of straps. She was thinner. At last. Grace buttoned her dress; all the while the woman watching, holding the child.

'You can't leave the child with me.' The woman leaned on her mop. Grace straightened her clothes and reached for her coat.

'Before you go,' the woman said, changing her tack and sitting down on the dusty floor in the corner of the storeroom. 'Before you go — you can leave him, but feed him first. It is late; it will be hours before I could find him milk. Feed him and he will sleep,' she argued. 'Then I will take him and find him a home. But feed him once before you go.'

186

Grace put on her coat.

'Sit.' The woman patted the ground beside her.

Grace sat down beside the door but not beside the woman. The room was bright, over-illuminated and painful to her eyes.

'Here.' The woman crawled over, cradling the baby. Grace sighed. Weakness came over her and the woman placed the child, which she had wrapped in linen, in Grace's lap. Grace sat like a cloth doll as the woman said, 'like this,' and, 'like this', arranging the child in Grace's arm. The child searched as if by instinct for the source of food. He was floppy and inert and Grace felt floppy too, and inert like a jelly. The child would do as it would with Grace's body, as her brother had done, and then Grace — separate, alone, herself again — would leave. Grace would belong to herself again. She sat there and the child searched and found, and lost and found where the food came from, wiggling in frustration.

'Help the child,' the woman urged, but Grace ignored her so that the woman took the bap of Grace's breast as if it were uncooked dough that she was moulding, until it was in the child's open mouth. Grace stared ahead, dispossessed. The woman said nothing, kneeling in front of Grace; one hand holding the child's head up, the other hand holding Grace's breast in the child's mouth. And there the three of them huddled, the child sucking, Grace exhausted and the woman at the outer realm of her skill and knowledge of what it took to make another woman give birth to herself as a mother.

187

* ★ *

Grace got off the tram at Piccadilly, by Eros, who was poised lightly on his pedestal, positioned to shoot an arrow at an unsuspecting mortal. She stopped in a dank doorway near the new Swan & Edgar department store, and rewrapped the swaddled baby so no one could see its face — so *she* could not see its face.

Grace felt weak. She leaned against the cold brick wall of the doorway. That morning, she had left the bakery then collected her suitcase from the Caledonian Lodging House, knowing she would no longer be welcome there. The landlady had made that clear. All afternoon she had wandered around the streets, finally catching a tram and sitting slumped on it until it terminated at Piccadilly Circus, the conductor shouting, 'The Angel of Christian Charity,' when they reached the statue which Grace had thought was called Eros. She should be hungry but she wasn't; her appetite had fallen away, and she needed to rest.

'Are you in trouble, miss?' a young man with an amputated arm asked, looking into the doorway where Grace was half-hidden.

'No.'

'You are unwell?'

'No. I am well.'

'Only asking, ma'am.' The man had spoken to her as an equal and not as a maid who tidied other people's mess. He walked away, turning round briefly to check on her. He smiled, and doffed his cap. All I need to know, Grace thought, all any woman needs to know about any man, is that he is kind. That's all.

It was late afternoon; the daylight was beginning to fade. She must find a convent and a cardboard box. She stepped from the doorway facing the new electric billboards on the front of the London Pavilion, their lights incandescent in the fog, and slowly trudged across Piccadilly. Her father said if a man stood long enough in Piccadilly Circus he would see the whole world go by, and meet everyone he knew. But Grace didn't want to meet anyone she knew and traipsed onwards, through the formal garden in Leicester Square then towards Trafalgar Square, to an imposing church with six pillars in its portico and a tall, sharp spire. Pulling her shabby coat around her, she stopped and read the black and gold sign: *Saint Martin in the Fields. Church of the Ever Open Door.* But she hadn't yet found a box, and if she left it here, there were people all around who would see her walk away, perhaps call her back. A huddle of unemployed men were camped on the stone steps, like a tatty, listless pack of dogs. One lay curled on newspapers, one with his back to the many pedestrians, the sun-missed skin above his trousers revealed. Their homelessness frightened her. The baby began to mewl and the men turned.

'Come here, love,' one of them called, but Grace walked quickly away.

She kept walking, passing the National Gallery where people were spilling out onto the pavement. They chatted, buttoned up dress coats and pulled on leather gloves before dispersing onto omnibuses. Grace stumbled down a lane behind the Gallery and through quiet, cobbled side-streets until she found a discarded cardboard box outside a closed butcher's shop. It was battered but clean. She waited a moment, looked around surreptitiously, took it and walked on. It was a large box and she struggled to carry it along with the baby.

Suddenly she felt overwhelmed and strangely hot, and all she wanted to do was sleep. She thought of Wilfred: strong and tall in his undertaker's suit, Wilfred in her bedroom, Wilfred holding her on the last night of their married life. He was the only man who had ever held her, or rather the only man who had held her with affection. Then she thought of Wilfred's da and his gentleness and how he had complimented her at the wedding breakfast on the honey from her hive. That was when she had Wilfred to love and bees to keep: when there had been hope.

She collapsed onto a muddy kerb. 'Excuse me,' she called out to a tall man coming down the lane. 'I'm looking for a convent.'

'A convent?' the man replied, taken aback. 'I don't know that there's a convent around here. This is near the picture houses in Leicester Square. Is there something the matter, miss?'

'No.'

He looked at Grace and he looked at his watch. 'There's a convent near Marble Arch, that way.' He pointed diagonally. 'But it's a walk. You'll need to take the omnibus to Oxford Street, past Selfridges department store, miss.'

Grace stood up tentatively. 'I'm well, thank you,' she said, not realising the man hadn't asked after her well-being, was already moving away. She walked slowly up the lane in the direction the man had indicated, but soon the child began to cry. Grace walked a little further until she found a hidden office doorway, which she crouched into. She put down the cardboard box, undid her coat and the buttons on her dress and tried to put her breast in the child's mouth without covering his nose. She saw his red and ugly face, pickled and raw. He was small enough to fit into a shoebox.

It was foggy and beginning to rain, steadily heavier. Grace sat in a damp huddle as the rain isolated her from the streets around. But she couldn't leave him here; he would get wet. And it might be a while before a passer-by found him. But there were childless people who wanted a child. She would give them a gift. The mother, the father and the child would be happy and complete. And her gift in return would be to walk away. She ought to do it quickly, the sooner the better. Someone would find him. When it stopped raining, she would look for somewhere sheltered and walk away.

'Miss. Come out of the doorway, please. May I offer you assistance?' a police constable asked, the imposing silver star on his helmet glinting in the dark. 'Would you like to come with me to the police box to get out of the wet?'

Grace shook her head, thrown by the police-man's presence, as if she was already guilty.

'Where are you heading?'

'Paddington.'

'Well, there's a surprise: a baby. My wife has a baby. I know these things can be awkward, but come out of the rain, please, Mrs . . . ?'

'Rice.'

'Rice. Let me move that cardboard box out from under your feet, I don't want you to trip.' The policeman offered her a brolly as she stood up. 'The Number 23 goes to Paddington train station. I will accompany you to the bus stop on Trafalgar Square, it's only two minutes away.' He guided Grace, his hand under her elbow, towards the end of the lane where Grace could see the silhouettes of streetlamps and passing motor cars. 'He is a small baby. Is it a boy?'

Grace nodded.

'How old is he?'

'Two weeks.'

'He's small for two weeks,' the constable said, the chain on his whistle rattling. 'Our little chap is a bit older; two months and a day.' The young man beamed, eager to talk. 'There's not much you can do to keep them quiet when they are that young but milk is the answer to everything. If they want milk, they have to have it, that's that. My wife has the same problem. But we can't have you out in the rain. Dear me, no. What are you doing in London with a Scottish accent? There's the number 23.' He ran to the kerb, waved a white-gloved hand and a red bus pulled over. Grace stepped tentatively onto the platform.

'She's going to Paddington railway station, conductor,' the constable shouted.

The conductor tinged the bell, then began punching the buttons on his ticket machine.

'Single?' he asked. Grace nodded.

The conductor quickly turned the handle on the machine, a ticket stuttered out and he handed it to Grace.

'Threepence, please. Dreadful weather. Wouldn't be surprised if there was a pea-souper,' the conductor commented chattily to Grace. The bus stopped abruptly — he bent down and looked out of the window. 'There'll be some drunks falling in the Thames tonight, but don't you worry yourself about that, miss. You and your baby get straight home to your husband and into the warm and dry. Have you got far to go when you get to Paddington station?' he asked, holding onto the back of a seat to keep his balance.

Grace nodded.

'Where's that then?'

'Narberth.'

12

A Good Home

Wilfred woke abruptly. There had been a tap on the front door. Who was it? Mr Probert! He looked at Flora Myffanwy, who was fast asleep beside him. He heard a knock again and quick, quiet steps. That was definitely a rap on the door. If he opened the curtains and looked out of the window, the light might wake Flora Myffanwy. And she needed to sleep. At least his da wasn't there; he'd gone to stay with Auntie Blodwen. His da had endured enough recently, and if there was any trouble, and if it was that Probert, he would deal with it alone.

He peered at the alarm clock. Twenty minutes to six. Who would knock on the door at this time of the morning? Someone must have died — that was the reason. He'd have to go and collect a body. In the pitch-dark, he got out of bed, pulled on his long-johns and padded barefoot down the winding staircase — avoiding the third step, which creaked loudly.

He peered through the bay window in the paint and wallpaper shop. No one. That was strange. He turned towards the ruins of Narberth Castle but there was no one to see there either. Wilfred felt sure he had heard someone. He was overwrought, that's what it was, and imagining things — what with the baby and his worry for Flora. Wilfred sighed, rubbed his forehead and turned to go back to bed. The brain could do things like that when one was frightened and on the edge, he thought to himself. He felt weary as he climbed the stairs.

'Come here,' he whispered to Flora Myffanwy as he got into bed. He moved over to her and put his arm around her now-thin body, closed his eyes and felt his own body relax around the contours of his wife. Then he heard something again. He opened his eyes. He could hear a sniffling sound — like a fox or a badger. But there wouldn't be a badger in town: they were too shy a creature to come so boldly into Narberth, even in the darkest night. He would go and check one more time. It could be someone who was grieving, and he knew grief made people behave strangely.

Wilfred opened the unlocked door.

'Hello,' he called cautiously. 'Is someone there?'

No one there. He was imagining things. He stepped out with bare feet, knocking a cardboard box on the doorstep. He bent down and picked it up with one hand and something, a weight inside, slid to one side with a small mewl.

It was an animal in the box. Why on God's earth was someone leaving a cat on the doorstep in the middle of the night? No accounting for folk, as his da said. Perhaps it was dying and they wanted Wilfred to bury it. He balanced the box in his arms and opened it. There, wrapped in a kerfuffle of blankets, was a baby, a wide-awake baby, its dark, moist eyes staring up at Wilfred. Wilfred blinked. He was seeing things. A baby was on the doorstep. It was . . . it was his baby! His and Flora Myffanwy's baby! The thought flashed through his head in a split second. No, it couldn't be. It wasn't their baby, it was another baby. Why would anyone give him a baby in the middle of the night?

The baby made a small sound, a whimper. It was alive. It didn't need to be buried; it needed to be cared for. The baby looked at him unflinching, acceptingly, as if it was perfectly normal to be lying in a cardboard box on an undertaker's doorstep in Narberth, in the middle of the night.

He took the box inside and up to their bedroom.

'Flora,' he whispered. She didn't move. The baby snuffled. Wilfred looked at the child: this unearthly creature with a wrinkly, raw face and flaking skin. This was a completely different sort of human being from him. It wasn't an adult and it wasn't a corpse, and so Wilfred was at a loss. The baby screwed up its eyes. Was it going to cry?

'Flora!' he whispered urgently. Flora stirred, brushing a mass of brown curls from her eyes. 'Look!' Flora looked at the cardboard box, puzzled, not understanding Wilfred's urgency. 'Look inside the box.'

'Is it a delivery?' she asked, half-awake.

'No. Yes.'

'Has the post been? That's early. Is it for me?'

'No . . . ' Wilfred said hesitatingly, whispering,

'I don't know who it's for.'

The lid of the cardboard box flopped forward. There was a sound from inside. Wilfred looked around, not knowing where to put the box down. It had occurred to him that perhaps he should take the baby out of the box, but he didn't know how to pick up a baby, wasn't sure how to hold it or lift it up. How did you pick up a baby? The questions raced through his head.

'Here, Wilfred, put it on the bed,' Flora suggested calmly, sitting up.

'I'll put the box on the bed, then?' It came out as a question.

'Yes, Wilfred,' Flora said, smiling, humouring him. Wilfred placed the box on the quilt and there was the sound of the baby slipping and hitting the side of the box. Wilfred gasped, utterly horrified.

'Is it a box of china?' Flora asked.

Wilfred was now in a state of panic. 'No.'

Flora looked in the box and caught her breath: 'It's a baby.' The baby gazed up at them with dark, fresh eyes; absolutely perfect eyes. Wilfred was mesmerised by the tiny human being lying in the box.

'Why has someone left a child with us?' Flora asked.

'We have a child,' Wilfred heard himself saying. Yes, he thought, Flora and I have a child. All the grief and loss and shock of the past months disappeared as Wilfred's world, the world itself, was righted. They had a child. All was well with the world. The earliest light began to filter through the curtains into the room

— somewhere a million miles away the sun was shining. The Earth was spinning on its axis and slowly, inexorably, the day was coming as faint sunbeams stretched and gently reached out into the room.

'No,' Flora said. 'This is not our child.' She looked at Wilfred. 'We must find its mother,' she said.

'But it has been abandoned!' Wilfred was taken aback by the force with which he heard himself say the words. 'Its mother doesn't want it or why else would she have left it with us? On the doorstep? The child has come to us, Flora. To *us*.' He looked around. No one could see them, no one could hear them, apart from the child in the cardboard box.

'No, Wilfred, a mother would want her child.'

Wilfred felt anger within him, something steel-like in his stomach, and he felt the strength in both his shoulders and his back as he spoke.

'But she wasn't looking after it. You don't leave your baby on a doorstep in a cardboard box if you want it.'

'You do.'

'You don't.' Wilfred heard himself contradict his wife. He had contradicted his wife. Flora looked at the counterpane. They had never had cross words before; they had never disagreed before. Wilfred had never before thought his wife was wrong. Wrong!

'But she's gone,' he continued, 'and we'll never find her, and she's left him here. With *us*. And she could have left him with anyone in Market Street, in Narberth . . . in Pembrokeshire! She could have put him on the steps of a . . . ' Wilfred tried to think of the places someone might leave their child . . . 'a shop! Or — or a church!' Wilfred urged, remembering the places he had heard that people left babies. 'She didn't leave him on the step of an undertaker's by accident.'

'The child wasn't left with us by accident.'

'No! She wanted us to have him. So she must not want it — him, her — the baby.' Wilfred realised he didn't know what sort of baby it was. Because it could be a girl. Or a boy. It definitely wasn't an 'it'. But that was beside the point. 'So, it's ours, then. That's all decided.'

Flora looked away. Somewhere in the depths of himself, Wilfred knew his grief was speaking, that his grief was being given voice.

'We'll tell everyone you've had the baby and it was all right.' He heard the fantasies of grief come from him.

The baby lifted a small, curled hand near his face. Flora and Wilfred watched as the baby tried to rub his eyes, yawned wholeheartedly and then appeared to fall asleep instantaneously.

He was right. Yes! He was right. The child was meant for them. Their family was complete. And now he was a father.

'Right . . . right.' Wilfred began to concoct a plan. They'd tell his da when he came back from Auntie Blodwen's that . . . the baby was — hadn't — was upstairs and Flora would be down with the baby soon, and he would be in the workshop today. Varnishing as usual. And his da wouldn't say anything. He would take it all as normal. His da accepted things, was dignified and kept his counsel. And they'd tell everyone else in Narberth that it had been a mistake and the baby hadn't died. These thoughts rushed through Wilfred's head in an instant.

He saw that Flora had put her finger into the box and the baby was holding her finger in its hand while sleeping; it looked as if it was renouncing itself to sleep. The baby was happy.

'The baby is happy with us,' he said. 'See, the baby is happy.' He gazed, awestruck, at the tiny child.

Flora thought for a moment. 'This is Grace's child,' she said.

Reality hit Wilfred. It felt cold. He closed his eyes for a moment. Yes, it could be Grace's baby.

'We must find her,' Flora replied, 'before she leaves Narberth.'

'Perhaps she is at her parents' house,' Wilfred suggested.

'Then she wouldn't have left the baby with us.'

Wilfred nodded. 'I'll go,' he said. 'I'll help her.'

★ ★ ★

Grace put her foot onto the Carmarthen train. The patent leather of her shoe was scuffed, the shine scraped away and she could feel the ridged ledge of the train step through her worn sole. Would Wilfred care for the child? He had been kind to her. But he had also rejected and divorced her; he might reject the child. But the child would be safer to leave with Wilfred than with a stranger in London. He would see that the child went to a good home.

Grace stood still, one shoe on the train, one shoe on the platform in Narberth, waiting for her foot to step into a carriage. Her body was perfectly balanced: her feet, her spine, her head, her shoulders, felt erect and in order, her poise perfect. She trusted that Wilfred would care for the child. The child would grow up in Narberth or nearby. He wouldn't be lost to the world. The train hissed. She would get on the train now.

'All aboard,' the guard shouted.

Grace looked at her shoelaces, frayed and knotted together. She stood still.

'Miss. All aboard!'

The driver blew his whistle. It was a certain sound. To Grace it meant only one thing — the endless forwardness of life.

'Miss!'

She saw the guard walking hurriedly towards her, along the carriages, eager to sort this out, restore order, to make the first train of the day depart from Narberth on the dot to arrive at Whitland the minute it was supposed to arrive. He lumbered towards her. She would get on the train now. Grace waited for her foot to lift her up and put her on the train. She waited for her body to rule and define her as it had done so expertly and inevitably while she was pregnant. Her body had shaped her life and she expected it to get her on the train and take her forward. And she would live like a dumb, empty ghost inside it, neither dead nor alive, merely functioning, merely residing in a body that decided her fate. But Grace saw her foot move backwards, step back on the platform.

'Miss?'

No, she wouldn't leave. Grace looked down, her two feet neatly on the gravel, facing the train, but no longer on it. No, she would make sure Wilfred had found the cardboard box, see that Wilfred had taken the box from the doorstep. The guard stopped abruptly, turned and hurried back to his cabin, arms and legs swinging in exasperation. The whistle blew and the train lurched and hissed like a great mechanised snake, then slithered round the corner ever eastwards.

* * *

Grace sat down on the wooden bench on the platform and swallowed hard, shaken that she had almost stepped onto the train and away. With each moment, the light grew stronger. Should she take the child back, the small, living human being she had left in a cardboard box on the doorstep of her ex-husband's house, which was also the funeral parlour, at half past four on this cold morning? Could she walk through the now dawn-lit streets, be seen and pretend she was visiting Narberth? She had been born here — she was the doctor's daughter and was part of Narberth; she could not visit, could only belong. Could she call at Wilfred's front door and ask?

She hugged her suitcase to herself. Did she want the child back? But she could have a fresh start, now that the child was finally separate from her. Where did someone go when they were lost? They went home. Her thoughts were muddled.

She could still walk away. She could be like virgin snow again, never trodden on. Her body would regain its integrity and bear no marks, though it was aching as if it had been punched and kicked or had the influenza. She might return to London — it was an interesting place — perhaps become a Suffragette, learn jujutsu. Although she might have to go back into service. Or she could go abroad. She was free and alone. She felt like a balloon untethered, with no one, nothing, holding her string.

Suddenly, Grace heard a motor car driving down Station Road. She hoped it was for one of the houses, but it approached nearer and she heard it stop at the dead end of Station Road. It would be someone for the train, whenever the next train was. Grace jumped up, grabbed her suitcase, ran to the end of the awning and hid behind its corner. She heard the door of the vehicle click shut, then footsteps come onto the platform. She didn't want to be seen. Grace scrambled up the bank of earth beside the platform and hunched down, her suitcase behind her. She would hide in the foliage, wait until the train had come and gone, then at night . . . then . . . she had no plan. Her mind froze. She would —

Someone was wandering around and going backwards and forwards. The footsteps stopped. Perhaps it was Madoc. No, Madoc was in London. At least, she thought he was in London. The stranger came nearer. A piece of bracken under her shoe snapped. She breathed shallowly and crouched, her head tucked down, her knees aching from being bent uncomfortably. There was silence.

The silence suggested someone was listening, sensed she was there. This was foolish, hiding in bushes in case a stranger found her. But she would not be a stranger to anyone in Narberth.

Moments passed.

Her suitcase slipped slightly down the rise and stopped, then Grace watched in horror as it slid further down the bank, tumbled off the small wall onto the platform, landed on its corner, the clasps zinging open. Her paltry belongings were flung out onto the black tarmacadam, her nightdress falling softly amid the clatter.

There was a silence after the clanging and hullabaloo. Grace closed her eyes. It was all over. Everything was falling apart. She put her head on her knees and waited.

'Grace?'

★ ★ ★

Wilfred opened the passenger door for Grace — he had moved the hearse right next to the station's wrought-iron gate — and looked around.

'Sit here on the floor,' he whispered. 'Stay crouching down.' Grace climbed quickly over the driving seat, into the space next to it and knelt down. Wilfred unobtrusively passed her her case, the nightdress still sticking out, so hastily had Grace repacked it. Grace knelt right down, her feet squashed to the side. Wilfred pulled a black cloth from under the seat. 'I'll put this over you.' He leaned into the hearse to make sure no one could see or hear him talking. 'Here,' he offered, placing the cloth over her head, then getting into the driving seat. He understood she wanted to remain hidden.

Grace heard the engine judder and the floor beneath her vibrated roughly as Wilfred kept trying to start the engine. She could hear his tense breathing. The engine didn't want to start. Wilfred tried again, and on the fifth attempt the engine clicked. She felt the hearse jump into life, reverberate and jerk forward. It turned at what she imagined was the top of Station Road and then a few minutes later turned again. She put out a covered hand to the side to steady herself as she was jigged around. It was humid beneath the cloth, dark and oppressive. The cloth was sumptuous, hung with bulbous tassels, and must be the material Wilfred used for covering coffins.

The hearse slowed down.

'You're up with the larks,' she heard someone call out.

'Morning, Jeffrey,' Wilfred replied. 'Can't stop.'

'Whyever not?' She heard Jeffrey's surprised reply. 'There's strange you are. Leaving me to walk when you could have given me a ride in the hearse. Not that I'm dead yet.' Jeffrey's voice trailed away. What if he had seen the oddly-shaped lump on the floor of the hearse?

'I'll come round later,' Wilfred called back.

Later. There would be a later, Grace realised. And then the rest of the day opened up. The child. In Wilfred's room, alone. They should hurry. Wilfred should drive faster. What if the child was crying on his own? But Wilfred slowed down. There was the clop of hooves on the road, and she heard the sharp crack of a whip on the side of a flank.

'Who's dead, Wilfred?' a male voice asked.

'Just running the engine,' Wilfred replied. She felt the hearse glide downhill: they were in Sheep Street. Soon the automobile stopped and the engine was silenced. Wilfred stepped out, the motor still purring, and she heard a door-bolt jolted open. Wilfred then jumped back in the hearse and Grace felt him precisely manoeuvre it into a garage, taking care to edge it in slowly, inch by inch. He switched off the motor and there was a moment's silence.

'You can get out now, Grace.'

★ ★ ★

Grace stood by the table, the lilac gladioli on the windowsill wobbling in the aftershock of the breeze from the door. It was odd to be back in Wilfred's kitchen, which was much cleaner and tidier than she remembered, and to see the Narberth-ness of it. There was the smell of coal that permeated the air — the deep wet smell of West Wales — and the sunlight, moist and soft, was streaming though the window. She felt a strange relief to be back in the town where she belonged, where she had been born and had grown up: the place that had been her home before her life had been truncated.

A woman came in carrying a baby. Grace stepped forward and took him from her. The baby opened his eyes and blinked, yawned lazily and curled into her, his light weight resting against her, unaware he had been left on a doorstep. Grace placed the blanket around the child's spongy head and wisps of hair. She felt her milk drip down her front, over her stomach and seep into the waistband of her skirt, two rivulets that were soaking her blouse and running downward in a thin, watery stream.

'Can I introduce you?'

Grace looked up. She had not seen the woman before; she must be from outside Narberth.

'This is Flora Myffanwy,' Wilfred said, 'my wife.' The woman smiled. She was beautiful, Grace saw, more beautiful than Grace would ever be, and she was married to Wilfred. Grace glanced at Wilfred. There was something proud in him when he said 'my wife', something unashamed and strong. He had said the words 'my wife', with certainty and meaning.

'Wilfred has told me a little about you. Would you like to sit down?' the woman offered. Grace sat down awkwardly, holding the child to her. 'We have looked after him this morning for you,' the woman said gently. 'I hope we have cared for him well enough.'

Grace nodded, unable to speak, unable to trust her voice not to break if she opened her mouth. Her tears might leak from her the way her milk was leaking from her. She felt heat in her face, the heat of early motherhood, bloom across her cheeks and redden them. Her leg jigged involuntarily and she felt a slight shiver over her body with the strain of the night before, and the days before, the days that lay ahead. Her

207

nerves had been stretched to breaking-point. The woman sat looking at her and Grace was aware of how charged the air was.

'We, um, gave it — him — milk,' Wilfred said clumsily. 'Well, my wife gave him warm milk,' he added, 'from a teaspoon.' His wife nodded and smiled. 'I thought he might get hungry.'

'He took the milk,' she agreed.

They sat in the kitchen, all three of them silent, and all unsure, all waiting for something to happen.

★ ★ ★

'I know — come upstairs,' Wilfred suggested, and began stacking the three kitchen chairs to take with them. Flora and Grace followed him up to the little landing.

'If I open the door to the linen closet we should have more space,' Wilfred said, pulling the door open and removing a pile of neatly folded pillowslips, quilts and blankets. He pushed a chair slightly into the closet.

'There! That should do it,' he announced, sitting down. There was just enough space on the landing for the three of them: Flora and Grace perched on chairs, Grace holding the swaddled baby in her arms — its mouth open, lost in sleep, while Wilfred was almost in the airing cupboard.

'At least no one can see us here,' Wilfred said. He noticed Flora glance at him and then at Grace, almost frightened.

'Got to see the positive in things!' he continued, holding himself together. The kitchen had been too exposed with its small low window and the path leading to Water Street; anyone could have looked in and seen Grace.

There was a long pause of unspoken words. Wilfred looked at Grace and rubbed his jaw, trying to take in her presence. He had hidden Grace in the hearse on the drive from the station. She would not want to be seen in Narberth with her child. Wilfred understood that. She would be the talk of the town and the shame would be overwhelming for her. If he could, he would try to allow Grace her secrecy because it protected her dignity and kept her from whispers and stares. Sometimes secrecy was necessary. It was the only way a person could pretend to hold their head up high. That's why they were crammed into the landing. At some point she would be strong enough to face her family and her town. But not yet. She looked pale and vulnerable. And he understood that Grace wanted protection from her brother learning where she was. There was no knowing what Madoc might do.

'How can we help you, Grace?' he asked. He didn't know what to suggest: maybe Grace knew what she wanted. Grace opened her mouth and closed it again.

'Your mother and father are only round the corner. You can go to your mother and father and brother,' Flora said gently, wanting to help. 'And I think your brother might be back on leave. They will be so pleased to see you, and the baby. He looks so much like your father.'

Wilfred looked at Flora. Grace said nothing.

'What do you need?' Wilfred asked.

'I think that I might be ill.'

'Your father is a doctor, he will be able to help you,' Flora suggested encouragingly.

Wilfred had buried several women who had recently given birth, one of whom had said she had the influenza but then entered an irrevocable slope towards death. Giving birth was a treacherous and life-threatening journey and it often wasn't over once the baby was born. Wilfred knew that Dr Reece wouldn't want his daughter sick, he wouldn't want his daughter to die; he knew now that no man would want that.

'Your father, can you not go and see your father?' said Flora, trying again to bring Grace back into her family and not understanding Wilfred and Grace's reticence.

'Grace, do you think that you are unwell enough that you need to see a doctor?' Wilfred asked.

'I think that I may be,' she answered.

13

The Last Days of Socrates

'Wilfred? It's Angharad Owen.' Wilfred had been expecting this telephone call, and it had come in the middle of his conversation on the landing with Grace and Flora. He had bounded down the stairs, three at a time, to pick up the receiver before the bell stopped trilling.

'Good morning, Mrs Owen,' Wilfred replied. Two weeks ago, Mr Owen, a strong seventy-two-year-old who still farmed vigorously, had woken up a lurid yellow colour. Well, that was it for him: no one could live if they were bright yellow. Wilfred knew that death heralded itself in colours, vividly shading its victims' faces before claiming them: a face that was too red or white, grey, blue or yellow usually meant only one thing.

'How are you, Mrs Owen?' Wilfred said into the telephone receiver. 'And the family?' Wilfred would have liked to visit Mr Owen — he knew him from the Bethesda Chapel choir and he was fond of him — but no one wanted to see the undertaker when they were very poorly. It was all too obvious a reminder of where they were headed, so Wilfred had to make do with reports from Willie the Post and Mrs Annie Evans, both of whom knew everything that happened in Narberth.

'Mr Owen has passed away. Dr Reece has been. I have my husband lying here on the couch and we are in need of a coffin,' Mrs Owen explained. 'I've wrapped a bedsheet around him but I want to put him in a coffin and lay him on the parlour table so the neighbours and family can come to visit him. Could you come by when you have a moment, Mr Price?'

Mrs Owen was pragmatic about death — some women were. Death was like another housekeeping chore, a task to be done that involved tidying away, the final tidying away. Mrs Owen's practicality encouraged Wilfred to be practical and businesslike too, and to ask what he would never ask the clearly distressed: 'I have a simple pine coffin for £1. Would that be acceptable?'

'Yes; Mr Owen had saved for his burial.'

'And my sincerest condolences.'

'Thank you, Wilfred, but we were expecting it.'

Wilfred placed the telephone receiver back in its holder on the hall wall and stood for a moment, thinking. It was easy when customers were unemotional: then undertaking was a simple business of box, hearse and hole. But when the bereaved were distressed, as most of them were, it was not as straightforward as providing a service and being paid. Then Wilfred's job was to uphold the wounded souls who cried as if they were burying themselves along with their beloved one, and were as raw as if someone had taken a potato-peeler to their skin and peeled away their covering, leaving them skinless and seeping, just tissue that smarted with the touch.

Wilfred looked at the telephone. It was made

212

of one piece of moulded Bakelite and a wonder to him; although it was silent now, waiting for the next call to come, telling Wilfred of another death. He leaned back against the wall. Undertaking was not an easy trade because it was the practical end of dealing with the ultimate mystery. When it was with unemotional people, those who saw death as a part of a whole where everything was one and there was no great divide — usually farmers — then Wilfred's trade was not much more than a shop for selling boxes to be put in the ground, altogether a very simple business. But when his customers were grieving mercilessly, then Wilfred sometimes felt like Hercules in an endurance test, with the weight of the world on his shoulders. On those days he could rename his business: *Wilfred Price, Purveyor of Superior Funerals. And Dealer in the Weight of the World.*

* * *

Flora dusted the rolling pin with white flour and then looked for the pastry cutter in the cutlery drawer. Grace, she thought to herself, who used to be married to Wilfred, was upstairs. Flora floured the raisin-speckled dough. She didn't know what Grace was hiding. Whatever it was, Wilfred knew. Why had she left her child with him? Flora sensed Wilfred's guilt towards Grace.

Flora flattened the warm dough, moving the glass rolling pin back and forth. Grace said she felt unwell but wouldn't see her father, a doctor. Flora flipped the dough over, and rolled it again.

213

When Flora had seen Grace's mother around Narberth, she looked sharp and unforgiving. Her family must have disowned her.

Flora dusted her hands with the smooth white flour and felt doubt worm into her. Grace had had a baby. There were explanations, ways of weaving this. Flora cut a baker's dozen of Welsh cakes, bevelling the cutter into the soft yellow mixture. She would have liked to talk to a friend about this, but she didn't yet have a close friend in Narberth, someone her own age she could trust. She had invited Mrs Probert to come round for a cup of tea, but Mrs Probert hadn't called.

She took the spatula and shifted each Welsh cake onto the slate bakestone. A foreign anxiety came and rested over her like a cloud of dust, almost imperceptible in its fineness, as if she was floured with a dust of doubt. Wilfred's ex-wife was upstairs with her child, and the dates of their marriage and the child's birth matched.

But no. She would see Wilfred's innocence. In her mind's eye she remembered Wilfred sitting and stretching out on the kitchen chair, his long large legs crossed at the ankle, his hands behind his head. She recalled the soft chalky-white folds of his linen shirt and the slight paunch of his stomach. The curtains behind him were gently billowing in the breeze. It had been a Sunday dinnertime and she was laying the table and talking. He was watching the way she opened the cupboard door, reached for the plates and wiped the teacup. He had been watching her in that deep, mature way he had: when he looked at her like that, she was conscious of the depth of thought within him. She had been chatting lightly, aware he was listening to her voice, the flow of her words. He had been attentive: he had been thinking about her, wondering about her at the same time.

Yes, that was Wilfred, that was her husband, and that was how she would hold him. She would see his kindness, his strength and his love for her. And that, she decided, was how she would always see him, always, as good.

Flora lifted a Welsh cake from the bakestone. It crumbled, as did the next: the texture was too dry. She had not been concentrating. Only when she lifted the last Welsh cake from the bakestone did it stay intact, its lightly tanned surface slipping smoothly off the spatula and onto the cooling rack.

Wilfred walked through the kitchen on the way to the library, a book under his arm, and reached for the one, whole Welsh cake.

'Hello, my dear. Smells lovely in here.' He examined the warm cake in his hand, saying, 'A well-cooked Welsh cake is the same colours as a giraffe.'

★ ★ ★

'This book, *The Last Days of Socrates*, is being returned a day late. Have you been busy with a funeral, Wilfred?' asked the librarian disapprovingly, putting on her glasses and folding her arms.

Wilfred nodded. He stifled a yawn.

'Even if there is Armageddon in Narberth, I expect my books back on time. If you wish to take another one of my books out of the Mechanics Institute . . . ' the librarian lifted her head up and looked down her nose at Wilfred, 'then you must return them before this day here.' She pointed a sharp fingernail at the date stamped in the front of the book. 'Place it back on that shelf, please, Wilfred, by *Merlin and the Afterlife.*'

Wilfred followed the librarian's instructions. He had not expected Grace to come back. She seemed changed, more worldly and faceted than when he had last seen her. She had a sophistication and a wariness, which was uncommon among the people of Narberth. Yes, Grace was different: she had had a child and there was nothing of the princess left in her.

'Not there! That's by *The History of Witchcraft in Carmarthenshire.*'

Wilfred felt unable to shake his worry about Grace. Perhaps it was only the strain of giving birth and the train journey, and just a few days of rest would surely put her right again. She had asked if she could stay. He had said yes.

'Not there! That's by *The Singing Trees of Wales.*'

'*The Singing Trees of Wales.*'

'You're going absolutely in the wrong direction: the Philosophy section with the philosophy book in it is on the weight reduction and fat-loss shelf.'

He was frightened that Grace was very sick.

'Wilfred, *The Last Days of Socrates* sits next

to Dr Lulu Peters's *Diet and Health, With Key to the Calories.*'

Wilfred went along the bookshelf, looking for the right place. And it must be a shock for Flora, too. He had told her about Grace, the barest outline, how the marriage was unconsummated. Flora knew that Grace had been expecting when she left Narberth. She must have thought about Grace over the months, but not mentioned it to him. It had been Flora who had realised that the baby on their doorstep was Grace's.

'You need to be looking at the shelf below,' the librarian ordered.

This was like when Mr Jacobs had been rotting in the workshop and covered in tarpaulin; there had been a moment of shock and revelation when Wilfred had removed the tarpaulin and seen the rot, seen how far it had gone, and didn't know what to do. What had been going on — brewing, building, hidden — had been revealed and left him floundering. Everything was exposed and nothing was neat. And Wilfred didn't know what to do. He had no idea what Mr Auden would say in this situation. And Socrates? As far as Wilfred could see, Socrates didn't have any problems to speak of, apart from owing a chicken to Asclepius.

'Put the book there, please, Wilfred — carefully!' the librarian ordered. Wilfred slotted the book on the shelf, then absentmindedly took it back off the shelf and flicked through the pages. Wilfred had tried to read *The Last Days of Socrates* — he really had. Socrates had done a lot of thinking about what a good man was.

217

Perhaps it would have been more helpful if Socrates had been married — or once accidentally proposed to a young Greek lady at an orgy in Athens — then he might have had some of the same things on his mind as Wilfred. But Wilfred supposed philosophers, unlike undertakers, didn't make mistakes in matters of romance. They were too busy thinking.

'Library's closing in twenty-three minutes,' the librarian announced to the empty library. Putting her date stamp in a cardboard box on her desk, she got up briskly. The librarian was English and had a different manner about her. 'Handle my books carefully, please. One crack of the spine and the whole book is broken in half. Ruined, Mr Price.'

'Yes,' agreed Wilfred.

'As you can imagine, I don't want my books in two halves. Not in the Narberth Mechanics Institute, thank you very much, Wilfred Price. So if you are considering borrowing that volume yet again from my library, then I would like to instruct you in the correct manner of handling a book: wash your hands first, seat yourself, do not read the book in direct sunlight — it bleaches the page — do not use a bookmark, store the book closed in an upright position on a bookshelf and dust only with a feather duster. The correct manner of opening a book is not fully, but like this.' The librarian demonstrated, opening the book very slightly, using both hands, taking the utmost care not to bend the spine. 'The spine is the backbone of the book.'

'Do you think it will be possible to read the

218

whole page if I only open it that much?' Wilfred asked.

'Of course. Library's closing in twenty-one minutes.'

★ ★ ★

'Let's sing 'Bread of Heaven',' Jeffrey said chummily to Wilfred and Flora, who were waiting expectantly on Narberth Moor for the annual Narberth versus Carmarthen tug-of-war to begin. They looked at him quizzically.

'It frightened the New Zealand All Blacks in 1905.'

'True enough.' Wilfred replied, trying to put thoughts of Grace and the baby from his mind. Grace had been in bed since she arrived yesterday morning, and the rest would surely do her good. He attempted to focus on the obligations of the day.

'Have you come straight from work?' he asked his friend.

'No, no, I took it into my head to have a swift half down the Dragon Inn before lunch,' Jeffrey said, tucking his shirt in his trousers. 'You should have seen that Probert — so drunk he could barely walk. There's a state he's in these days. He's no more dependence than a baby's arse.'

Wilfred had not the heart to readily say words against Probert — he remembered how, when Probert was a boy, he'd played the violin in chapel — but he put his arm around Flora, to reassure her at the mention of Probert's name.

'Mr Owen passed away,' he said sadly,

changing the subject.

'I hear he was the colour of a banana. Is that right, Wilf?'

'Aye, aye, he was yellow,' Wilfred replied, 'yellow' seeming too weak a word for such a lurid colour.

'There's sudden his death was. But Mr Owen was always a busy man and not one to waste time dying.' Jeffrey stroked his thick red moustache. 'But it comes to us all,' he stated.

'So it does.'

'Aye, comes to us all. At least you benefit — at least one bugger benefits from it, eh, Wilfred?'

'Wilfred Price, over here!' Tiny Evans shouted.

'He's come to bury us!' someone called from the crowd.

Wilfred took off his tweed jacket, handed it to Flora and rolled up his shirtsleeves. The crowd clapped.

'Come on, Wilf. Let's beat those salty buggers from Carmarthen this year.'

Wilfred strode into the middle of the muddy town moor, where a line of twenty beefy men were standing each side of the fat coiled rope, with more joining them.

'Move away from that puddle,' ordered Tiny Evans, the referee, 'and Eynon Cadwallader, come here.' He beckoned to a man in the crowd, who rubbed his hands together, took off his glasses using both hands and gave them to the child standing next to him.

'Now, gentlemen!' announced the referee, trying to call order among the rabble of men jostling along the rope. 'Welcome to the one hundred and nineteenth Annual Gŵyl Mabsant Narberth' — he waited for the applause to die down — 'versus Carmarthen' — there was weak applause — 'tug-of-war. On the left we have the blue team all the way from Carmarthen Town,' a handful of arms went up in the air and some children cheered, 'and on the right, the red team led by Mister Jeffrey Evans.'

'He butchers kittens!' a voice shouted.

'I'm fit as a flea,' Jeffrey retorted.

'Are you ready for the off?' Tiny Evans continued. 'On the count of three. Stand back, boys and girls. I'm going to blow my whistle and — '

'Get on with it, man! If it doesn't happen quick, it won't happen at all.'

The referee flushed. He blew the whistle urgently. There was a moment's silence and then the children erupted, jumping up and down, and the women talked animatedly among themselves, the brims of their hats bobbing. Soon the men were at a slant to the rope, the muscles of their forearms rippling, their teeth clenched, pulling hard against each other and roaring like heated bulls.

'Go on! Keep belting,' the excited crowd called. 'Put your backs into it!'

For several minutes, the tag slipped to the left then slightly to the right, the referee bouncing up and down on tiptoes in front of it, shouting, 'It's even-stevens!' There was intense strain in the faces of the men. With the sudden release of the rope, the Carmarthen team catapulted forward, tumbling and scrambling, arms swinging, while the triumphant red team from Narberth collapsed on top of each other in a bundle. In the celebration the children surged forward, finding their fathers, uncles and older brothers, and some running to Mr Jones, the schoolmaster.

'Well, what with you carrying those coffins and me chopping meat, we've got a bit of muscle between us,' said Jeffrey exuberantly, dropping the rope and slapping Wilfred on the back. 'Serves them right for coming from Carmarthen.'

Wilfred smiled, wiped his brow and looked around for Flora.

★ ★ ★

Flora left the tug-of-war on the town moor and ran along Moorfield Road, past Narberth School, slowing down into a brisk walk as she reached the corner. Her long, brown hair was flying from its bun and her cheeks were flushed. She didn't want to cause a comment or for people to notice. She would quickly warn Mrs Probert that she had heard Mr Probert was drunk, let her know, so she could leave the house, go for a walk and keep herself safe. Then Flora would return to the tug-of-war. It would only take her a moment, and it was the kind thing to do.

She nodded at Mrs Cadwallader.

'Aren't you watching the tug-of-war?' the other woman asked. 'Mind those eggs in your shopping basket, rushing like that.'

'Good morning, Mrs Cadwallader.' Flora Myffanwy smiled politely and kept walking to reach Mrs Probert's before Mr Probert came home.

At the big house she turned right into the row of small cottages on Spring Gardens. It was a dark street, made dank by the springs under the road. The houses were close to each other so that sun and light rarely penetrated the lane, and the brickwork was dirty, splattered with mud from the horses and the odd car that passed close to the walls.

When she reached Mrs Probert's house she had sudden doubts, hoped she wasn't being too forward or interfering, because she hadn't seen Mrs Probert for a while. But surely the woman would want to know, and there would be no harm in telling her. She knocked on the door, its red paint chipped and worn.

'Mrs Probert!' she called in a loud whisper. 'Come quickly.' She waited for the door to open and knocked again urgently, louder and more boldly. 'There's something I would like to tell you.' She heard the latch being lifted slowly on the other side and the door opened.

'Well, well, well, what have we here?' Mr Probert stood filling the doorframe with his stout body. His shirtsleeves were rolled up to his elbows. 'Good day, Mrs Price. And what can we do for you?' he said, looking her up and down. He leaned against the doorframe. 'Something to tell the wife? Spit it out.'

Flora could feel him looking at her. She put her hands across her chest. She had her shopping basket with her; the eggs had broken with all her rushing and were seeping through the wicker.

'Good afternoon, Mr Probert.' She tried to

think of something to say, but in her panic could think of nothing but difficult truths.

'Got more lipstick for my wife, have you?'

'No, Mr Probert.'

'I told her to have nothing more to do with you. Told that husband of yours too.'

Flora Myffanwy was too scared to move, to walk away, to say, 'I'd better be going now.'

'Well?' Mr Probert said eventually. 'Is there something I need to go and see that undertaker husband of yours about?'

'No, Mr Probert.' Their eyes met. Flora Myffanwy looked down quickly at the ground. She must go.

'I'll . . .' she said.

'You get going, Mrs Price. And don't you be coming back here . . .' The rest of the sentence hung in the air as an unsaid threat. 'Good day to you, Mrs Price.'

'Good day to you, Mr Probert.' The door closed firmly, almost slamming.

'Phyllis,' she heard Mr Probert shout through the closed door. 'Come here.'

★ ★ ★

Flora and Wilfred stared down at Grace, who was a livid red colour and appeared to be sleeping deeply. It was evening and the streets outside were empty after the bustle of the tug-of-war. Grace had been in bed all day.

'I bought some milk with the money in the tea caddy,' Wilfred whispered to Flora, noticing how tense Flora looked. He summoned up his courage and said, 'Would you mind me asking if this is perhaps a strain for you, my dear?'

'No,' replied Flora, but the usual tone of serenity in her voice was absent. 'I saw Mr Probert today,' she admitted quietly.

'At the tug-of-war?'

'No, outside his house. I don't like to see him.'

'I understand.' Wilfred put his arm around Flora. 'He's an idiot to a multitude of people.'

The baby wiggled on the bed. 'We can put some milk in the teacup and feed him with the silver spoon again,' Wilfred suggested.

Flora picked up the baby and took it to their bedroom and, with Wilfred standing by, she changed the baby's sodden clothes, wrapping him in a blanket. Wilfred watched and thought, This is how it would have been if we had had a baby. We would have stood together, hushed, while Flora gently cared for our child. He wondered what Flora was feeling. He wanted to talk to her about Grace arriving with a baby, but he didn't know how to broach the subject. He didn't want to cause her pain or for her to move away from him, inside herself. He wondered if or when they would talk about what was happening.

'I will wash it out,' Flora said, taking the tiny white vest, 'and dry it by the fire. He needs a change of clothes.' Then she added quietly, 'This is the cleaning and tidying I wanted to be doing.'

Wilfred understood: she wanted to be caring for a child. He was grateful for her honesty, for the insight into her feelings. It reassured him more than those weeks of endless, silent cleaning. She was cooking more now, and eating again too. Cooking seemed to give her a sense of peace and comfort her — and it comforted Wilfred to watch her.

Together they stepped back into his da's room to check on Grace. Wilfred knew death could be sudden, happen quickly, that an adult in rude health could be fine at breakfast and dead by supper. And here was a woman with all the warning signs of death: the flushed red face, she had recently given birth, and her spirit was broken. He rubbed his jaw firmly. It was easy to see how her spirit was broken. He had read in the *Daily Express* that when healthy young African men, savages who lived by their instincts on the Serengeti in Tanganyika, were captured by the white plantation owners and locked over-night in one-roomed prisons, the next morning they were found dead, when, the day before, they had been perfectly healthy. That's what hap-pened when you imprisoned a human being: they died — and Grace was in a prison, of sorts.

There was the sound of careful footsteps coming slowly up the stairs.

'Your da,' Flora whispered. Grace was lying in Wilfred's da's bed. 'Did you tell him?'

'I haven't told him — I haven't seen him. I hoped he would stay a few more days at Auntie Blodwen's.'

The door creaked open and Wilfred's da looked startled to see so many people in his simple cell-like room.

'Wilfred?' he said. Then he looked at the woman in the bed. 'Is that Grace Reece, Wilfred, in my bed?' The blankets lifted up as the baby kicked. 'And . . . ?' he uttered, dumbfounded.

'Yes, Da, yes, it's Grace. And a baby,' Wilfred admitted in a whisper. Wilfred's da looked uncomprehendingly around his tiny, crowded room.

'I think we'd better talk in the scully,' Wilfred suggested.

By the time they had reached the scully Wilfred's da was holding the back of the chair to steady himself from the surprise.

'Well, Da. It's Grace. She came back. We don't know why. She hasn't said.'

'She must be in trouble,' Wilfred's da stated in his bewilderment, then added, 'The child is the spit of Dr Reece.'

'She's ill,' Flora said. 'She has a fever.'

Wilfred's da looked frightened. 'We must get Dr Reece. Straight away!'

Then it occurred to Wilfred: it was suddenly obvious what his da meant. His own mother had died four days after he was born. Wilfred grasped the full enormity and reality of what he was doing: hiding a sick woman and a new baby in his home.

'She could die, Wilfred, like your mother.'

'I don't think she will die,' Flora said quietly. 'She has her child to live for.'

'But we don't know,' said Wilfred's da. 'We must help her.'

Flora began to wipe the draining board and to clean. Wilfred didn't know what to do. He wanted to do what was right, what was good, but he didn't know what that was. He had been like

227

that child: a helpless human being with a mother who was very ill. He tried to remember something of his mother, anything of those four days they spent together, but he couldn't: it was only blackness or fantasies, not even a shell of the sensation of her. The infant lying helpless on the bed upstairs was on the precipice of his life changing irreversibly, and embarking on life without a mother. Would he let that child — a boy — *help* that small child lose its mother? And this child only had a mother, he could not be said to have a father he could count on.

Wilfred's da slowly, as befitted his age, began to take his coat from the back of the chair to prepare to leave for Dr Reece's.

'Wait, Da, wait. No one knows she's here. Her father doesn't know she's here.'

They stood silently for a moment until Wilfred's da said, 'A family feud is not important at a time like this.'

'No,' Wilfred replied. 'But — '

'There is something else, isn't there?' said Flora.

'Yes,' admitted Wilfred.

'Tell us, Wilfred.'

'No,' he said, honestly.

'But it isn't as it seems?' Flora asked. There was a pause. 'Could we get another doctor to give Grace a prescription?' she suggested.

'Dr Williams in Carmarthen. But he drinks,' Wilfred said. 'So he'll talk. What about Jeffrey?'

'Jeffrey's a butcher!' his da exclaimed. 'There's a retired doctor in Stepaside.'

'He died.'

'Could we get some medicine from the apothecary?' Flora said.

'We don't have a prescription,' Wilfred replied.

'Is there no one we could get a prescription from?' his da asked. 'Are you sure about not going to see Dr Reece, Wilfred?'

'Would you wait the night, and see how Grace is tomorrow?' asked Wilfred.

Each of them stood there, each with an answer, but Wilfred wrestled with himself, not knowing what to do or who to ask or whose experience to trust: his da, who had lost his wife, his wife who had lost her child, or himself, who knew what it was to lose a mother as an infant.

14

Still Life

'So you say you have been feeling unwell?' Dr Reece put his hands behind his back and rocked on his feet. 'And this has been since the birth?'

'Yes, Dr Reece.'

'And you said you feel hot? Fevered?' Dr Reece looked at the stuccoed ceiling as if it was a repository of all answers. 'The symptoms you described to me sound very much like those of infection.'

'Yes.'

'But I have examined you, Mrs Price, and you seem to be in good health and don't have a temperature. The baby was born, or rather arrived, a while ago. And I feel that if you were going to have poor health, you would have experienced these symptoms in the first few days. That is the common time for an infection to appear.' Dr Reece put a hand to the stethoscope around his neck. 'Mrs Price,' he turned and faced the large bay window, 'what happened was a very unfortunate Act of God.'

Flora nodded.

'And these things happen.' The doctor looked out of the window, his face silhouetted in profile. 'Events happen for which science has no explanation.'

Flora Myffanwy shifted uncomfortably on the upright chair. She had described Grace's symptoms as Grace had described them to her, though Dr Reece was too experienced and knowledgeable to hold any concerns when he had been unable to find any evidence for the symptoms.

'My dear, you are a healthy young woman whose nerves are strained. I can think of no other explanation. Although it does happen — and it is peculiar to the female sex and the hysterical — that there are those women who can believe they are pregnant or indeed suffer the symptoms of pregnancy although they're medically unproven to be pregnant. It is rightly called a phantom pregnancy. As if the woman is pregnant with a ghost. Do you understand my meaning?' Dr Reece stood with his back against the surgery wall that was wallpapered a confident peacock blue.

Flora had hoped it would be simple to describe Grace's symptoms, receive advice and expert opinion and, most importantly, a prescription for some medicine. Wilfred had had the idea early this morning that she should visit Dr Reece as a way to get a prescription for the correct medicine for Grace. She watched the doctor slowly pacing his surgery. She didn't know who the child's father was, but she saw the strong resemblance to Grace's child in the eyes and the shape of the brow.

Dr Reece glanced at Flora quizzically and sceptically. She could see him thinking, perhaps putting two and two together.

'Dr Reece, if I was unwell, what medicine

231

would you recommend?'

'I recommend none at all, Mrs Price. You are a nervous, perhaps neurotic woman.'

'Yes, but if I was, you would recommend perhaps that I . . . ' Flora held out the sentence for him to finish it. She attempted to look hopeful and expectant so as to encourage the doctor to say the name of a medicine, any medicine that might help Grace, his own daughter.

'Well, had you had an infection, I would prescribe *Ovedoxs* three times a day, although it's rarely efficacious, and complete bed rest and very skilled medical supervision. Infections can be extremely serious, most notably in post-partum women — that is, women who have recently given birth, Mrs Price.'

'*Ovedoxs?*' Flora repeated the name.

'Yes, but I don't recommend those things to you. Grief can disturb the mind, Mrs Price, and make us think what is not there is there, if you comprehend my meaning.' He sighed. 'You are to go home and put your feet up, smoke — modern science is showing that smoking cigarettes is beneficial for health — do your housewifely chores and care for your husband. And in the fullness of time you will have another child; children invariably come to a young and healthy married couple. Because an unfortunate experience happened to you once doesn't mean it will happen again.'

Flora could feel the thin cover of her pretence slipping and tears rise in her eyes. The grandmother clock on the mantelpiece chimed half past three. Dr Reece looked pointedly at the imposing clock to signify the appointment was over.

'Now, Mrs Price, if you will excuse me. If there is any situation of medical concern, I trust you will not hesitate to telephone me immediately,' he said sternly. He sat back down in his chair. 'It won't be necessary to charge you for the consultation.'

'Thank you, Dr Reece.'

★ ★ ★

When Wilfred arrived that same morning at the Owens' farm on Providence Hill, he was expecting Mr Owen to be heavy, but when he saw how much weight the man had lost in the days since he'd turned yellow — and he was truly yellow — he knew he would be able to lift him in the coffin easily.

'I have a clean bedsheet here,' Mrs Owen said. 'I ironed and starched it four days ago in preparation. It's for a winding sheet.'

'Very well done, Mrs Owen.' Only two weeks ago, Wilfred had seen Mr Owen in the Salutation Inn, leaning on the piano, drinking stout. He was right as rain and certainly not this extraordinary colour. It had been a quick death.

One of Mr Owen's sons came forward. He had a stunned look as if he'd been slapped in the face by a plank. Wilfred could have cradled Mr Owen alone and lifted him into the coffin, but didn't want to do anything ungainly with the corpse in front of the next-of-kin, so it was best if the sons helped.

'You take the feet.' Wilfred guided and put the young man's hands under the wasted body.

'That's right,' he encouraged, although Mr Owen's arms flopped against the side of the coffin with a bang. One son gasped.

'My sons are shocked,' Mrs Owen said simply. She stepped forward and arranged the winding sheet. Then the pine coffin with the body in it was placed on the parlour table.

'We have visitors coming this afternoon,' she explained.

'Of course. I'll leave the lid there,' said Wilfred, propping it up next to three lucky horseshoes tacked to a beam.

'The Reverend Waldo Williams said the funeral would be this coming Thursday. Is there anything I need to do with the body?'

'Keep the room well ventilated and the lid on at night and when you haven't got visitors. Anything untoward or leakages, then do telephone my office immediately.' Wilfred didn't have an office: he had the Bakelite telephone screwed to the wall by the front door, he wrote invoices on the kitchen table, and did his thinking — well, everywhere — but 'office' sounded formal, and formality was what one wanted from an undertaker. 'Good day to you, Mrs Owen. And my sincerest condolences.'

As Wilfred stooped to leave the parlour, he glanced back over his shoulder and saw the family arranged as if in a photograph, in what Flora would call 'a still life' — with Mrs Owen standing beside the coffin, her sons side-by-side at its foot and the father laid out, still, and at peace.

Wilfred got into his hearse, touched the walnut veneer fondly and put the key in the ignition.

Mrs Owen, particularly, had the wisdom and the years to accept death, to take it in her stride without adding drama to it. But Wilfred couldn't help feeling a new sadness, one that he'd had since his own baby had died, an understanding that as he buried one person it was as if, in some intangible way, he were burying his child. He had been an undertaker for almost nine years, and it wasn't until now that he understood what a funeral was.

He sighed. All those *B* words — *baccivorous, bice-blue* and *biliverdin, bilateral, bimanous, Baconian, bathykolpian* — for nothing. How could their baby be born dead? It was as if birth and death were stuck together, when they should be separated: birth at the beginning of life, death at the end, and seventy years in between. 'And the days of our years are threescore years and ten,' the Bible said. That was the time allotted to man.

Then he thought about Grace and wondered if Flora had got a prescription from Dr Reece this morning. Wilfred turned the key and started the engine of the hearse. At least he could be kind to Grace now, make amends for his unkindness to her; at least he could lift that weight from his mind. As long as he didn't have to bury her.

★　★　★

'This is it,' Flora said.

Grace was lying in the bed in Wilfred's father's room.

'It says 'To be taken three times a day'.' Flora

unscrewed the small jar of medicine and spooned the pink powder into a glass of water. 'He didn't say what it did; only that this is what he would prescribe. I bought it in the apothecary.'

'Thank you,' said Grace, drinking the powdered water.

'And you need bed rest.'

There was a knock at the door downstairs. Grace and Flora Myffanwy looked up and waited. There was a knock again.

'Wilfred has gone to collect a body,' Flora Myffanwy said. 'I had better go and see who it is. It might be a customer for the wallpaper shop.' She looked at the baby, who was fast asleep in the bed. 'I won't be long.'

Grace heard Flora call hello and her feet running lightly down the stairs, heard a woman's voice say something. Grace tried hard to listen but didn't recognise the softly spoken voice. She wondered if the woman downstairs would know her; she surely would. Grace huddled very carefully under the blankets, not daring to disturb the baby, who was sleeping with his curled hands either side of his head.

Her father. Flora had seen her father this morning. Grace remembered the last time she had seen him. It was at Narberth station. He had given her an envelope and she had opened it on the train. *Write*, it said, that's all. She hadn't written. She had wanted to but didn't know what to say. If she couldn't speak the truth then she couldn't say anything, and felt condemned to silence. Only truth would loosen her tongue.

Grace pulled the blanket up. Her hipbones

ached, her head ached and she was continually hot then cold. Her mouth was dry and so she drank some water, but as soon as she took a sip, one mouthful was too much. She pulled the blankets over her head and buried herself under them. She moved restlessly onto her side and wrapped herself round the limp body of her small child, his chest moving up and down rapidly. Even her eyelids ached. Something was raging through her body, wracking her with heat, then making her shiver. Her teeth ached and her hair felt thin and flat to the touch. She needed to see a doctor. She needed her family; she needed to see her father. She knew he would be alarmed if he knew how sick she was, and he was rarely alarmed. She needed medicine. Sitting up clumsily in bed, she drank some more of the powdered water then lay down and fell into a fetid, drugged and disturbed sleep.

* * *

'Mrs Probert!' Flora said with surprise, opening the door.

'Is it an awkward moment? You said if I ever wanted to visit ... ' Mrs Probert asked hesitantly. 'I know it was months ago now.'

'No, not at all,' said Flora with feeling, but with some anxiety. 'There's lovely to see you again.' Mrs Probert had a fresh bruise on her face.

'Please sit down. Would you like to take a cup of tea?' asked Flora, topping up the teapot with boiling water from the copper kettle. She hoped that the baby wouldn't cry, or that Mrs Probert wouldn't hear it. And if the baby cried, Flora thought, she would say nothing and smile.

'I made a pot of tea now just; it should still be hot.' Flora placed the teapot, which was round and friendly in shape, on the clean tablecloth. Her mother had given her the tea set for their wedding present. She upended the teapot and the leaves span outwards in a steaming circle of boiling water.

'Would you like some milk? Oh . . . would you mind if we had black tea, as I have hardly any milk,' she said, remembering the milk was for Grace and the baby. 'Perhaps you would like sugar in your tea?'

Mrs Probert nodded gratefully.

Flora opened the door so that the bustle from the street outside might mask any sounds from inside.

'Your kitchen is very clean,' Mrs Probert remarked, looking around, spotting the ball of dough resting in a bowl on the kitchen table. 'Don't let me interrupt you with your baking. Or shall I help you?' So the two women stood side by side making and patting Welsh cakes, placing them on the bakestone, turning them when they were golden, and filling the kitchen with the warm aroma of butter, allspice and nutmeg.

'Thank you for coming to warn me, on the day of the tug-of-war,' Mrs Probert began. Flora looked at the woman's battered face. Wilfred had told her that Mr Probert had played violin in chapel when he was young. He seemed so angry and brutish, Flora couldn't imagine him having the sensitivity to play music.

'I walked around Narberth today,' Mrs Probert continued, with some hope in her voice.

'Are you getting stronger?' Flora asked, remembering why Mrs Probert was walking around the town. She noticed that the woman's fingernails were bitten down to the quick.

Mrs Probert nodded. 'I have a plan. I walk around Narberth every day, and when I am in the house and Mr Probert is out, I wear the lipstick you gave me. I want to stay strong for the future and I want to feel like a woman, even if only a little.' She patted a stray sultana into the Welsh-cake mixture.

'I'm so sorry for giving you my lipstick and the trouble it caused you,' Flora said.

'No, sorry I am. I only hope Wilfred can forgive Mr Probert. I heard he gave Wilfred a bloodied nose and made a terrible mess of the new shop.'

'It was all easily tidied,' Flora replied. She put some more uncooked Welsh cakes on the bakestone. There was a spark and a refinement to Mrs Probert; Flora could see it, even though her clothes were old and she was so thin and worn.

'And you have had troubles of your own,' Mrs Probert added.

Flora paused, not knowing how to talk about what had happened to her.

'Would you like to help yourself to a Welsh cake?' she asked, still unable to talk about the experience she'd had. 'They will be ready to eat in a minute or two.' There was a cough from upstairs.

'Is Wilfred here? Mrs Probert asked, surprised. 'Am I disturbing you?'

'Not at all, only doing the things that need to be done,' said Flora, putting some freshly-baked Welsh cakes from the cooling-rack onto a cake-plate.

'May I tell you something? Between you, me and the doorpost?' Mrs Probert asked.

'Of course.'

'Could you shut the door?' Flora went and pulled the back door to and sat at the table with Mrs Probert.

'Mr Probert gets very angry, and into blind rages,' she began. 'And when he's drunk too much beer at the Dragon Inn he gets terrible headaches and sits with his head in his hands, crying. Dr Reece says he drinks too much.'

Flora nodded, listening. She heard a sound from upstairs that she pretended not to notice.

'He does drink too much,' Mrs Probert added. 'Dr Reece is right.' She pushed a lank strand of hair behind her ear. 'Dr Reece says he should stop.'

Flora didn't see how Mrs Probert could have a better life if Mr Probert didn't stop drinking.

'So if I am strong and feel like a woman, I could marry again,' she said unexpectedly.

Was Mr Probert seeing another woman and Mrs Probert was going to divorce him for adultery?

'There is something wrong with his brain and he can't control himself when it comes to drink. He sees red so quickly these days,' she explained.

'But I wouldn't want you to make too many

excuses for him,' Flora said, then added quickly, 'I'm sorry, I have been too forward.'

Mrs Probert shook her head. 'Dr Reece said there is a growth in his brain. The rages are because of it.' She looked down and said quietly, 'So I came to ask if Wilfred would be willing to bury him when the time comes.'

Flora nodded, taken aback. She didn't know what to say.

'Dr Reece said there is no cure because it is the brain.'

Flora expected Mrs Probert to cry, but she didn't.

'I can endure it because I understand, and because Dr Reece said it won't be very long. But I have had enough. I hope, one day, I can marry again.'

'I understand.'

'I'd rather nobody knows, Mrs Price. And Mr Probert would be humiliated to think that Wilfred knew his difficulties. He doesn't like pity.'

'Certainly, Mrs Probert.'

'I don't want to wash my dirty linen in public.'

'Of course.'

'Only it would be reassuring to know that Wilfred will be able to provide his services when they are needed. Before he was ill, Mr Probert always spoke very highly of Wilfred.'

★　★　★

'You cannot imagine the state it is in,' Mrs Estella Newton-Lewis said, leading Wilfred

241

through her elegant hall into the parlour, where a five-foot strip of wallpaper was hanging from the ceiling and swinging loosely. 'I'm confident you will be able to sort it out, Wilfred.'

Wilfred didn't know what he was doing; he had unthinkingly embarked upon a paint and wallpaper shop without any knowledge or particular skill. Him and his fancy ideas. He had been impulsive again. And now he was having a baptism of fire in the art of wallpapering.

'My sisters Eugenie and Cecilia are here again from Llanddewi Velfrey, and Mrs Prout is reading our tea leaves,' exclaimed Mrs Estella Newton-Lewis.

Wilfred saw the three women gathered eagerly at the tea table, which was laid with starched, embroidered linen and set with a porcelain china tea set. Mrs Prout, like an old tortoise, was hunched with a teacup in her hand, contemplating the tea leaves.

'Good afternoon, ladies. I hope I won't be in your way,' declared Wilfred, putting down his stepladder.

'Things aren't sticking together for you, I see,' sneered Mrs Prout, narrowing her eyes. She pulled her Paisley shawl around her shoulders.

'There's dreadful,' confessed Wilfred, examining the large flap of wallpaper that was hanging from the ceiling almost to the floor. He spread out a piece of white canvas and put a pot of glue and his toolbox onto it. It had been difficult decorating Mrs Newton-Lewis's parlour in the first place, trying to work among so many lamp-stands, chairs, antique cut-glass decanters and Chinese vases. It was even more difficult to decorate during a tea-party.

'Mmm,' muttered Mrs Prout. 'I see your mother . . . ' The three sisters gasped, grasping each other.

'She is well.'

They sighed.

'And there is a birthday coming.'

'That will be mine!' cried Mrs Newton-Lewis delightedly. 'What do the tea leaves say about me buying a copper warming-pan with a fruitwood handle from the Golden Sheaf Antiques? Perhaps for my birthday?'

Mrs Prout examined the teacup, drawing back her head to squint into it. 'I see a shop.'

'Oh!' the sisters cried in unison.

'With . . . with . . . with . . . ' Mrs Prout slumped as if asleep.

'Is she all right?' Mrs Newton-Lewis mouthed to her sisters.

' . . . furniture, small ornaments and oil paintings,' Mrs Prout continued.

'Oh, yes!' said Mrs Newton-Lewis. 'I have always longed to have a shop like that.'

'Selling wallpaper and paint,' stated Mrs Prout.

'And where is this shop?'

Mrs Prout indicated that more tea was to be poured into Mrs Newton-Lewis's teacup. It was, and Mrs Newton-Lewis drank quickly and delicately from it.

'In Narberth.'

The sisters gasped. 'Oh, how exciting! I always knew you should have a shop selling beautiful objects for the home,' said the older sister. 'Then there would be two wallpaper shops in Narberth!'

'And you'd be so very good at it,' encouraged the younger sister.

Wilfred was listening, all the while spreading paste on the underside of the hanging wallpaper. He set out his wooden stepladder, climbed up, then carefully pressed the wallpaper against the ceiling. A paint and wallpaper shop in Narberth — owned by Mrs Newton-Lewis. Wilfred knew Mrs Newton-Lewis would have a wonderful wallpaper shop, the eel's hips — he only had to look around her beautiful, considered parlour to see how stylish she was. Whereas Wilfred didn't know anything about style. He was a man; his favourite colour was blue. He only knew that red and green should never be seen except with a colour in between. And he didn't know much about decorating either.

Wilfred patted the wallpaper — it was barely sticking to the ceiling and was full of bumps. He had spent four hard years as an apprentice learning to become an undertaker, but had only ever glimpsed at *Home Decorative Interior Suggestions* on how to decorate. Even so, perhaps he should advertise. *Narberth's very best wallpaper shop.* That was a good sentence to put in the *Narberth & Whitland Observer. All tastes catered for.* Although, on reflection, he didn't think there were many tastes in Narberth. Everybody liked their houses the same — indeed, everybody copied Mrs Newton-Lewis and did what she advised them to do.

Wilfred examined the crumpled wallpaper stuck wonkily on the ceiling. He took a small hammer and a tack from his dungaree pocket, placed the tack discreetly on the edge of the wallpaper and knocked it in as quietly as he could. The sisters stopped their excited chatter.

'Are you knocking nails into my plasterwork, Wilfred?' Mrs Newton-Lewis asked, with a note of surprise.

'Well, you see, Mrs Newton-Lewis, it helps it stay on the ceiling.'

'Is that usual? I have never seen *that* in my French magazines.'

'It is the Welsh way, Mrs Newton-Lewis.'

'Wilfred, come and have your tea leaves read,' enjoined Mrs Newton-Lewis's younger sister. She poured a cup of tea for him.

'I have just had a cup of tea,' said Wilfred.

'Oh, come on, Wilfred,' said Mrs Newton-Lewis, strolling over to the ladder and putting her hand on his leg flirtatiously. Wilfred climbed down, drank the cup of Japanese tea and handed the remains to Mrs Prout.

'I see a tall tower,' stated Mrs Prout.

'I can't think of a tower anywhere in Narberth,' the younger sister said.

'No, this is not in Narberth.'

'Perhaps you mean the church-tower — a funeral,' said Mrs Newton-Lewis helpfully.

'This is the tallest tower in the world.'

The four tea-drinkers looked puzzled. The tallest tower in the world wasn't in Wales.

'It is in America.'

Wilfred wondered how he, an undertaker in

Narberth, could drink a cup of tea and create a tower made of tea leaves that was in America. He didn't know he was capable of it.

'I expect you're going to receive a postcard of a tower from America,' suggested the eldest sister.

'Wilfred is *in* the tower in America,' declared Mrs Prout.

'Well, I can't see that,' Wilfred rejoined.

'Well, I can,' snapped Mrs Prout.

'I had better get on with the wallpapering then, before I cross the Atlantic!' said Wilfred and the sisters laughed.

'I told you Mrs Prout was wonderful,' said Mrs Newton-Lewis. 'She knows everything.'

'And there is death around you, Wilfred Price,' Mrs Prout murmured into the teacup. 'Much closer than you know.'

15

Relinquish

'What can we do for you?' Wilfred asked Grace
with some despair. He was standing next to the
bed, Flora beside him.

For three days, she'd lain in a stew of blankets
with lurid dreams seducing her away from the
world. She woke on her side from dreams where
she had been trying to run, the blankets kicked
off. Where could she run *to*? She knew what she
was running *from* — a meeting with her parents,
or rather her mother, in which any semblance of
hope she had of her mother forgiving her would
be crushed. And away from the devastation of
her life.

Flora pulled the curtains and opened the
window. Grace was aware that the room was
fetid and the air was thick. She breathed in the
acidic odour of smelling salts and the milkiness
of the baby, who had slept and fed throughout
all of this.

Wilfred looked down at her gravely. Grace
noticed he looked like an undertaker even in his
paint-splattered dungarees. If she was going to
die, she would feel safe at the thought of him
burying her. Grace thought how her mother
wouldn't forgive her and how Wilfred understood a little — not that his mother had rejected

247

him, she had died — but it was an experience of living without a mother and Wilfred knew, too, how hard that was.

Grace stared glassily up at the tapestry on the wall at the end of Wilfred's father's bed. She had spent hours, days, looking at it: the careful stitches, the gentle lilac flowers, the pink lettering: *Cleanliness is next to Godliness*. It had been created with great patience and an eye for detail. It was the opposite to the wall she saw in her mind's eye when she remembered Madoc at his most violent towards her. All of which was held in the memory of the wallpaper. The tapestry was the only thing on the wall. She thought Wilfred's mother must have sewn it.

'Take some more medicine,' Flora encouraged, pouring a glass of fresh water and tapping some of the powder into it. There was only a little left in the medicine bottle now; Grace had taken most of it.

'There's not much left in that bottle,' Wilfred commented. He asked again. 'Grace, what can we do for you?'

The sound of Wilfred's voice pulled her away from her thoughts. Wilfred was being considerate. This is what Grace had needed she realised, kindness. Kindness healed the spirit and the spirit came first.

'Although I understand — we understand — it might be difficult, what with your parents so close,' Wilfred wrung his hands, 'but you can stay here with us as long as you need to.'

Lady Lytton had said it was foolish to reject friendship. For months Grace had been unable

248

to take any gifts from anybody. She had been forced to receive from her brother what she hadn't wanted and she had responded by closing, receiving nothing from anyone. For the first time, in a long time, she felt able to accept the love offered to her. Grace felt able to open herself up and willing to receive what Wilfred — and Flora — offered. Grace reached out a hand and both Flora and Wilfred put their hands forward and there was a muddle of fingers and wedding rings and hands held tightly in response to the words that were so clearly felt.

★　★　★

Flora Myffanwy turned the steering wheel to the right with effort and drove through the archway and down the winding lane towards Pleasant Valley. She wasn't very practised at driving but Wilfred had been certain she should take the hearse this morning, insisting it was too cold for her to bicycle to her mother's. The vehicle felt elephantine, many times more powerful than her bicycle. It was a quiet lane, and she doubted she would meet another motorist.

The lane was frosty and icy. Winter had bitten in a while back and the ground was hard and the landscape stark. The trees looked dead, like jaggedy black lines against the white, winter light.

When she had driven a mile or so she pulled over, folded down the top part of the window and took from the wicker basket next to her a round ball of mud the size of an apple, and gently threw it out of the window into an empty part of the verge. The ball of mud disappeared in the foliage and she heard it land with a gentle thud. She drove forward a few more yards, took another ball and threw it out of the window, then kept driving and stopping until all five balls were thrown. She pressed the accelerator down with more confidence than before and drove towards Wiseman's Bridge.

Flora had made the mud balls that morning in the kitchen. She'd collected handfuls of earth from the vegetable border in the yard and then rolled the muddy balls in seeds taken from packets she'd bought in the hardware shop: forget-me-not seeds, foxglove, honesty, baby's breath, pansies, love-in-the-mist and daisy seeds and poppy seeds, small as full stops.

She wanted to make more of these globes full of seeds and scatter them, when she visited her mother, in the green hedgerows of the road to Pleasant Valley. In the spring she would bring Wilfred along the pleached lane and the hedge-rows would be full of flowers: lilac foxgloves, dark blue love-in-the-mist, white baby's breath, scarlet poppies and the pearly flowers of honesty. There would be colour and scent among the green horse-chestnut trees and hawthorn hedgerows, where now there was only bracken and sparse grass.

She shifted from first gear into second, and drove bumpily over a small bridge crossing a lively stream. For dark, unsatisfying days she had cleaned and cleaned, but as the bleak winter days had begun to lighten, the thought had dawned on her that it wasn't enough for the world to be clean, it must be beautiful too. It might not be the world she wanted it to be, but she knew, for her own sanity, she must find her world beautiful. These seed globes were hope for the spring; that the winter would pass and there would be flowers and birds singing again.

The hearse rolled down the hill and she saw the vista of Wiseman's Bridge, the great cove spread in front of her, the gulls larking in the air, and was unexpectedly reminded of the dream she'd had when she was very newly married, of a stone angel, or archangel, striding across the sea, armless, legless, her body delicately draped. The angel had been moving forward, parts of herself missing, striding alone and across the sea on faith. Flora understood. The dream had been prescient. She felt as if part of herself was missing now, had been lost and died prematurely, but that now she could move forward, in the place she loved, to what lay ahead of her in her life. She had lost her child and she had lost a freedom in marrying. Flora gazed at the great cathedral space of the cove. Now she would find something for herself. She looked up at the serene sky. She would become a photographer.

* * *

When Flora came back from her mother's she went to check on Grace, and stood outside the closed door to her room. She could hear small sounds coming from within: the baby was awake but Grace must be asleep. Flora paused, clean bedlinen in hand, listening. Perhaps the baby needed attention.

Flora waited a moment outside the door, gathering her thoughts. Grace was not getting better, the medicine was not working. For four days she had mostly slept, whispering fragments, moving her mouth in soundless words, talking, almost angry — trying to wrestle with something bigger than her, which made her arms and legs twist and turn with heavy effort. She was lost in a netherland, where the way is decided.

Grace was trying to make her peace with something; Flora had seen it in her blinking, closed eyes, the white saliva at the corners of her mouth, her lips that were dry and cracked. Flora heard the odd fragment of sentence: 'No,' and the name Madoc, and she heard her say, 'Mother,' then, 'Daddy.' And once, '*the beds are made . . .* ' Then the words faded, lost in oblivion.

Flora came in every hour to check on Grace. She knew Grace's life was in the balance, that Grace, in her dark dream, was weighing her life against death. When she woke — if she woke — then she would be a different woman, one who had walked through a dark night of the soul.

Flora put her hand on the door handle. If Grace died? Perhaps Flora and Wilfred could have the baby for their own, and bring up the child. If Grace died? Wilfred would have to tell Dr and Mrs Reece and there would be uproar and intrigue and consequences, perhaps legal consequences too complex for Flora to contemplate. They were hiding a very sick woman, a doctor's daughter who hadn't seen a doctor.

Flora pushed open the door. Grace lay oblivious. The baby was on its back, kicking its little legs. Flora walked tentatively around the small iron bed and picked up the child, cradling its loose head. She carefully carried the baby from the room, past the now-discarded bedlinen and into her bedroom. She lifted up his shift and saw that his nappy needed changing so she fetched a clean piece of towel and began to change him. Once downstairs, she put the baby on the clean kitchen table. She poured boiling water from the copper kettle into an old baby's bottle she had found under a dirty frying pan at the back of the crockery cupboard, when she'd been cleaning everything. She'd remembered about it yesterday. It was an old-fashioned baby's bottle; perhaps it had been Wilfred's.

Once the warmed milk was poured into the sterilised bottle, she fed the baby, who seemed to prefer the spoon to the teat, small silver teaspoons of milk tipped from the bottle. Flora had not cared for a baby before but it came easily to her. She had played and helped on the farm around White Hook as a girl, and a baby was much like a lamb or a calf or a foal. They all inspired gentleness, they all demanded milk and they all needed a mother.

Milk dribbled down the baby's chin and Flora dabbed it with her hanky. The baby drank easily and with contentment, as if he wanted for no more than milk, then blinked slowly, rubbed his nose and, mid-sip, fell asleep, the small neat hole of his mouth open. Flora looked at him as if there was nothing more beautiful than this child, as if the child was a great magnet from which she couldn't pull herself from.

Wilfred was right; they could have kept this child. If Wilfred hadn't gone to find Grace. If she hadn't told him to find Grace before she left Narberth, before Grace broke the first bonds and ties of her motherhood. In a perfect world, they could have kept this child. Yet, in a perfect world their own child wouldn't have died. She knew it took great generosity of herself to care for the child and not possess him, not wish to own him, but to relinquish him. She had welcomed the child with reverence, was caring for him with love and she would, if Grace lived, relinquish him with freedom.

And if she was to relinquish the baby back to Grace, she realised, in a light, bright moment of hope, then she would like another child, another child with Wilfred. And so when he next came to her, she thought with warmth, she would be ready now, to make love again.

The sunlight caught the lens of her camera on the sideboard. Flora carried the sleeping child through the sitting room and laid him on the arm-chair, where he flopped contentedly and looked full, congested almost, with milk. He was sleeping deeply. Flora, walking on tiptoes so her shoes didn't clack on the slate floor, went to the kitchen and took her camera. She smoothed the dust from it. It had been a long time since she last took a photograph. She held the Box Brownie in her hands and a sense of expansion blossomed through her. Her camera; her way of seeing.

Hope and excitement surged through her when she held the square leather box.

In the sitting room Flora knelt down in front of the child to arrange the blanket around him so the fabric was like a scalloped shell. She looked through the lens at the baby, who filled the viewfinder. But in the comer of the frame was the side of the armchair and the antimacassar, its frill hanging down. She stood up and took it off the chair. The picture was clearer now — a sleeping child in a white blanket, an oval of innocence and purity.

Flora clicked the shutter; there was the certain sound of a moment captured in form. She clicked again and again. The purification of the image demanded to be multiplied. She would relinquish this child, but she would keep a photograph. That was what a photograph was, a smithereen of someone's soul that could be kept forever.

★ ★ ★

Wilfred and Flora were kneeling on the floor of the wallpaper shop, untying the two large boxes that had arrived in the post. The cardboard creaked loudly as Wilfred pulled up the lid. Inside the first box were twelve pots of paint.

'I ordered them from Arthur Sanderson & Sons months ago, thinking I would surely be needing to replace the first tins of paint by now,' Wilfred explained to Flora Myffanwy. 'But I doubt there will be much room for them on the shelf, I have sold so few.'

Flora took out the tins and read the labels:

Old Gold, Pear Green, Isabella Yellow, Great White. 'Paint has such lovely names,' she said.

'It hasn't been the busiest shop in Narberth,' Wilfred sighed, sitting back and looking round the somewhat stark shop. 'Times are hard. People can't afford to buy paint.' He had hoped his paint and wallpaper shop would be like Mrs Annie Evans's Conduit Stores, bustling with customers and open till midnight serving them. Apart from Mrs Newton-Lewis, he'd had very few customers.

'Are we in need?' Flora asked.

'No, my dear,' Wilfred reassured her, taken aback by her question and aware that they hadn't spoken about the matter of their finances before. 'I opened the shop because I thought it would help bolster our savings.' He leaned towards her and confided, 'I keep our savings in an empty coffin in the workshop. No one would dare open and look inside a coffin in a chapel of rest.' They both laughed, then Wilfred added, 'I thought if I opened a wallpaper shop and read *The Last Days of Socrates*, I would be prepared for fatherhood.' He hoped he hadn't upset her by mentioning the baby. She was much calmer now, and cleaned so much less. If only she would start taking photographs again.

'I understand.'

'But it wasn't to be,' Wilfred said with a sad smile, stacking the tins on the shelf one by one. 'Perhaps it's not a wallpaper shop and a philosophy book that makes a good father,' he reflected. He took the last tin from the box, a pot of Old Gold. 'I don't know what makes a good father,' he remarked, thinking aloud. He looked around at the empty shop. 'It had better not be having a busy wallpaper shop.'

Flora smiled.

It was kindness, he realised. That's what made a good father. And husband. And friend.

Wilfred began removing the string from the second box, opening it to reveal twelve tight rolls of dark pink Arthur Sanderson & Sons' wallpaper, jammed hard into the box.

'Wilfred . . . ?'

He recognised the distinct tone of voice Flora used when she was going to ask something. 'Yes, dear?'

'Are you very worried about Grace?'

Wilfred nodded.

'So am I.'

Wilfred could not bear to think about the risk he was taking.

'Will you tell me something?' she asked.

Wilfred looked at this wise young woman who was his wife. 'Do you want to wait until we next go for our drive?' he suggested, sensing what Flora was intending to ask and uncertain of how he would explain. 'But,' he pulled a roll of wallpaper from the box, 'if there is something you want to know . . . '

Flora put a small tin on the back shelf and asked, 'Why has Grace not gone home?'

Wilfred smoothed back his hair. 'If she went home, her mother wouldn't want to know her because she is unmarried and has had a baby. Mrs Reece would choke on the shame. She would throw Grace out of house and home. And

257

that would be a dreadful thing for anybody from Narberth, to know that your own mother doesn't want you. I don't think Grace could bear that.'

'And why did she leave the baby with you?'

'Because she has no family — no family to speak of — and I am her friend.'

'But everyone would think . . . '

'I know.'

'Do you know who the father is?'

Wilfred nodded.

'I don't,' Flora said. 'The baby looks so much like Grace and Dr Reece, it makes it hard to see a resemblance to anyone else.'

Wilfred nodded again and leaned back on his hands. 'If there is anything you want to know, ask, my dear. We cannot have secrets between us.' Wilfred watched while Flora arranged the tins on the shelf, and gathered her thoughts. He knew the shallows of this woman, but not yet the depths; he doubted he would ever fully know her, but he would spend his life trying.

'Why do you feel guilty about Grace?'

He sighed: she had seen him, and what he struggled with. He rubbed the stubble on his cheeks: it was hard to put what he felt into words. 'I am sorry to have to talk to you about such personal matters from my past, only I do not want to hurt you.'

Wilfred heard himself talk with the formality of an undertaker. He began again.

'Those weeks when I was married to her, I was not kind. I lay in bed, I am ashamed to say, hating her and certain I was right. Yet she was alone and suffering more than I knew or understood.' He put his palms on his thighs. 'I understand more now. I thought I was right, but I was wrong, and these things have bothered me. I have been wrestling with them in my mind.'

'Can you forgive yourself?'

'I can if I can make it up to her.'

There was a pause. Flora went over to the two miniature pink roses in terracotta flowerpots sitting in the bay window. She gently pressed down the earth around them with her fingertips.

'Wilfred?'

'Yes, my dear.'

'With all this paint,' she said with a hint of flirtation, 'you could decorate our bedroom.'

'Anything for you.'

★ ★ ★

Fear began to rise in Grace like a wave. The candle was too bright and the room was too dark. Her head was heavy and hot on the pillow. She felt light-headed. Everything and its opposite were true. Her thoughts were both mushy and vivid, flipping around her mind as if they themselves were alarmed by their contents.

She felt unhinged, loosened from the earth, held only by a tether that could break or strengthen, and she would fly or sink, die or live. The only constant was the fear coiling up within her. She tried to focus; she was worried for her life. She hadn't known it mattered to her.

The candle flickered and a bee — one of her own, in her sickness she was certain it was one from her own hive — landed on the handle of a teaspoon dunked in the lurid pink medicine. Even when she had wanted to end her life, when she had found out she was pregnant, she had felt alive. Now she had a weak grasp on life, as if her knuckles and fingers were too frail to hold on. She feared her weakness. So this was death: resolution, an answer, arriving of its own accord. Unchosen. When she was suicidal, death was a thought and a choice. Death unbidden was something to fight, for death made life show its value.

The bee flew to the curtains. Grace thought of the curtains in her recent lodgings in London, the small dark room on a busy road, and how the black grit on the windowsill settled only half an hour after she had wiped it.

Heat flowed over her in a great wave and she opened her eyes and pushed away the quilt with what strength she had left in her limbs; she was fighting for her life yet she was barely strong enough to move a quilt.

She thought of Madoc and his mad, war-created arrogance. Then of Wilfred: the pain she had caused him through not stopping their marriage, the generosity he had shown her when she told him the truth. And how safe she had felt when he held her. She thought of her father, whom she missed. Then London, the food she'd eaten there, the lumps of stale bread, and porridge from old oats. And her small piles of notes in her suitcase, how she had counted them: there was the £10 note, with its cottony paper slightly torn in the corner by the King's head. How precious it was, representing safety. She'd dared not break into it, turn it into change and fragment it into coins.

The bee hovered around the room. Grace's mind hovered aimlessly and she remembered the Ritz, and Hilda, who knew how to survive, and the hopeful, battling Suffragettes and their desire to vote. Grace couldn't vote, yet the Suffragettes had touched her and inspired her, although to what, she didn't know. She could return to London, perhaps approach Lady Lytton and find a new way in life, perhaps leave the child here. But first she would have to make her peace with what had happened to her — and that she couldn't do.

Grace watched the bee walk delicately down the spoon into the pink liquid. Its feet were touching it. She must rescue the bee; she didn't want it to drown. She reached out, but her hand was heavy and she knocked the glass. The spoon, the medicine and the bee fell off the bedside table and onto the floor, the glass smashing, the bee entrapped within the sticky liquid, trying to free itself from the goo that was clogging the frantic movement of its legs and wings.

She saw the bee stagger drunkenly to its death and spent a minute, or an hour, she knew not which, watching it struggle, relinquishing itself to stillness, then death. That was her bee. She was its keeper: how much more was she her child's keeper? This child who was conceived by a dark act, in an unholy alliance.

There was a gentle tap on the door and Flora came in and sat down on the bed. She handed Grace an envelope. Grace took from it a softly focused photograph of a baby. The photographic card was thick and scalloped and edged with white and gold. It was of a newly born baby surrendered to the deepest sleep. She saw that he had grown in the day or so since the photograph must have been taken.

'I didn't know you had taken a photograph,' Grace commented, pushing away the bedcovers.

Flora looked away, almost embarrassed, and Grace saw that her child meant something to Flora. Flora and Wilfred didn't have children yet, and she wondered if perhaps Flora Myffanwy was hoping for a child.

'I took it when you were sleeping. I . . . I like taking photographs.'

There was a pause and Grace knew for certain that Flora wanted a child. Grace ran her palm over the smooth surface of the image.

'Thank you,' she said, accepting the gift, accepting the friendship.

'I thought you would like it,' replied Flora.

Then Wilfred knocked and came into the small bedroom.

'You have taken a photograph!' he exclaimed, looking with astonishment at Flora.

Grace put the picture back in the brown envelope and handed it to Wilfred, who looked confused. She prompted him to take it again.

'Would you take this, please?' she said. Wilfred looked at her. His face fell into solemnity and he nodded.

'If anything happens to me, will you give this to my father?'

16

The World is a Wedding

'I've come to see Grace Price.' It was a black night with no stars, and Wilfred, night-blinded, couldn't see the woman who was speaking.

'I'm sorry, you've made a mistake,' Wilfred lied, into the darkness.

'I know you have her,' the voice uttered, 'so let me in.'

The woman came forward onto the step and Wilfred, taken aback, stood aside. Mrs Prout lifted the cloak from her face and then brushed past Wilfred through the sitting room and up the staircase as if she knew where Grace was.

'Stay here,' she demanded. 'Let me be.'

Wilfred saw Mrs Prout look at the two closed doors at the top of the landing, lift the latch on the door of his da's room and disappear inside, shutting the door resolutely behind her. Wilfred stood flabbergasted. The charmer had come, and the smell of sage and thyme about Mrs Prout's shawl and matted hair lingered in the air.

* * *

It was night again. Grace heard the latch on the door lift and she stirred slightly; it must be Flora Myffanwy checking on her. She waited a few moments before she summoned the strength to open her eyes and smile her welcome at Flora, before falling back to that ineluctable warmth and that paradoxical sensation that she was gigantic, her body floating above the earth yet at the same time, minute in the universe. She felt Flora Myffanwy's hand on her upper arm, then tough nails pinching her very hard.

'Oh! Ow!' Grace exclaimed on an in-breath, her mind yanked back into her body from the cloudy landscape it was spreading itself thinly across, like a vapour. Grace opened her eyes in alarm, jerked her arm towards herself and away from the pain, but the hands held on and the fingers pinched harder, the sharp nails digging into her flesh, cutting into it, so the pain didn't go. A woman swayed into form.

'Let go!' Grace pleaded weakly, but with all the strength she could muster. 'Let go!' Her eyes filled immediately with tears. Her right hand went to pull the pinching hands off. 'Stop!' she begged.

Mrs Prout laughed. 'So you're awake now?'

Grace, her senses alert, saw it was Mrs Prout in the shadows. She swallowed and roughly brushed the plentiful tears from her eyes and looked at the mark on her arms that had been administered so vehemently and was now bleeding.

'I will do it again,' Mrs Prout claimed, her eyes wild and staring.

'Go away.'

'If you fall into that sleep again, and dream of that other Heaven, I will come in the depths of the dark night and I will needle you.'

She's a witch, Grace thought.

Mrs Prout looked at the child who lay wrapped in a blanket.

'This is the child. I saw you with him in the street at night,' the woman whispered, and bent and kissed the baby's fragile forehead. Grace took the child in her arms. Mrs Prout lunged, grabbed Grace's forearm and bit down hard. Grace yelped, upright now, eyes open. The baby stirred and slumbered.

'I bit you, Grace Price, with my old yellow teeth in your firm fleshy arm.'

What was this woman doing here? How had she got in? I could call for Wilfred, Grace thought; if I call for help, someone will come, but she didn't. Something inside her let the apparition stay.

'I will not let you sleep like that again.'

I am dreaming, Grace thought. This is a dream, a nightmare. She would wake. Flora would be here in the morning, soft and consoling, and Wilfred standing at the foot of the bed, worried and making hapless jokes, trying to make it all better than it was. The night would pass. The dark would pass, second by second. The woman would fade from her mind like a bad miasma.

'Lie down,' Mrs Prout ordered. Grace lay back knowing it was all a dream. The woman put her hand to the edge of her shawl and pulled out a very long, very fine needle, then clamped the needle horizontally between her teeth. She folded back the bedclothes at the bottom of the bed and held Grace's left foot in both hands. Grace looked in alarm at this woman, while Mrs

265

Prout stroked her foot tenderly, took the needle in her right hand and stabbed it hard into the skin over the joint of Grace's big toe. Grace leaped. The needle was wrenched out. Mrs Prout then jabbed it into her little toe. And out. And in her heel beside her ankle. And out. Then she licked the needle with her fat tongue.

The dream will fade, Grace told herself, going to turn over on her side. I will wake up; it will be normal again.

Mrs Prout clasped her other foot and speared the needle in again; then again until Grace felt clarity return to her thoughts, as if her mind had shrunk down to fit her skull. Air, fresh and sharp, reached deeper into her lungs, her tongue gathered back its muscularity and waves of soothing undulated through her.

'What you want you cannot have,' the image of Mrs Prout muttered. 'Grace, open your mouth.' Grace obediently tilted her head back. Mrs Prout shrugged off her shawl, produced a vial and dropped liquid onto Grace's tongue. Grace tasted brandy burning the inside of her parched mouth and the cracks in her lips — then something, some essence of herself, seared back into her body.

'This is the child. This is your brother's child.'

Oh, Grace thought, someone has said it. The truth had been spoken aloud, and she had been set free. She nodded, meaning, Yes, this is my child and my brother is the father. Mrs Prout pushed her face up very close to Grace, their noses almost touching so that Grace could see the perfect black in the centre of the irises of the woman's ancient eyes.

'Now you listen to me, you girl, you woman, you whore, you slut, you mother, you wife. You queen, you virgin, you sacrifice, you listen to me.' Grace felt vehement fingers jab hard and sharp on her between her breasts.

'*Live*.' And with that, the woman turned, jigged a jig, and was gone.

★ ★ ★

Wilfred lay in bed wide awake and full of fear for Grace. Mrs Prout had come and gone, having stayed only briefly, but still he couldn't sleep. Perhaps if he checked on Grace and knew she was passable well, he might be able to fall asleep. He stood up and went and knocked very lightly on the door to his da's bedroom; there was no answer. He carefully lifted the latch. There was Grace, breathing, sleeping on her side, a white sheet pulled up to her shoulders, the baby asleep besides her. She seemed undisturbed by Mrs Prout. Somewhat reassured, Wilfred turned to go, but then instead pulled the wooden chair from the foot of the bed and put it as silently as he could next to Grace. He sat down, his legs apart. He was wearing only his long-johns — he still didn't own pyjamas. He sat there in the pitch-black, absorbed in his thoughts.

His da was sleeping downstairs on a roll of blankets, and had been since Grace arrived. His da hadn't said anything, beyond that brief, heartfelt conversation in this room and his almost pleading request that they get Dr Reece to come and see to his daughter, to save her, the night he had found Grace, like Goldilocks, sleeping in his bed. Wilfred knew he disapproved profoundly of the fact that Dr Reece hadn't yet been called, but his da kept his counsel, stood back, and let Wilfred unravel his own adult life, and his own predicaments.

The baby shuffled slightly. Wilfred noticed how the child had grown since yesterday, and appeared to grow every day.

Wilfred looked at Grace. 'I am sorry,' he whispered. He put his head in his hands. 'I am sorry I proposed to you at the picnic. I am sorry I took so long telling you I didn't want to marry you, and that I told you in the street, in front of those tennis players. And I'm sorry I didn't say anything when your father came to tell me we were getting married. And I'm sorry I stood there in such a black mood on the day of our wedding, and for all the nights I lay there hating you. And I'm sorry I loved Flora Myffanwy, and not you: that when I knew what it was to love Flora, I knew what it was to not love you. I'm sorry I divorced you and humiliated you in front of everyone, so that you had to leave. I didn't understand what you were enduring. I am sorry I didn't understand. I am sorry I didn't get Madoc by the throat and throttle him. And I'm sorry I let you leave in such a hurry. I thought I was a good man, but I had never been tested.

'I spent months worrying and wondering where you were. I thought you would have gone to Swansea — it never even occurred to me you would go as far as London. I didn't know where you were, Grace.' Grace moved slightly, her eyelids fluttering. Wilfred sighed.

'All these things I have wanted to say to you. They have been on my mind, and weighed upon me more and more heavily, so that I haven't known what to do. Since you left I have been wrestling with my conscience. The more I understood, the guiltier I have felt.' He rubbed his chest back and forth.

'I thought you had given the baby to us,' he whispered ruefully. 'I wanted to keep him. I would have, if you hadn't come back. And I saw the hurt in your eyes when you met Flora and realised that she was now my wife, and I saw hope fade from you.

'Tomorrow morning, Grace, if you are not better, I want to go to your father and tell him, get him to see you and take care of you. I can't wait any longer. I will ask you first, but that is what I want to do. Your father is not a bad man, Grace, if you can forgive him. He is a kind and caring doctor, but he is weak. Your mother is cruel. And you, Grace,' he reached out and stroked her hair, 'were innocent. Then Madoc . . . The deeper the rot, the shinier the front, eh?'

'Please forgive me, Grace. I am so sorry for the hurt I've caused you.' Wilfred got down off the chair, knelt at Grace's bedside and took her two roughened, hot hands in his and put his forehead down on them.

'Please don't die, Grace. Please don't die,' he begged.

* * *

Wilfred finished eating his breakfast pensively, as if he was waiting for something portentous to happen. He must get Dr Reece this morning; he would leave immediately. He watched Flora open the cutlery drawer, the knives and forks rattling, and search for a pastry brush. Wilfred finished his cup of tea and looked towards the window.

'Are you waiting for someone?' his da asked.

'Hello?' a faint voice called. Wilfred jumped up and searched out of the window, but the voice was coming from inside the house. Flora looked into the sitting room.

'I wondered if I could have a scrambled egg?'

Wilfred went through to the sitting room and saw Grace in her white nightgown and a long shawl, the baby in her arms. Grace: frail, thin, but alert. Alive. Yes, she was alive. There she was, standing on her own two feet, the baby in her arms. There was a smile on her pale face, dark circles under her eyes, but a light in her eyes. Whatever journey she had taken was finished.

Wilfred stepped forward. He loved her. He loved this woman, his friend, and he was grateful from the depths of his heart that she was alive. He hadn't had to bury her, nor see the tragedy of a child without a mother. This woman had been sent to test him, and test him she had — but she was alive. Whatever risks he had taken, whatever foolishness he had shown this woman, and he knew it was a lot, something had been surpassed; something within her had risen to meet the hardship life had brought to her.

Wilfred stood there, both hands on Grace's

upper arms, his eyes closed tightly, nodding as he thought these thoughts. When he opened his eyes, he saw the child's face, lying in its mother's arms.

'You have a beautiful child, Grace,' he said.

★ ★ ★

Grace was lying on the bed, resting through the morning. She had dreamed, or thought she dreamed, that Mrs Prout had come during the night, disturbed her sleep and reordered her thoughts. And she thought she remembered Wilfred speaking to her in the night. Peace and a growing sense of health was flowing through her, as if after a battle. She stretched out her feet, pointed her toes and felt her legs tingle with life. She closed her eyes and sighed, then she heard a voice say something, a voice she knew. She listened. As if summoned by the voice, she stepped weakly out of the bed, picked up the child, wrapped it in a blanket, then she took the envelope Flora had given her and walked barefoot downstairs gingerly but purposefully to the kitchen.

There was Madoc. Standing facing Wilfred. They both turned abruptly when she entered, their charged words interrupted.

'Come to see the father of your child?' Madoc sneered.

Flora came in, followed by Wilfred's da, both silenced by the air of threat in the room.

'I said, 'Come to see the father of your child?' I knew you'd come back, Grace. I knew you'd return,' he continued arrogantly. 'Mrs Prout told me you were here and I came to find you.' He straightened the belt on his uniform. 'So it *was* Wilfred, not some rotter at a dance! So Wilfred here is the child's father,' he goaded.

'No,' Grace said loudly. 'Wilfred is not the child's father.' Her hair was loose and swung as she shook her head. Her eyes met Flora's. Then she saw Wilfred look at Madoc.

'So it was some farm lad from Pembrokeshire, then. Don't look at me like that, Wilfred Price. You couldn't even consummate the marriage. You're a country undertaker who doesn't know anything about the world, least of all women.'

There was a moment of uneasy silence. The silence grew into something darker, leaden and frightening.

'No! It wasn't me!' Madoc shook his head and took a step backwards, unintentionally hitting the wall so that his back was against it.

'It's not *my* child!' Madoc said with disgust.

Wilfred hung his head. And Grace saw Flora and Wilfred's da look horrified, disbelieving, and then grasp the truth.

'No,' Grace said clearly. 'He is not your child. He is *my* child. He belongs to me.' Yes, he was her child. She looked down at the child in her arms. She would care for him as she had cared for her bees, with the same wonder and reverence; show the same nurturing, patience and attention, learn the skills of motherhood as she had learned the skills of beekeeping. She could take this strangely conceived and unexpected child, as she had taken that unexpected and unwanted hive in the Ritz, and care for him.

Grace was aware that they were all looking at her, as if they were listening to her thoughts. The door rattled in the breeze. She would leave Narberth; she would go to London. And she would work. She had learned that she could do a job from working in the Ritz. In a week or so, when she had rested and was stronger, she would ask Wilfred if she could use the telephone and she would call Lady Lytton and ask if she needed a maid. Or if any of Lady Lytton's friends might need a servant. Maybe Mrs Garrud needed a new maid. She would find a woman to care for her child during the day, and lodgings for herself and the baby to live in. It would be hard. She pulled her child to her. She felt the enormity of the journey ahead, the mountain of work. But she had made her decision. She had made her commitment; she had cast her vote.

She looked at Madoc, hard and smart in his light brown uniform, the gold buttons catching the sunlight. There was one more thing to do. She looked down at herself. She was wearing her nightdress; she was not wearing jujutsu clothes. She had not even ever practised any jujutsu moves, but she could still practise Suffragettes' self-defence.

Grace turned and gave the child to Flora, then went to the kitchen table around which they all stood silently, intently, opened the cutlery drawer and took out the meat cleaver. The baby began to cry. She walked up to Madoc and he stepped back, hitting the wall again.

'Grace!' he exclaimed, a look of horror on his face, his hands raised, backed into a corner.

Despite his greater size, Grace saw he was frightened; that he understood the power of her intention. Grace walked right up to him and quickly put the knife under his throat. He gasped. She could feel his breath on her face, see the individual bristles of his moustache. Would someone stop her? But no one did. Out of the corner of her eye she saw Wilfred put his hand out to tell his da and Flora to stand back. Wilfred wasn't going to stop her. Grace pushed the knife-edge against Madoc's throat. He looked down in absolute terror, frozen. His throat clicked.

'If you touch me again, I will kill you.'

There was no doubt in her words. She had found her voice, she had used her tongue; she had said the words. He gurgled and pushed himself right back against the wall. And the terror in his eyes told her he believed her. She stood back. Madoc rushed to leave.

'Wait,' she said. Wilfred stood in front of the door. Madoc waited. Grace went to the crying child, unwrapped a fold of the blanket and took out the photograph Flora had taken. She turned it over and put it on the kitchen table. Wilfred handed her a pen, anticipating her need.

To Father, she wrote, *from Grace and Abel. Narberth 1926.* She waved the photograph to dry the ink. 'Please give this to Father,' she said to Madoc. 'Does he know I'm here?'

'I think so,' Madoc replied, his throat dry, his voice cracking. She would not go to her father; she would leave him to his cowardice. She would care for herself and her child, and when she was much stronger, she would seek him out.

'I want you to go now, Madoc. You are never to come and find me again,' she said, loudly and clearly.

He nodded. He understood. She had made him understand. Madoc looked at the floor, then turned and went.

★   ★   ★

There! He'd done it. Wilfred hadn't thought of Stanley Baldwin once.

They had come back from Bethesda Chapel and found that Wilfred's da had gone to visit Auntie Blodwen and Grace and the baby were in bed sleeping deeply after the strain of the morning. Flora had left the washing up — the dirty teacup on the table, the dishcloth hanging easily and unfolded over the sink, the newspaper ruffled on the armchair, the blade of the butter-knife yellowed with butter, and dropped her coat over the chair, and Wilfred had led his dear and beautiful wife up to their small bedroom, full of hope and excitement. Please don't let her say, 'I'm too tired,' he thought. Please don't let her be too tired. And then in their bedroom they crumpled the clean sheets and had conjugal relations until the bolster fell from the mattress, their clothes were strewn in the blankets and Wilfred's socks had been jigged to the bottom of the sheet and found their resting place. And so, to Wilfred's great delight, Flora, who these last few months had seemed like a sodden rag doll, regained her musculature, coming back to him with a new strength, bringing fresh facets of herself to those hot, humid minutes. Yes, minutes, Wilfred thought to himself. This was minute after minute of pleasure, held back from its conclusion.

When the events had reached their — almost long-awaited — conclusion, Flora looked up and smiled at him. He smiled back and put his forehead against her forehead and they rested there together, Wilfred lying like a collapsed heavy lump. Then Wilfred rolled off Flora and silently, wordlessly, pulled her to him and, holding her, they fell asleep enveloped in a peace of their own making.

★ ★ ★

'Flora!' Wilfred called. Flora came out of the scullery in her green pinny; she was doing the washing up she'd willingly abandoned earlier. Wilfred beckoned to her; he was standing stooped by the wall and looking at the flagstones in the yard.

'Look what I've found.'

Flora came up to him. There in the corner, its head pushed into the wall, was a fat-bellied toad. It was trying to get down a crack between the flagstones and the wall but it was too fat to allow any more of itself to disappear down the gap. Still, it tried: fear propelled it.

'It's frightened,' Flora observed.

'It's a long way from a pond,' Wilfred stated. 'It's lost on these flagstones and it's very dry.'

'Oh,' Flora said, and a moment later came out with a teacup of water.

'Is it taking tea with us, dear?' Wilfred asked. Flora smiled. She crouched down and poured the cold water on the toad, which moved flatly to the left and to the right, aware of Wilfred's shadow.

'Well, it won't find a pond outside an undertaker's workshop,' Wilfred said. He picked up the toad, plopped it in the teacup and put his large hand over the delicate bone china with its intricate border of gold flowers.

'That's from the tea set my mother gave us for our wedding present.'

'I don't think she expected we'd put a toad in it,' Wilfred replied. 'It's like a witch's brew. Would you care to take a walk with me, dear?' Flora glanced upstairs to where Grace was. 'It will only take a moment.' He held out his arm and Flora took it, while Wilfred walked ceremoniously through the High Street with the teacup held out in front of him.

'Good afternoon, Mrs Bell Evans.'

'What have you got there, Wilfred?'

'A toad, Mrs Bell Evans.'

'Is that your best bone china, Mrs Price?' Mrs Evans asked, scandalised.

'Yes,' Flora admitted.

'By damn, you can never trust a man with a tea set,' Mrs Evans proclaimed, shaking her head regretfully. 'Mind you wash it out properly.'

At the town moor they turned down the gentle lane that led from Narberth, where the sycamores spread their crinkly branches out over the stream. It was late winter, almost spring. They walked past a bank of croci, with flowers like purple pixie hats; Wilfred picked one and gave it to Flora. The birds sang overhead. Some late snowdrops scattered among the blackberry brambles were drooping, as if weighted down by their beauty. Even the nettles looked noble with their upright stems and broadly spread leaves. Wilfred stopped before the kissing gate.

'I'm going to bob my hair,' Flora Myffanwy said. Wilfred swallowed. His wife's beautiful hair.

'Yes, dear,' he replied. When they reached the stream, he stood at its babbling edge, then took a few steps towards the clear, clean water and lifted his hand from the delicate teacup. 'Here you are, toad; you're moving to a new residence on the outskirts of Narberth.' He shook the teacup. 'Bugger won't come out now! Come on, toad, you have to do better than that.' He waited but the toad clung to the teacup even when the pure water swirled around it.

'It prefers the teacup to the pond,' Wilfred commented.

'You've found something really spiffing,' said a small child, who had suddenly appeared. 'Is it dead?'

'I was hoping it wasn't.'

Suddenly the toad jumped out, plopped into the stream and swam, as if startled by the cold, then held on to a twig. The little boy crouched on his haunches, peering closely into the water.

'It's like a swimming pool and the toad's holding on to the side,' he observed. Wilfred held the teacup out to Flora, who was listening bemusedly to the child's chatter now about a grass snake he had found. 'And I don't even want to tell you what happened next!' the child exclaimed.

Wilfred walked a short way up the path and looked through a small oval gap between the fence and the moss-hugged branches. On the green hill two sheep were eating grass, their heads bowed in humility. Beyond the swathe of green grass there was the faint blue sky. A sheep bleated. Wilfred bleated back; the sheep bleated again. Flora and the child looked up.

'Talking to a sheep,' Wilfred told them, while the sheep continued chewing, its face to the earth.

The air and the trees were still and Wilfred felt at one with his surroundings. Sometimes as a child he had wondered what it would be like to have the mighty hand of God, written about in the Bible, a gigantic hand with which he could reach out to touch the fields of barley and feel them swaying, or ruffle the top of a tree as if it was the hair of a small child. If he had the hand of God he would stretch out to the stars and pick them up as if they were marbles. Mercury would be a hot ball-bearing, Mars, a big India rubber ball, Saturn, a dust-covered ball like one found months after it had rolled under the furniture. Then he would reach beyond the solar system and feel the emptiness between the stars. He didn't know what filled that enormous incalculable space: he hoped it was God and he felt it was love.

Wilfred looked up the valley at Narberth. Narberth was a green, living world that — happily, contentedly — saw only itself: this was a blessed circle of a small town that looked inwards. Narberth was his world and it was a world in itself. And in Narberth, as far as he could see, there was everything. It was all here in this town of nine hundred years: the funerals and the babies, the dead and the living, the pure and the ill-intentioned, the sick and the well, the contented and the grieving, the winners in the dog competition and the losers, the rotting and the neatly buried, the happily married and the violently married, the beautiful and the bruised, the humble and the arrogant, the guilty and the forgiven, all joined together like the dovetail joints on a carefully made cabinet, or a coffin. It was wedded, all of it — everything was wedded in the world and to the world, and there was no escaping any of it.

Wilfred threw his head back, stared upwards and sighed. So instead of wrestling, like Jacob struggling with the angel, he would attempt to accept what came his way with a little more grace, because this was the way it was, the violence and the love, the living and the dead, the good and the weak . . . and there was no escaping any of it. No, there was no escaping any of it.

Wilfred looked back into the stars where he hoped his child rested and then to the field, where his wife stood. Only the dead didn't hold hands, only the dead weren't wedded. The living were intermingled and knotted like the roots of trees in the earth. Only the dead let go fully. Everything living was knitted and wedded to the world. This was the wedding of the world.

'I've got a dog beetle on me,' the child said, coming up to him. 'It's a fur-male,' — he pointed to its waist. 'It's very fat downwards. That's where it keeps its wings.' The iridescent beetle crawled across the child's chubby knuckles, unaware of the fascination and learning it was inspiring. 'Even when it goes upside down, it can still walk. You can have him after me,' he said to Wilfred.

Wilfred saw Flora Myffanwy approach him in that quiet way she had.

'The toad has gone,' she said.

'Into the river,' Wilfred replied. He looked at his wife. Then he bent down and whispered to her, 'You are as beautiful as the day.'

Wilfred held the translucent teacup up to the sun and the light streamed through it. 'Right, let's go home. Fancy a cup of tea?'

Acknowledgements

I would like to thank Jenny Hewson, James Gurbutt and Sam Evans, who make a bright, valuable and strong team. I would also like to thank the early readers, in particular, Sally Furnival, Jacqueline Wilson, Laura Edwards, Helen Fox, Helen Cleary, Gaelle Lemoine, Anita Patel, Kristen Palazzo, Rachel Stegall, Hilary Duggan, Jacqueline McCann, John Cribb, Beth Rees, John Perkins, Livia Franchini, Joanne Hislop, Dee Benham, Paula Nightingale and Adrian Cross.

Thank you to Julie and Colin, and Austin Price.

My thanks again to Gwyn and friends, to Isabel Clementine Evans, and to Solly.

We do hope that you have enjoyed reading this large print book.

Did you know that all of our titles are available for purchase?

We publish a wide range of high quality large print books including:
Romances, Mysteries, Classics
General Fiction
Non Fiction and Westerns

Special interest titles available in large print are:
The Little Oxford Dictionary
Music Book
Song Book
Hymn Book
Service Book

Also available from us courtesy of Oxford University Press:
Young Readers' Dictionary
(large print edition)
Young Readers' Thesaurus
(large print edition)

For further information or a free brochure, please contact us at:
Ulverscroft Large Print Books Ltd.,
The Green, Bradgate Road, Anstey,
Leicester, LE7 7FU, England.
Tel: (00 44) 0116 236 4325
Fax: (00 44) 0116 234 0205

Other titles published by Ulverscroft:

THE THOUGHTS AND HAPPENINGS OF WILFRED PRICE, PURVEYOR OF SUPERIOR FUNERALS

Wendy Jones

In 1924, in the Welsh village of Narberth, undertaker Wilfred Price proposes to a girl he barely knows at a picnic. Almost instantly he knows he has made a mistake — he does not love her. He thinks it will be easy to extricate himself — but a chance meeting at a funeral and the revelation of a long-held secret complicate his world beyond recognition . . .